EDUCATING ELLA

He was in front of her again, picking up the leather strap. He held it out towards her face. 'Kiss the agency of your correction,' he ordered.

Ella turned her face away and pulled back. The chains on her nipples stopped her with a jerk and she felt the supple leather brushing her cheek. She shuddered. Soon, that leather would slap across her carefully prepared bare bottom, that naughty part of her body in which most of her sinful desires were concentrated. Another electric thrill ran through her. She submitted to his charismatic will and her own craving.

EDUCATING ELLA

Stephen Ferris

This book is a work of fiction.
In real life, make sure you practise safe sex.

First published in 1997 by
Nexus
332 Ladbroke Grove
London W10 5AH

Copyright © Stephen Ferris 1997

The right of Stephen Ferris to be identified as the Author
of this Work has been asserted by him in accordance with
the Copyright Designs and Patents Act 1988.

Typeset by TW Typesetting, Plymouth, Devon

Printed and bound by
Caledonian Books Ltd, Glasgow

ISBN 0 352 33189 5

One

The parcel was small enough, but unusually heavy for its size. Ella picked it up off the mat and turned it over in her hands. There was no return address and no stamp, indicating that it had been delivered by hand while she was out. She went into her tiny kitchenette and put the kettle on before she opened the brown, padded envelope. She tipped it up and a pair of shiny handcuffs slid out into her palm, causing her to shiver for a reason other than their cold contact with her skin. She squeezed the sides of the envelope to open it further and extracted a blindfold. It was made of shaped, heavy black velvet and was intended to be secured by an elastic strap, rather like the sleeping masks favoured by airlines.

She delved again into the envelope; she extracted the short note at the bottom and read it. This time, there was no touch of cold metal that she could use to explain the larger shiver that shook her body as she read, 'Tomorrow evening, at precisely seven twenty-five, you will unlatch the door of your flat so that it can be pushed open from outside. At precisely seven-thirty, you will be standing completely naked just inside the door. You will wear the blindfold. You will fasten your hands behind your back with the handcuffs.'

Ella sat down rather shakily on the kitchen stool

and turned the note over in her hands. There was no signature and nothing else to read; just those terse instructions which, by their very tone, brooked no refusal. She had expected an invitation but never in her wildest imaginings had it taken this form. Her first instinct was to burn the note, throw away the parcel with its contents and forget all about the crazy scheme on which she had embarked. But could she do that? After all the care and effort she had put into coming this far along the road to her goal, could she just turn her back on it and walk away? Even as her brain formed the question she knew what the answer had to be. Whatever the risk, she just had to see this thing through.

Next evening, her bathing was even more meticulous than usual. It was a token of her nervousness that she checked her watch against the speaking clock at least three times after seven o'clock. As she unlatched her door, she could hear her heart thumping loudly enough to disturb the neighbours. She was wearing only a bath robe and she slipped out of it, hanging it tidily on its hook in the bathroom before stepping out into the narrow hallway with blindfold and handcuffs in her hands. She felt her fingers trembling as she put the elastic strap of the blindfold over her head and pulled the velvet down over her eyes. She had not worn it before, but wished she had so as to be able to get used to the complete absence of any chink of light. She clicked one link of the cuffs around her right wrist, then put her hands behind her. As she groped for the spare cuff, she knew that her courage was ebbing fast. Even in the warmth of central heating, her teeth were chattering and she could feel her knees giving way. If she didn't get that cuff fastened quickly about her left wrist, she would not be able to go through with this bizarre procedure.

Her groping became desperate as seconds ticked by and she failed time and again in her attempts. When she finally heard and felt the metal click about her wrist, she heaved a sigh of relief that rapidly turned into a shaky laugh. What was there to be relieved about? She had just made herself totally vulnerable to anything that might be inflicted upon her by the person or persons who would soon come through her door.

And they would come, she was sure of that. Not for the first time, she speculated about the identity of her visitors. Would it be just one person, or more? Would it be male or female eyes that would feast themselves on her helpless nudity? What were they going to do with her? Her breathing was rapid and shallow, but she knew that was only partly due to apprehension. Lewd fantasies were painting themselves on the eyes so totally deprived of other sensory input and those fantasies were churning her stomach, erecting her nipples so that their gold rings hung clear of her breasts and making her vagina tingle and moisten. She shifted uneasily, rubbing her thighs together in an attempt to squeeze her clitoris. If she had been able, she would have touched herself and her very inability to do that was a further stimulus which could be increased, she found, by pulling against the secure restraint of the cuffs.

There was no sound to give her warning that her visitors had arrived. Her first inkling of their presence was when she felt material descending on her shoulders, causing her to give an almighty start of surprise.

'Who is it? Who's there? What are you doing?' she called, a little annoyed with herself to find her voice so thin and reedy with pent-up emotion.

The fact that there was no answer at all was both sinister and erotic and Ella found her arousal

3

mounting to match her apprehension. By the way the material brushed her body and was being manipulated she guessed that she was now wearing an all-enveloping cloak, buttoned at the front. Hands grasped her upper arms on either side and she was pushed forward. She had not really expected to be taken out of the flat so quickly and she gasped at the way her stomach squirmed as she realised that she was going to be paraded in public without knowing exactly how well covered her body was. She stumbled a little on the wide staircase, but her captors supported her and hurried her onwards. She felt the cold stone of the pavement beneath her feet, then a hand on her head bent her forward. She heard a car door open and realised that it was intended she get into it. She did so with some difficulty, grateful now for the hands that helped her. She judged it to be a large, luxury car because of the sound of the door as it closed and because she found that she could stretch her legs in front of her without touching the front seat.

She could feel someone on either side of her, still supporting her, and she leaned back as far as she was able with her hands still cuffed behind her. Suddenly, she felt movement in the material that covered her breasts and a cool draught told her that her cloak was being unbuttoned. She panicked, bending her body forward in an effort to prevent what was being done, but strong hands yanked her upright and held her pressed against the back of the seat while the unbuttoning continued. She was going to be stripped naked and there was no way for her to know who might be able to see her in the back of the car.

'No! Please don't!'

She might as well not have spoken. Her tormentors took not the slightest notice, maintaining their eerie and unnerving silence. Now the cloak was completely

4

open and she felt them tugging at it, sliding it out from underneath her. She pressed her bottom down as hard as she could, but it was a futile gesture. The cloak rasped against her soft skin, then she was nude, unable even to cover herself with her hands. Even without being able to see them, she knew that her nipples were in full erection. That was humiliating, because she understood only too well that it was not cool air alone, but sexual arousal, which provided the stimulation. Lustful fantasies filled her mind and she shuddered under the impact of them.

She was riding off into the night with strangers to some unknown destination. She was completely naked. She could see nothing and was powerless to defend herself. What was going to be done to her? This was insanity! How had she contrived to get herself into such a fix? She thought back along the strange trail that led to her present predicament. When had it started? It seemed a lifetime ago, now, but was really little more than a few weeks ...

No one could doubt that Nature had looked upon Ella Costello with favour. Between the long, blonde hair that framed her pretty face and the delicate toes that ended her long, shapely legs, there reposed a body for which 'gorgeous' was a considerable understatement. Fate, aided and abetted by Ella's natural talent, had similarly blessed her with an employment that she enjoyed. Already, at the age of twenty-one, she was established in the writing career she had always hankered after. True, she was as yet only a junior reporter on a local paper, but there was every chance that greater things awaited her. *The Globe* had a respectable circulation, was financially stable and had proved to be the jumping-off stage for several writers who were now famous in other spheres. If there were one tiny cloud in her otherwise blue sky, it was to do with sex. As might be expected, Ella had no difficulty in attracting young men. She had gone through the stages of back-seat gropes and heavy petting, and, with a couple of very favoured 'possibles', had progressed to what was alleged to be the ultimate delight of full-strip penetrative sex in bed. All these experiences were pleasant enough, but had left her strangely unmoved and with a restless feeling that there must be more to sex than that.

For *The Globe's* success, the paper's management had to thank competent staff like Ella's immediate superior, Paula Matheson. Wise beyond her thirty years, Paula could recognise latent talent and smell a budding story several miles away. It was she who had influenced the editor's decision to take on Ella and had guided her natural abilities through those difficult early stages. It was she who curbed her protégée's gauche impulse to wax lyrical over the inevitable weddings which were her first assignments and steered her towards the proper format of Who, Where, When, How, stressing the importance of recording the name of every single guest, because every name sold one more paper.

On the morning it all started, Ella was at her desk, tapping busily at her keyboard. She was intent on her work and did not notice Paula come into the office and stand behind her. Paula did not immediately announce her presence, content to stand for a while and admire the way the sun, streaming through the window, amplified the shining gold of Ella's hair. Paula knew that there was much office speculation about her sexual preferences but was confident enough about herself to be able to ignore them. Let them wonder about the reasons for her unwed status and the reported absence of boyfriends. That blonde hair would be so soft and silky between her fingers – completely unlike the texture of her own, which was short and dark, tending to frizziness.

'Morning, Ella. Is that your piece on the Flower Show?'

Ella looked round, raising her arms and rotating her neck to ease the stiffness. 'Hi, Paula. Why is it always the sodding anterrhinums that win prizes? Why can't people grow prize roses? I can spell those.'

Paula laughed. 'Never mind. I think I've got a story for you to cover that will be even easier for you to spell. Just three letters.'

'Dog Show?'

'No; better than that. How do you feel about sex?'

Ella frowned at her, unable to decide if she was serious. 'Is that a personal invitation, or what?'

'It's a real story. Or at least it could be if it develops. You know I keep my ear to the ground and people tell me things. Well, it seems as though there might be an interesting new club on the go in the town. A place where goings-on are going on that wouldn't please the vicar, if you know what I mean.'

'A sex club? In sleepy little Arton? I don't believe it!'

Paula nodded. 'If what I hear is true, it's not just sex, but kinky sex. Bondage and spanking; that sort of thing.'

'Ooh! How splendid! Tell me more!'

'That's just it. There is no more. Just rumour and speculation. No one can or will tell me where or who. If it's going to be a story, someone's got to winkle it out.'

Ella paused in thought. 'You can't mean what I think you mean? I should cover it? It's a bit out of my league, isn't it? I'm weddings, whist-drives and funerals.'

7

'Not any more. I'm sure you can do it. It would be your big chance. If it's true, this story would go national.'

'Golly!' Ella considered the implications. If she were successful, her career would be enormously enhanced. She knew that was not the only reason for her interest in this particular story. Somewhere inside her, a little imp was twitching and jumping, hinting at possibly exciting and different pleasures of the flesh to which she was by no means averse. She was aware of her perverse tendency towards voyeurism, although that had, so far, been confined within the pages of magazines and books. 'I'm grateful for the chance,' she said. 'I'll certainly do my best with it.'

'I'm sorry I can't give you a more promising start,' Paula said. 'I'll be very interested to see how far you can get.'

Over the next few days, Ella concentrated all her efforts on obtaining information, lingering in the places where the juiciest gossip might be heard and talking for hours on the telephone to contacts who might be able to increase her knowledge. If such a thing as this mysterious club existed, it was a well-guarded secret, a fact that she was obliged to report to Paula.

'Absolutely no one admits first-hand experience,' she said. 'The best I've been able to do is to establish that most of the best rumours come from clients of that new fitness centre, Bodytrim, but even those are not specific. I was going down there this afternoon to see what the management can tell me.'

'Hmm,' Paula said, doubtfully. 'If people are being as cagey as that, I doubt if anyone's going to talk to a reporter. Better perhaps if they don't know who you are.'

'You think I should disguise myself or something?'

Paula laughed. 'Reporters only do that in books. I

8

don't really see you as a plumber with a big, droopy, walrus moustache and jeans that show cleavage at the back.' She paused, reflectively. 'Oh, I don't know, though? Might be rather fetching! A much easier way would be to join. That gives you the perfect excuse to lurk about and listen. Tell you what; I'll join, too. Two pairs of ears are better than one. Your body couldn't be any trimmer, but mine could. I could do to lose a pound or two and I wouldn't mind putting the fee down to legitimate expenses.'

It was, perhaps, surprising that an establishment like Bodytrim had seen fit to set up in a little town like Arton and even more surprising that it seemed to be doing so well, attracting customers from further afield. Perhaps the secret of its success was that it was not the usual dreary conversion of a house or shop, but had been purpose-built from the ground up, so that it was equipped with every modern gadget and conveniences like swimming pools, saunas and Jacuzzis, as well as the more normal treadmills, bicycles and other implements of torture. Paula and Ella visited regularly and worked out; sometimes together and sometimes separately, engaging as many people as they could in idle conversation. After every visit, they compared notes, being disappointed at obtaining only hints and half-truths from people who knew someone else who had once heard a stranger mention something. It was exasperating.

The obligatory exercise was a spin-off benefit for Ella, who had been getting a little soft from hours spent at the keyboard instead of on her feet. It toned her up and made her feel sexy. She found the Jacuzzi particularly stimulating. To peel off her sticky leotard and go naked down the steps into the hot water was delightful. Often she would be alone and that offered the opportunity to snuggle up to one of the underwater outlets and allow the bubbling water to play with great force between her legs. She told herself that the reason for this was purely hygienic, but knew that was not the truth. The jet of water that vibrated her labia and rushed against her clitoris was a delight and such a stimulation that it did not require a great deal of fingering on her part to bring about orgasm. She was doing just that one day and had arrived at that crucial point in the proceedings when she became careless. Half-crouched, facing the side of the pool so as to obtain maximum benefit from the water-nozzle, her left elbow was on the tiled surround so as to give her arm support as her fingers tugged and manipulated her right nipple, while her right hand was busily engaged between her legs in attempting to finish the job the water had started. Her eyes were closed in rapt concentration as she bit her lip and grunted softly. Her climax was approaching and her breathing became faster, her nipple-tugging frenzied. Some sixth sense intruded upon her concentration and caused her to open her eyes. Right in front of her face was a pair of bare feet. With a gasp, she tore her hands away from her body and tried to assume a casually innocent pose. Her gaze travelled up the long legs to find that they belonged to Paula. She was standing with her hands on her hips, a knowing smile playing on her lips.

'Well, well! Who's a naughty girl, then?'

Ella blushed scarlet to the roots of her hair and ducked lower, as though the transparent water would hide her body. 'I wasn't . . .' she stammered.

'Weren't what? Doing yourself? Of course you were, and why not? Oh, come on! Stop looking so guilty. It's something everybody does and we've all been caught at it at some time or another. Got room for another one in there?'

Still speechless with embarrassment, Ella could only nod. Paula wriggled her leotard down over her hips and stepped out of it. Her body was hard and lithe, with an all-over tan. Ella had noticed before that Paula's claim of needing to lose excess pounds was unnecessarily modest. She watched her walk around the Jacuzzi and pause on the steps, dibbling one toe in the water to test the temperature. Her pubic hair, like the hair on her head, was dense and frizzy, her breasts full and firm. Ella noticed the glint of metal and was surprised to see that each of Paula's nipples was pierced and adorned with a gold ring which perfectly complemented the brown tint of her breasts. She came down the steps and waded into the water. Was it Ella's imagination, or was there something faintly threatening and aggressive about that tigerish body and the breasts which seemed to be pointed directly at her? She looked away quickly, uncertain whether that was because she did not wish to seem to be peeping, or whether from embarrassment at the sudden surge of sexual excitement at seeing another woman's body naked and close to her. Paula bent her knees so that her breasts were submerged. Ella felt able to look at her again, not knowing whether she felt relief or disappointment at this concealment.

Paula made her way over until she was beside Ella. 'Well? Carry on! Don't mind me.'

'What? Oh no, I couldn't!'

'No?' Paula said casually. 'Oh well, please yourself. I'm going to.'

'You are?'

'Sure! These jets are much too good to waste.' Paula turned towards the side of the Jacuzzi and positioned herself so as to achieve the optimum flow between her legs, a dreamy smile on her face. 'Mmm! That's good!'

Ella watched her, severely aware of unfinished business. 'Do you do it often?' she enquired shyly.

Paula opened her eyes and looked at her. 'At least once a day; sometimes more. It's good for you. Don't you?'

Ella surprised herself by saying, 'Yes. Usually once a day.'

'Ever have anyone do it for you?'

Ella blushed again. 'No.'

'What? Not even your boyfriends?'

'No!'

Paula nodded, closing her eyes again. 'Men are such selfish pigs, aren't they? All they think about is their own pleasure. It's very different, you know. When someone else does it, I mean.'

'It is?' Ella was well aware that what she was experiencing here was a lesbian advance. She had heard rumours about Paula, but they had seemed incredible. Ella had no experience of lesbianism. All her preconceptions were based on the biased views of her contemporaries. Lesbians, everyone knew, were butch and hairy women with deep voices who smoked pipes and wore men's clothes. Paula simply did not fit that stereotype. If she had, Ella had no doubt that she would have abruptly ended the conversation and hastily got out of the Jacuzzi. Perhaps it was the fact that she had been so close to orgasm when deprived of it that detained her now and gave her the frisson of excitement she was feeling.

She watched the shadowy outline of Paula's hand beneath the disturbed water as it moved to and fro between her legs, her fingers buried in the black pubic hair. 'Well, if you're doing it, perhaps I will just finish what I started,' she said.

'That's the spirit! Want me to help you?'

The jolt that shot through Ella's vagina at those

words was like a lightning bolt and she came almost as close to orgasm as she had been before. 'Help me?'

'Do it for you. I'm very good at it.'

'No!' That refusal was automatic and too fast. Ella regretted it as soon as the monosyllable had left her lips. What was on offer was sinful, thoroughly wicked and infinitely exciting. 'What if someone comes in?' she temporised.

'No one will. We're the last ones in the building.'

'I'm afraid.'

'Don't be. Nothing bad is going to happen. Here; touch my breast.' Paula supported her left breast clear of the water, the nipple erect.

Tentatively, Ella reached out and stroked the soft flesh. It felt good. 'Why do you have those rings?'

Paula laughed. 'It's a long story. I'll tell you one day. Touch the ring! Go on, pull on it! There! You weren't struck by lightning or anything, were you?'

Ella shook her head.

'There you are then. Now I'll touch yours. That's only fair, isn't it?'

Ella felt Paula's hand under the water caressing her breasts and teasing her nipples. She knew that she ought not to have allowed this familiarity, but it felt so good that she couldn't bring herself to pull away. She felt the hand slide down over her stomach and automatically clamped her thighs together.

'There, there!' Paula soothed. 'It's all right; really it is. Come on, open up for me and I can give you a special treat.'

As in a dream, Ella relaxed her muscles and permitted her legs to drift apart, allowing access for that teasing hand. It went down through her sparse, fair, pubic hair and she gasped as she felt a finger intruding between her labia, opening them like pink petals and rubbing insistently up and down her slit. Paula

13

was behind her now and she could feel the soft breasts and their golden rings pressing against her back. Paula's left hand was around her body and began to tease her left nipple, rolling it between finger and thumb, stretching it at the same time.

Instinctively, Ella threw back her head and rubbed the side of her face against Paula's. 'Yes! Yes!' she breathed. Now the hand between her legs altered its position slightly, coming up to the top of her slit and searching for her clitoris.

'Open your legs really wide,' Paula ordered. 'Now bend your knees.'

Ella obeyed, held in the thrall of pleasure. She felt Paula pushing her forward until she was squeezed close to the wall of the Jacuzzi, which effectively prevented her from closing her legs again, even if she had wished to. Her vagina was gaping open from the effect of her unnaturally strained pose and she jumped as she felt Paula's fingers grope for the hood over her clitoris and retract it so that her long clitoris popped out.

'Down!' Paula insisted, putting her weight on Ella to emphasise the command.

Exactly below Ella, a jet was gushing bubbly hot water. Already she could feel the disturbance on her exposed thighs.

'Further down!'

Suddenly Ella realised what Paula intended to do to her. She was going to force her down to the point at which that rush of water would impinge directly upon her vulva at a much closer range than she had ever been able to bear when alone. Worse than that, Paula was going to continue to hold back the hood of her clitoris so that it was fully exposed. She struggled weakly, but Paula had her in a firm grip and she could not wriggle away.

'No! Please not that!' Ella begged. 'I won't be able to stand it, I know!'

Paula was implacable, her weight irresistible and her grip vice-like. 'Down!'

The sensation of being forced towards the inevitable had a huge erotic effect on Ella. As one hypnotised, her knees bent under the volition of her sex-urge, rather than her will. Suddenly her crotch was level with the jet and the solid wall of water hit her with tremendous force. She felt it expand her gaping vaginal canal and thrust inside, heating her. That was as nothing compared to its effect on her clitoris. A million tiny teeth composed of water and bubbles battered and nibbled at the tender morsel with all the power of heavy-duty hydraulic pumps. She shrieked loudly and came to orgasm at once, her stomach undulating in huge waves. It was like nothing she had ever felt before. Her teeth were chattering in spite of the heat of the water and her knees would not have supported her if Paula had not held her up.

Paula not only supported her, she held her in exactly the same position, so that the jet continued its work.

Every part of Ella's sex was over-sensitised by her previous orgasm and the continuance of this stimulation was unbearable. She writhed helplessly, her face contorted as though in agony. 'No, please! Not again! I can't do it again!'

Paula was remorseless; her grip just as tight. 'Yes, you can!'

'I can't! Really! Oh God! What's happening? Oh! Oh!' The second orgasm was even more violent than the first, the hiatus before it infinitely prolonged so that she hung on the edge of the abyss of pleasure for a long time before plunging down into jerking, wriggling rapture.

Still Paula did not let her go, but held her even more tightly through a third climax that drained her so thoroughly that when Paula did, eventually, relent and release her, she would have drowned if Paula had not dragged her over to the steps so that she could sit on them and recover.

'Well?' Paula said. 'Was I right? Is it different when someone else does it?'

'My God, is it ever!' Ella replied with feeling, still getting her breath back. 'But what about you? You said you wanted to do it and you haven't.'

Paula leaned over and kissed her lightly on the cheek. 'No matter. You can owe me. It'll leave you feeling guilty and I like to have guilty women about the place. Come on; let's get dressed, otherwise we'll find ourselves locked in.'

For some days afterwards, Ella's mind was in a turmoil. There was no doubt that she had enjoyed that interlude in the Jacuzzi far more than any previous sexual experience, and that was worrying. Was that a sign of latent lesbianism? It was a comfort that Paula did not mention it. In fact, nothing about Paula's attitude towards her changed. There were no knowing looks or sly touches. The incident might never have happened. Gradually, the significance of it faded into the background. After all, Paula had not really masturbated her, had she? All she had done was to hold Ella in a position she could easily have adopted herself, had she been brave enough. That didn't really count as lesbianism, did it?

It was almost a week later that the matter was brought again to the front of her mind. When she was a little late for the office, it was Ella's habit to scoop up her mail from the doormat as she went out, then open and read it in the office. That day, one of the items was intriguing. It was a large, brown envelope bearing no stamp and no postmark. She tore it open and pulled out the sheaf of papers it contained. The words on the first sheet were so startling that she let out a little cry of astonishment.

Paula, who was in the office sorting her own mail, looked up. 'What's that? A big bill?'

'No. Listen to this. "Your obvious enjoyment of a Jacuzzi has been noted with interest. We wonder if you would care to make application to join Interplay, a club which can provide even greater pleasure in the company of like-minded friends." Oh, Paula! Do you think that means that someone was watching us? How dreadful!'

'Not dreadful at all,' Paula said, cheerfully. 'I'd say you'd struck pay-dirt, wouldn't you? This must be the mysterious club we've been trying so hard to find out about. What's the address?'

Ella riffled through the pages. 'There isn't one.'

'There must be. How are you supposed to send in the application?'

'I don't know. Wait a minute; here it is. I have to leave it in locker seventeen at Bodytrim and it'll be collected.'

'Crafty! What's the fee?'

Ella searched again and held out the relevant page.

Paula whistled. 'Jeez! Old Flatt will have a fit. Never mind. He won't be able to resist the story.' Mr Flatt was the paper's accountant who scrutinised every penny of expenses, allowing not even the cost of a pub's arrowroot biscuit to go unchecked. His great age and the parchment quality of his skin had led to rumours that his last job had actually been chief accountant to the court of Rameses II and that he had been de-mummified when *The Globe* started up near the beginning of the century.

Ella was staring in horror at the papers. 'Oh, Paula, I can't possibly do this!'

17

'Do what?'

'Fill up this application. Look what they want. I have to write a thesis on the relative pleasures of sexual encounters, as expressed through the media of masturbation, penetration, bondage and spanking.'

'Well?'

'But I can't!'

'You claim to be a writer. Of course you can.'

Ella thought about that. 'I suppose so,' she said, pensively. She blushed a little. 'The first two aren't so bad. I could do them. But the last two? I mean I've never . . . I mean I don't know . . . I mean I could invent something, but I couldn't make them sound authentic.'

'What? Never been tied down or had your bum smacked?'

'No. What do you take me for?'

'Someone who's missed a lot,' Paula said unsympathetically.

Ella looked at her incredulously. 'You mean you have?'

'Sure! At the right time, with the right person, either is delicious.'

Ella pushed the papers at her. 'All right, then. You fill it in.'

Paula smirked. 'Not addressed to me, are they? If you're worried about the thesis and you want to stay on the story, it seems there's only one thing you can do and that's to get some experience.'

'And how do you propose that I do that?'

Paula took her time over replying. She took out a cigarette and lit it, inhaling deeply before allowing the smoke to trickle in a slow stream from between her lips while she stared at Ella from narrowed eyes. 'I could teach you.'

Ella's vagina twitched so violently that it caused

her to wriggle in her seat. Her recollection of the Jacuzzi came rushing back from the cubby-hole where she had thought it safely locked away. She could feel her nipples erecting themselves. 'I don't know,' she said.

'Can you think of someone you trust more?'

That was definitely a point to be considered. Paula already knew more about her than she would care to have spread around the office and Paula had said nothing; not even to her. If she were going to experiment with these perverted practices, she could think of no one more suitable to share in that experimentation. 'Let me look at the rest of the application form,' she said, knowing very well that this was a ploy to delay a decision.

'Oh my! Just look at all these questions: "Who is the most exciting person with whom you have had sex and why? What is the most unusual place in which you have had sex? Does the prospect of being tied up for sex excite you and why? Does the prospect of tying someone else up for sex excite you and why?" It goes on and on like that. I can't answer those. And see here at the bottom, it says, "Only if your thesis and application form are arousing will your application be proceeded with. If it is dull, you will hear no more." '

'Well, we can make it exciting,' Paula said. 'We'll just use a bit of artistic licence.'

'Oh, my God!' Ella exclaimed.

'Oh, come on. A newspaper reporter shouldn't get all het up over a few little fibs.'

'It's not that. I've just seen this bit. "Applications from women must include a signed declaration that their nipples and labia are pierced and ringed." Well, that's it. Mine aren't. We can't tell lies about that.'

'You could make it the truth.'

Ella stared at her, her hands moving subconsciously to protect her breasts. 'You mean ... You mean, have it done?'

'Why not? I did.'

'I don't know. I've never thought about it.' That was a black lie. Ella had thought about it a lot, and even more since she had seen Paula's breasts and been aroused by those pierced nipples. Even now, she could feel her own nipples pressing against the flimsy material of her brassiere as she imagined how such ornamentation would feel. 'Doesn't it hurt?'

Paula shrugged. 'For a couple of days, maybe. It would have to be done by someone who knew what they were about. I could arrange that for you.'

'Yes, but ... but it's not just my nipples, is it? I mean they want rings in ... in another place.'

'Have them done at the same time. I did. It costs less.'

Ella was amazed and a little shocked. 'You've got rings there, too?'

'Well, I'm not going to prove it to you in the office. You'll have to wait until you come round to my place.'

'Your place?'

'So that you can learn enough to write a convincing thesis and answer the questions.'

Ella opened her mouth to speak but Paula held up her hand and silenced her. 'Don't rush into a decision. It's a big step. Take a night or two to think about it. If you decide that it's all too much for you, forget about it. I'll just give the story to someone with a bit more experience; and I don't mean writing experience. I won't think any the less of you if you say you don't want to do it.'

That was sound advice and Ella took it. For a couple of days, she wrestled with herself. She tried hard to be objective and make a decision based solely on the newsworthiness of the story that might be obtained by the sacrifices she would have to make. She didn't fool herself for a second. She knew very well that what was driving her towards acceptance of the idea was her inner sex urge. Ever since she had read the extraordinary letter and even more extraordinary application form, the prospect of bizarre, exciting sex with many unknown partners had dazzled her; blinding her to the obvious pitfalls along the path she was considering.

One thing was crystal clear. She would never be able to write a convincing thesis with her present limited knowledge. She deliberately closed her mind to the possibility of getting Paula to write it for her. Was that artistic integrity, or was it the enticing possibility of being forced into another encounter with Paula; this time a decidedly kinky one?

Two

Ella had not visited Paula's home before. Following the directions she had been given, she found it located in a modern apartment building in a pleasant part of Arton. She parked her tiny car outside and switched off the engine. She did not immediately get out, but spent some time just looking at the front of the building, trying to make up her mind whether she was ready for this. Finally she won an internal argument and shrugged her shoulders. With a last check in the driving mirror to make sure her make-up was to standard, she got out, locked the car and went inside, past the uniformed porter.

Her courage lasted well all the way up in the lift and even took her along the softly carpeted corridor to Paula's door. She had to act quickly then as she felt her resolve disappearing. The huge effort of ringing the bell drained the last ounce of her bravery and she would have run away had she not been afraid of being caught in the act of doing so. Paula opened the door almost at once. She was dressed in a long, dark green satin robe that looked good against her dark skin. There was no reason for Ella to leap to the conclusion that Paula was naked beneath the robe. Nevertheless, she was at once certain that was the case. She gulped nervously and just stood there, staring. Paula had to reach out and physically take her hand to start her moving forward into the flat. She led Ella into the living room.

'Why don't you sit down before you fall down? You look as though you need a drink.' Paula indicated a long, black leather sofa and Ella sank into it gratefully.

'Thank you. I think I do need a drink.'

'A restorative cognac or a drop of Mother's Ruin?'

'What? Oh, I think I'd like a gin and It, please.'

While Paula busied herself at an elaborate glass cocktail cabinet, Ella looked around the room. It was large enough to confirm the impression given by the façade of the building and the uniformed porter. This was not a cheap place to live. The furniture, too, was expensive and tasteful. Still, there was something a little odd about it. It was a while before Ella realised that the style of decoration was plain enough to be almost mannish. The black leather and chrome of the sofa and chairs stood out starkly against the dead white of the deep pile carpet. There were no natural wood colours in the room at all. Even the glass-topped coffee table had chrome supports while the plain grey walls bore two abstract, flat-backed sculptures in stainless steel. There were no feminine frills. This was definitely not a chintzy room, she decided.

Paula came back with two drinks, handed one over and took her seat beside Ella on the sofa. 'Well?' she demanded.

'Well, what?'

'Well, what do you think? We both know why you're here. Still think it's a good idea, or has your nerve gone?'

Ella took a big gulp of her gin. 'No! Well ... I mean, not really. The thing is, I'm a bit out of my depth, I suppose. I've never done anything like this before. I don't know what's going to happen and, to

24

tell the truth, it feels just a bit ridiculous to be here at all. A bit like the little heroine in a Victorian melodrama, if you know what I mean.'

Paula laughed. 'You think I'm going to bind you hand and foot, twirl my black moustache and say, "Aha, me proud beauty! At last I have you in me power!" '

Ella eyed her warily. 'You're not going to do that, are you?'

'No, I'm not. What we are going to do is to sit here quietly and have a few drinks and a gossip, like friends do. When you've relaxed a bit and come down off the ceiling, we might go into the bedroom, if you're ready by then. Once there, we will do our best to please one another and you will have a marvellous time. On the other hand, if, after our gossip, you don't feel ready for the bedroom, then you will just say goodnight and go home. Does that sound reasonable?'

Ella nodded, much reassured to find herself still uncommitted. She finished her drink and accepted another. As Paula had promised, they sat for quite a while, chatting about everything except the reason for her visit. Ella found that relaxed her as much as the gin, and she became aware that her guard was lowering, along with her inhibitions.

Finally, it was Ella who carried the matter forward. 'I feel much better now. Quite ready for the bedroom, in fact.'

Paula put her drink down on the table. 'Good choice! First, though, there's something I need to find out about you and you need to find out about yourself.'

'Oh, what's that?'

'Something I half-felt when we were in the Jacuzzi. Stand up.'

Puzzled, Ella rose to her feet, suddenly aware of the amount of gin she had consumed. Paula stood in front of her staring into her face, then reached forward and took hold of both her wrists, holding them tightly.

'Feel anything?'

'Only you, holding my wrists. Why? What am I supposed to feel?'

'Pull against me! Try to get free!'

Feeling rather foolish, Ella tugged half-heartedly at her wrists. Paula's grip just tightened. Ella tugged again, harder this time, trying to twist her arms up and away. Paula was amazingly strong, she found. However hard she tried, she could not break free. Suddenly, there was a sexual ingredient in being held captive by another woman and Ella detected something deep inside herself that was hoping her struggles would not free her. It was most peculiar.

'Feel anything now?' Paula was still staring intently into her face.

'No!' Ella lied, feeling her face reddening under that close scrutiny.

Paula released her suddenly, stepping back with a faint smile on her face. 'Since you didn't get any pleasure from that, I take it that you don't want to explore any further?'

Ella rubbed her wrists, unwilling to look into that smiling face. 'I wouldn't say that. After all, I've come here to learn, haven't I?'

'Indeed you have. The next step would be for me to tie your hands instead of just holding them. How do you feel about that?'

A sudden jolt of lust hit Ella between the legs and she knew, without understanding, that being tied by Paula was something she wanted very much. Nevertheless, she sought to conceal her feelings. 'All right,

26

if you think I should. But shouldn't we go into the bedroom first?'

'No! You either go in with your hands tied or we don't go in at all.'

There it was again. That pleasurable twitching in Ella's vagina. This time there could be no doubt that it was being brought about by Paula's assertiveness. She was taking charge, commanding and compelling obedience, searching out that submissive element which she had known about, but Ella hadn't. Ella's recollection of the pleasure of being held against the jets of the Jacuzzi suddenly took on a fresh aspect. It occurred to her that it had not been simply the bliss of orgasm which had moved her, but her own surrender to the dominance of a stronger will than her own. That notion, when it came into her mind, was bizarre and freaky, making her a little afraid. For an instant, she contemplated drawing back, then capitulated, drawn onwards by curiosity and sexual arousal. That arousal was compounded by the sight of Paula taking a length of soft, white cord from the pocket of her gown and she struggled to keep her voice normal as she said, 'What do you want me to do?'

'Turn around, put your hands behind you and cross your wrists.'

Ella was glad that she was not obliged to speak as she obeyed, being certain that her voice would have betrayed the powerful emotions that coursed through her as she submitted to this domination, revolving dutifully and adopting the required pose. She felt the cord being passed around her crossed wrists, binding them tightly together. Paula seemed to take a long time over it, wrapping the cord repeatedly, then passing it between the trapped hands several times. Each pass was accompanied by a little tug, as though to affirm the impossibility of escape and those small movements communicated themselves directly to Ella's vagina as tiny, electric shocks. By the time Paula completed the final knot, Ella's pulse-rate had risen considerably and she could feel herself lubricating freely.

Her task completed, Paula walked around in front of Ella and draped herself on the sofa. She picked up her drink and sipped at it casually. 'Now pull at your wrists and try to get free.'

Ella was already well aware of the impossibility of that, but tried, nevertheless, each effort increasing her sexual expectancy.

'Feel anything now?'

Far too embarrassed to reveal her innermost feelings, Ella shook her head, not daring to trust her voice.

'Liar!' Paula said equably. She got up and approached her helpless captive, her eyes fixed on her face. Slowly and deliberately, she reached out and unfastened the top button of Ella's crisp, white blouse. 'Let me know when you start to feel something.'

Ella looked down at the hands which were unfastening the lower buttons, squirming impotently in an effort to reach out and stop this intrusion. When the buttons were all undone, Paula tugged on the blouse to free it from the black skirt so that it hung open, revealing Ella's bare stomach and breasts encased in a light brassière. Almost casually, she hooked the fingers of her right hand into the top edge of one cup and dragged it down. With her left, she reached inside and grasped Ella's soft breast, lifting it up and out so that it protruded obscenely over the top of the material.

'No! Please!' Ella wriggled her body in an attempt to prevent what was happening, but there was nothing she could do to stop the other breast from

28

receiving the same treatment. When Paula returned to the sofa and resumed her seat, Ella stood there, crouching a little in shame, looking down again at the vulgar exposure of her breasts. The fact that her nipples had leapt into erection did nothing to calm her. She looked into the face of her tormentor and, following the direction of her gaze, was well aware that this evidence of sexual excitement had not gone unnoticed.

'Still feel nothing, I suppose?'

Precisely because she did feel a great deal, Ella shook her head again, knowing the transparency of that unspoken lie as she told it. This combination of humiliation and captivity was a powerful cocktail, combining with the gin to produce powerful urges. She knew that at least a part of her reason for lying was to provoke Paula into further degrading actions and that knowledge increased her shame. When she saw Paula get up and come towards her again, the cringing stance Ella adopted was only partially due to apprehension. The violent shocks coursing through her vagina were making her bend a little, something she hoped Paula would mistake for an effort to protect her naked breasts.

'Please don't . . .'

Paula stopped, an amused smile playing around her mouth. 'Please don't what?'

'I . . . I . . .' The images whirling in Ella's head were frightening. Paula could, if she wished, maul her breasts, finger her nipples, lift her skirt and pull her knickers down. There would be nothing she could do to prevent those things. Knowing that was disturbing, but the frightening part was the feeling growing in her she would find such abuse madly stimulating and highly desirable.

It was almost with a sense of anti-climax that she

heard Paula say, as if from far off, 'I think you're ready for the bedroom now.'

'No . . . I don't think . . . Perhaps . . .'

For answer, Paula gave her a hard shove which overbalanced her and sent her tottering in the required direction. For Ella, that shove was a clear signal of dominance which rekindled all her previous excitement. Her nipples were now so rock-hard that they were hurting her. Quite deliberately, she dawdled so as to receive a series of smaller pushes between her shoulder blades, each one reinforcing her mounting lust. The bedroom door was closed and Paula pushed Ella hard against it, laying her weight on her so that her bare breasts were pressed against the cool, painted surface, reminiscent of her entrapment in the Jacuzzi. Once again, Paula's face was close to the side of Ella's own and she could feel her breath, warm and soft, in her ear. Then Paula unlatched the door and Ella fell through, stumbling a few steps into the bedroom.

The room was as stark and mannish in its decoration as the one they had just left. Walls, ceiling and carpet were of a whiteness that hurt the eyes, matching the modern white furniture. Only the coverlet on the huge, brass bedstead was black, making it the focal point of the room, so that Ella's eyes were drawn to it as to a magnet. Ominously, thick, soft, white ropes were coiled at each corner, already fastened to the tubular brass frame of the bed and distinct against the contrasting blackness of the material on which they lay. Ella knew at once what they were for and her fevered imagination provided for her a picture of herself, spread-eagled and naked.

'I am going to unfasten your hands, now. I am releasing your body, but I am not releasing your mind, which belongs to me. You will not speak. You will not move without being told to do so. You will obey all orders without question.'

'Yes.' Packed into that monosyllabic acquiescence were all the powerful emotions pent up in Ella's body; her acknowledgement of and submission to her new-found desire which placed her squarely under the domination of this forceful woman. When she felt the last of the rope coils leave her wrists, she made no attempt to cover her breasts, but stood, like an automaton, her hands dangling loosely at her sides.

'You may start undressing now. Take your blouse off first.'

Ella allowed the unfastened garment to slide down her arms and dropped it on the floor.

'Now your brassière.'

Mechanically, Ella reached behind her and unfastened the clip, allowing her bra to join the blouse on the floor.

'Now your skirt.'

Unbuttoned and unzipped, the black skirt joined the growing pile.

'Now just stand while I look at you.'

There was no doubt in Ella's mind that it was a sex-driven caprice which had caused her to elect to wear black stockings and suspenders instead of tights, for her visit to Paula. Only her knickers were white. The part of her mind which still belonged to her was glad of that as she watched Paula stalk around her in a circle, devouring her semi-nudity with her eyes. Bound by the force of Paula's will, as securely as by ropes, she made no protest, except to utter a short sigh of surprise when Paula, behind her, grasped the material of her knickers in her fist and, gathering it into a thin strand, pulled it viciously upwards so that it jerked against her crotch at the same time as it exposed both cheeks of her bottom. She still did not

31

move when Paula came in front of her again and, hooking her fingers into the waistband of the white knickers, pull it outwards, then leaned forward to gaze down inside. Looking down herself, Ella could see her own fair bush of pubic hair. Somehow, the knowledge that this was what Paula could see, too, was wildly exciting.

Paula released her grip, allowing the knickers to ping back against Ella's bare stomach. 'All right. Lie down on the bed now. On your back. Exactly in the centre, please.'

As though hypnotised, Ella obeyed, first sitting on the bed, then swinging her legs up and squirming over until she was in the mathematical centre, where she lay staring unblinkingly at the ceiling.

'Right arm!'

Without moving her eyes, Ella stretched out her arm towards Paula, feeling the rope being coiled many times around her wrist and secured.

Then Paula was on her left. 'Left arm!'

Ella felt the same process being played out. With the slight jerk of the last knot being secured came an overwhelming sense of security and rightness, as though her time unbound had been some sort of ordeal to be endured before reaching the safe haven of bondage once more. She pulled against the securing cords to test their restraining power before relaxing with a deep sigh, feeling able to look now at Paula, who had taken her seat on the edge of the bed and was regarding her with a knowing smile.

'What are you going to do with me?'

'Anything I damn well choose, wouldn't you say? What would you like me to do with you?'

Ella shook her head, colouring slightly. 'I don't know.' She knew perfectly well what she wanted Paula to do. She very badly wanted to be brought to orgasm as quickly as possible, but was too shy to say so.

'If you don't know why you're here, perhaps I should let you go?'

'No!' The speed of her reply, forced from her by lust, embarrassed Ella greatly, causing her blush to deepen.

'You'd better say what you want, then. Unless you do, you're not going to get it.'

'Must I?'

Paula nodded. 'You must.'

Ella turned her face away in shame, her voice almost a whisper. 'I . . . I'd like you to make me come.'

'You mean you want me to masturbate you?'

'Yes.'

'Say it, then.'

'I'd like you to . . . to masturbate me.'

'But that would involve taking the rest of your clothes off. Do you mean that you want me to strip you naked?'

Ella's voice was even fainter. 'Yes.'

'Say it then. All of it.'

With her hands tied, there was no way Ella could relieve the tensions she was feeling. Her burning desire swept through her deeply frustrated body, raising her voice to a scream. 'I want you to strip me naked and masturbate me until I come! Please! Please, Paula!'

'All right. All right,' Paula said soothingly. 'Shoes first?'

Ella nodded and Paula removed the black, high-heeled shoes one by one.

'Stockings now?'

'Yes please.' The sensation of having her suspenders unclipped and the filmy material of her sheer blacks stockings rolled down her legs was exquisite.

33

'Suspender belt?'

Ella nodded.

'Lift up, then.'

Paula's hands groping underneath her arched back, feeling for the clasp of the belt made Ella shudder. When it was cast aside, she knew that only her knickers stood between her and the complete nakedness she longed for. She looked down between her breasts, anxious not to miss any part of the sensation of this final act of submission. With tantalising slowness, Paula hooked her fingers into the waistband, the backs of them pressing against Ella's bare stomach and making it twitch. Little by little, she tugged at them until the tuft of golden hair was fully revealed, although the panties were still wedged high against Ella's hips at the back. Ella squirmed, raising her body high off the bed in an effort to dislodge them. Finally, her frantic movements succeeded and the white knickers shot down to her thighs and were then drawn completely off. She was completely naked.

'Left leg!'

Ella let out a long, shuddering sigh. So, the ropes at the foot of the bed were going to be used, after all. Paula tugged at her leg, stretching her before securing her ankle.

'Right leg!'

Now Ella's legs were very widely parted, the tendons inside the top part of her thighs strained and prominent as Paula stretched her out like a great white starfish and secured her in that position. If Ella had found excitement in having her hands immobilised, this total restraint was profoundly more moving. She felt Paula's hand on the inside of her thigh, stroking upwards, and knew what was to come. She was more than ready for it. Paula had to do no more than lay the tips of her fingers on Ella's bulging clitoris with a light stroking movement. The instantaneous orgasm that it provoked was both pleasurable and frightening for Ella. She bucked and heaved as far as the ropes allowed and that restraint seemed to amplify everything she felt. It was as though her inability to move freely, to touch and stroke herself, concentrated all her pleasure in her head and her vagina. She screamed and grunted loudly, thrashing her head from side to side before relaxing, panting a little.

Paula was grinning at her. 'But we both know you can do more than one, don't we?'

Ella nodded. 'Are you going to do me again?' she asked, hopefully.

'Not right now.'

'Oh!'

'I mean, what do I get out of it? What's in it for me?'

Ella was puzzled. 'I don't understand. What do you want?'

'Pain!'

'What?'

'It's very simple. I'm a sadist. I enjoy inflicting pain. You give me a little of what I like and I'll give you a little of what you like.'

'I don't know if I'd like that,' Ella said doubtfully.

'I sincerely hope you won't, otherwise there would be no fun in it for me.'

Ella's apprehension was battling with her need for another orgasm. 'What sort of pain and how much?'

'Nipple-pinching. As much as you can stand. No more. But certainly no less. I wouldn't expect you to cheat on me by giving me short measure.'

Ella found one corner of her mouth twitching and puckering and knew it for what it was – sexual tension which desperately longed for easement, at war with her fear of the price which must, inevitably, be paid for that benison. She licked her lips nervously in an effort to conceal her inner emotions, looking down at her bared nipples. They were still stiffly erect and she could feel them throbbing in time with her pulse, standing out from her firm, young breasts like twin monuments to passion. What would it feel like, she wondered, when Paula gripped them between her strong, brown fingers and pinched hard? Her stomach griped as her vagina communicated its wanting readiness to the muscles just beneath the skin and she knew that, come what may, she was going to agree to this bizarre torture. Her need for climax was overriding all sense and reason. She could not bear the thought of being released, of meekly abandoning the intense pleasure she was experiencing from her confinement. With her hands and feet separated and bound, there was no way she could masturbate or even rub her legs together. She was Paula's possession. A sex toy to be abused or pleasured at her captor's whim. With that realisation came wild excitement and another wave of lust.

'Yes, yes! Do it now, pinch me!'

Ella gulped as she watched Paula's hands reach out towards her unprotected nipples. The hands moved with agonising, sadistic slowness, so that Ella was able to feel them on her body long before they actually touched her. When they did so, she gasped with the release of tension. She continued to watch, fascinated, as Paula's fingers and thumbs settled around the brown knobs of flesh, moving a little and shifting to find the best possible grip on them. When the squeezing began, it was a hardly discernible pressure; certainly a pleasure, rather than a pain. The pressure increased to become a definite pinch and Ella grimaced a little at the unfamiliarity of the sensation.

Now Paula's grip was very firm, enabling her to pull upwards, extending the brown skin of Ella's aureolae into volcanic points. The pain rose up in her until she was forced to grunt through gritted teeth at the force of it. Yet, with a part of her mind, Ella noticed that the pleasurable sensation she had first experienced did not diminish, but increased to keep pace with the pain. Paula was not only pinching and pulling, now, but rolling the trapped, abused flesh very slightly between her fingers and thumbs, multiplying the torment enormously.

Ella's teeth were chattering and her breath whistled between them in long sighs. She could feel another orgasm approaching and knew that it was going to be magnificent. Even while part of her mind was screaming, 'Enough! Stop!' she heard her own voice imploring, 'Go on! Don't stop – more – harder! I'm coming ... Oh God, I'm ... coming!' She bucked and wriggled in her bonds, her vagina making vain, empty thrusts at nothing before she flopped and relaxed. Paula had released her grip at the instant of climax and now, deprived of the confusing, masking lust the aftermath of the pinching was making itself evident. Ella moaned softly, not simply because of the ache of returning circulation, but with astonishment at her body's reaction to what ought to have been torture. Paula lowered her head and allowed her lips and tongue to circle each nipple in turn, briefly, then blew on them.

Ella regarded her with adoring, submissive eyes. 'Thank you! Oh, thank you! That was so good. But I don't understand. Why was it so good?'

Paula smiled down at her. 'It was certainly an interesting reaction and more than I could have hoped for. Some people are made that way. You just happen to be one of them. I take it you didn't know that before?'

Ella shook her head wonderingly. 'No, I didn't. Is that bad?'

Paula laughed aloud. 'Certainly not! Not from your point of view or mine. It means that you love taking the things I enjoy giving. It also means that I suspect you are going to enjoy what comes next.'

'Are you going to hurt me again?'

'I promised you something in return for letting me pinch you and I'm going to give it to you. I'll just do it in a slightly different way from the one I planned.' Paula went to the foot of the bed and began to untie Ella's spread ankles.

Ella protested. 'What are you doing? I thought being tied down was part of the fun, for me.'

'If you just shut up for two minutes at a time, you'll see what fun really is,' Paula said equably, and went about her work. She took the cord and passed it around the leg she had freed, just above the knee. Moving up the side of the bed, she rummaged under the bedding until she uncovered the bed frame alongside Ella's right breast, then passed the cord around that too, so as to form a continuous loop, before drawing it tight and knotting it.

Ella found her right knee pulled upwards and outwards so that her legs were spread even more widely than before. When Paula did the same thing on the other side, her victim was secured with knees bent and fixed on either side of her body, her bottom slightly raised by the strain of this new position. Ella watched Paula take a small packet from a bedside drawer and open it. The object she withdrew was like a condom, but smaller than Ella had ever seen.

It was only when Paula fitted it onto her right forefinger and smeared it with clear gel from a tube that Ella divined its purpose. 'It's all right,' she said. 'You don't need that. I didn't mind you touching me without it last time.'

Paula sighed patiently. 'Dear little Ella! So innocent! Last time, I didn't put it where I'm going to put it this time. My fingernails are long. Trust me; you wouldn't like it one little bit if I didn't use this.'

'What do you mean? I don't understand.' Realisation dawned. 'You can't mean ... You're not going to ... Oh God, no, you mustn't! Really, I mean it.' Ella began to struggle and kicked out with the only part of her legs she could move, understanding now why she had been fixed with her bottom raised, but there was nothing she could do to change the way she had been positioned.

Paula took not the slightest notice. She sat down on the edge of the bed alongside Ella's hips and reached across casually with her rubber-tipped finger.

'Please! Please don't, I implore you. I should be so ashamed. I won't like it, I know. Oh!' Ella felt the coldness of the gel touch her bottom between the stretched cheeks and slide upwards. It centred itself on her sphincter and pressed, gently but insistently. 'No, Paula. You mustn't, really! You ... Agh! Ah!' The shock of penetration came as a small pain, instantly submerged in a wave of huge delight as she felt the tip of Paula's finger inside her. It wiggled tantalisingly, sending tremors of lustful bliss into her vagina, from where they stretched electric fingers to her stomach and nipples. Ella puffed out her cheeks in her effort to stay calm under this intense stimulation. 'Ooh! Ooh! Wait a minute. I can't stand it. Don't move it for a moment, for pity's sake. Wait, please wait. I can't ... Oh!'

For Ella, the sensation was incredible. As with the pinching, there had been some pain. The increasing thickness of the finger as it progressed had seen to that. Swamping the discomfort, however, was a far greater sensation; not just sexual arousal, although there was plenty of that. The humiliation of what was being done to her against her will was a large part of what she felt. It emphasised her helpless captivity. She was a sex toy again; Paula's plaything. The finger far inside her was pumping gently now, with wriggling movements which created paroxysms of purest pleasure. Somehow, knowing that Paula was making those movements just to see how much Ella would writhe and moan added enormously to that pleasure. Each tiny twitch set the muscles in Ella's vaginal walls afire, creating sucking waves of contractions. Her thighs were wide apart; the entrance to her love-canal gaping open between the inflamed labia. In spite of that, it seemed to her that she was still not open enough and she tried hard to part her knees even more. She most desperately wanted something; anything to fill that aching void. Briefly, a fantastic vision drifted across her mind in which Paula clenched her fist and drove the whole length of her forearm into that hot, wet, empty space. It felt so open and wanting that even such a huge intrusion would be barely sufficient to damp her fire. That finger was turning her into a bucking, shivering jelly of desire, yet the orgasm she longed for just would not come.

Ella turned unfocused, imploring eyes on her tormentor. 'Please,' she gasped, 'I can't stand it. Finish me, for God's sake.'

'You mean touch you between the legs?' Paula enquired innocently, as though such a thing were a completely novel idea.

'Yes, yes! Oh, please – put your fingers in me and do me now!'

'Oh, I'm not sure I could do that. I could pop your clitoris for you, if you like. It does look a little confined.'

That was an understatement. In spite of her

stretched position, Ella's clitoris was still trapped beneath its protective hood. In her doubled-up position, she could clearly see the rounded hump of pink flesh beneath which it bulged like a tent-pole. 'Yes – please!'

The fingers of Paula's left hand, reaching down between her thighs and lightly brushing her pubic curls were a blessing which provoked a long, shuddering sigh, which rapidly became a sharp gasp as the hood was twitched back, allowing her clitoris to spring to full erection. 'Do it, do it – rub me!'

'No, I'm not going to rub you. I'm enjoying watching you wriggle far too much. I'm going to stroke the tip of it very gently – just enough to drive you crazy and keep you on the edge.'

Ella stared. 'You wouldn't be so cruel.'

'Indeed I would. I love being cruel, remember?' Paula suited actions to words, teasing and exciting with touches so light as to be exquisitely stimulating, yet insufficient to induce orgasm.

Ella felt herself lapsing into hysteria. The plunging, irritating finger in her bottom was still at work, filling her mind with crazy fantasies. She wanted that finger to be thicker and longer, for it to cause her the exquisite stimulus of the pain she longed for. She wished Paula had a free hand so that she could pinch her nipples again. Suddenly, another image rushed into her mind. Paula would lean forward and sink her teeth into her clitoris, biting, gnawing and hurting. That fantasy was just too much for her overburdened sex-drive to endure. With a great shriek, she jerked into an orgasm which lasted longer than any she could remember. Groaning and heaving, she heard her teeth grinding together until she feared they would break. Even when at last it was over, she continued to heave and sob with the effects of its aftermath, utterly drained. When Paula released her, she rolled over and sat up on the edge of the bed, her head bowed and her arms folded over her breasts, rocking to and fro.

Paula stroked her hair fondly. 'It'll take you a while to come down off that high. I'll be in the other room. When you feel ready, get dressed and come to join me.'

When Ella, now fully dressed and a little more composed, went through into the living room, she found Paula sitting once more on the black leather sofa, quite at her ease, with a glass in one hand and a cigarette in the other. At her gesture, Ella seated herself beside her and picked up the drink which had been poured and was sitting on a side table. She sipped cautiously, happy to feel the fiery spirit warming her and restoring some semblance of normality.

Paula surveyed her over the rim of her glass. 'I guess you can do it now, can't you?'

'Sorry. Do what?'

'Fill up the application form. You were required to know how bondage feels. Now you do. What did you think of it?'

Ella blushed. 'It was very . . . strange. I felt things I'd never felt before. Does that mean that there's something odd about me?'

'Goodness no, child! Like I told you, some people are built that way. Just be thankful you found out about it. Some never do and go right through life not knowing what pleasures there are to be had.'

Ella nodded thoughtfully. 'I suppose you're right. I feel a bit guilty, though.'

'For enjoying bizarre sex? No reason to.'

'No . . . Not that. I mean it all seems to have been a bit one-sided. I've enjoyed myself so much and had orgasm after orgasm, but you haven't. I haven't done anything to please you.'

Paula laughed. 'Yes you have! I gave your nipples a good seeing-to and I really enjoyed watching you squirm when my finger was right up –'

'Yes, yes,' Ella interrupted hastily, suddenly overcome with fresh embarrassment at the recollection. 'But I've been with you twice now, and you haven't had a thrill yourself. Shouldn't I do something about that?'

Paula shook her head decisively. 'Not today.' Seeing Ella's obvious disappointment, she added, 'Don't worry. I'm writing it all down in a little notebook and keeping track of what you owe me. One day, when I feel in the mood, I'll collect from you. In the meantime, it pleases me to keep you in suspense and wondering.' She locked eyes with Ella, staring intently. 'You know that you belong to me, now, don't you?'

Ella licked her lips nervously and tried to look away but felt trapped and held by those eyes. 'Yes,' she whispered.

'Then show me!'

'I don't understand.'

'Kneel in front of me. There, on the carpet.'

There it was again, thought Ella. That sharp stab of excitement she had experienced when held and then bound by this woman. She was holding her with her will just as surely as with ropes. She got up and stood in front of Paula before dropping to her knees in the place indicated by the imperiously pointing finger.

'Your body is mine to do with as I please, isn't it?'

'Yes.'

'Any time I beckon, you will come running and do exactly as I tell you to do. Pleasure me in all the ways I can think of, and I can think of many, I promise you.'

'Yes.'

Paula relaxed, releasing Ella from that compelling gaze, and leant back, drawing on her cigarette. 'Very well, you may get up and go home now to think about what has happened here today. The call will come. Think about that too.'

'Yes, Paula.' Meekly, Ella did as she had been ordered, getting up and letting herself out of the flat. All the way down in the lift, she felt herself still to be under the spell of Paula's dominance. Even after she had driven home, the feeling hardly diminished at all. Her life had changed dramatically. Strangely enough, that was not disturbing. To know that the promises she had made on her knees were valid and binding, that she was now a possession; that she would, any time Paula ordered it, become her toy again, was oddly comforting – like belonging to a family: part of a greater whole.

Life in the office went on exactly as before, still with no change in Paula's demeanour towards her. Ella went along with this petty deception, although she was secretly longing for Paula to make some demand upon her. Disappointingly, the only faintly sexy thing Paula did was to take her along to the surgery where she herself had been pierced and ringed, so that Ella could receive the same treatment in sterile, painless safety. In a surprisingly short space of time, these adornments became part of herself so that she hardly noticed them unless she became sexually excited.

Another disappointment was the length of time it was taking Interplay to respond to her application, which she had duly deposited in locker seventeen. She had been able to write about bondage in what she thought was a sufficiently arousing way. With Paula's help, she had concocted a fiction about her enjoyment

44

of spanking and being spanked, although she had experienced neither. Perhaps the biggest disappointment of all was the discovery that self-help methods were only a pale imitation of the pleasure she had found when her bottom had been interfered with by Paula's finger. Her own finger, even in combination with enthusiastic masturbation, did not have nearly the same impact. Neither did any of the slender dildos she invested in particularly for that purpose. It was all most unsatisfactory and she longed for another session with Paula which would enable her to recapture the joy of that particular encounter.

Three

So much time had elapsed since Ella had deposited her application in the locker that the Interplay story had diminished in significance. There was other routine work to be done; no new leads had been forthcoming and there had been no further sexual encounters with Paula which would have served to renew her interest in the subject. Ella put Interplay on her mental back burner and assumed that her application had not been deemed satisfactory. Consequently, it was the last thing on her mind when she went to answer her doorbell late one evening.

She stared without recognition at the tall woman on her threshold. 'Yes?'

'Miss Costello?'

'Yes.'

'I have come in response to your application for membership in Interplay.'

'What? Oh yes.' Now the stranger had all Ella's attention. She judged her to be in her mid-thirties. She was wearing a white raincoat. Her hair was jet-black and arranged in a curiously old-fashioned way, drawn back severely from her face into a large bun. Her very pale face, like the rest of her body, was thin and angular, with high cheekbones. Her mouth provided the only colour, being a thin, unsmiling gash of deepest red.

'Well? When you've seen enough, are you going to

ask me in, or should I stand on the doorstep all night?'

Ella blushed, suddenly aware that she had been staring. 'Sorry. Of course, won't you come in, Mrs ... Miss ...'

'Miss Doyle.'

Ella stood back to allow her visitor to enter. 'May I take your coat?'

'Thank you.' Miss Doyle stopped and placed her executive black briefcase on the floor in the hall before shucking off her raincoat and handing it over.

More cautious, now, about being seen to stare openly, Ella surveyed her out of the corner of her eye as she went to hang up the coat. There was nothing artificial, she decided, about the silk outfit Miss Doyle was wearing. It did, however, seem decidedly old-fashioned. The severity of the black blouse with its high mandarin collar and long sleeves was unrelieved even by the frivolity of buttons. If there were any, they were concealed beneath a layer of the material. The tight, black pencil skirt came well below the knee – almost to mid-calf. The black stockings and black high-heeled, patent-leather shoes made a totally black ensemble from which her white face and hands stood out in stark contrast. It was rather strange. That colour and style ought to have given an impression of drabness. It did not. Instead, it seemed to radiate an atmosphere of sexual danger and appetite. Ella wondered whether that was entirely due to the costume or the rather odd person inside it.

'Won't you go through into the living room?' Ella followed the silk skirt from the hall, observing a smoothness in the material which bespoke either incredibly well-made underwear, or no underwear at all. She moved some magazines from an armchair. 'I'm sorry it's a bit of a mess. I wasn't expecting you.'

'No.'

Miss Doyle took the proffered seat in the armchair, put her briefcase on her lap, opened it and began to sift through the papers inside. Ella hovered uncertainly, wondering how to improve contact with this taciturn person.

'Can I get you a drink, Miss Doyle?'

'No.'

'Oh.' Ella tried again. She held out her hand. 'My name is Ella, but I expect you know that. What do I call you?'

Her visitor settled a pair of steel-rimmed spectacles on her nose and regarded the outstretched hand with distaste. 'You call me Miss Doyle.' Ella noticed that the steely greyness of her eyes outdid the steel of her spectacles. Thoroughly deflated, she took her own place in a chair opposite and waited.

Miss Doyle reached out and handed over a sheaf of paper and a pen. 'Here is the contract you must sign. I have little time to waste so I must ask you to read it quickly. The most relevant parts, you will find, are these. Please pay attention. You must agree to deliver your body and your mind completely and absolutely into my care and custody. You must permit any intrusion into or abuse of your body by partners of my choice, male or female. You will never discuss with anyone who is not a fellow member any detail of what takes place at Interplay or reveal the club's location. Anyone you meet for the first time there must be treated as a total stranger if encountered anywhere else. The contract must be renewed with a fresh signature every time you enter the club, otherwise admission will be refused.'

Ella allowed her eyes to run down the various clauses, a little stunned by the implications of them. 'It's a rather unusual contract.'

'It's a rather unusual club.'

'It means that I would be virtually a slave while I was there.'

'Of course, what else?'

Ella was conscious of conflicting emotions. To sign such a contract would be an act of folly, but the images the conditions of that contract had conjured up in her mind were acting as a powerful aphrodisiac. It would mean, perhaps, a repetition of the intense pleasure she had experienced with Paula, of which she had now been deprived for some considerable time. She knew that if she hesitated longer, she might easily lose her nerve. Quickly, without further thought, she scrawled her signature and handed the papers back.

Miss Doyle took them from her and put them back into her briefcase, closing it with a snap that seemed to Ella to be symbolic of the way she was now entrapped. 'I presume you have been ringed, as was required of you?'

Ella coloured again. 'Oh, yes. I've had that done, thank you.'

'Show me.'

'What? You want me to show you the rings?'

'Naturally. I take nothing on trust.'

Ella tried to prevaricate. 'But I've only just met you. I don't know you. I would be embarrassed.'

'What of it? You have only to lift your sweater and pull down your brassière – if you're wearing one, that is.'

Ella became acutely conscious of her casual evening wear, of the loose-fitting wool garment that covered her otherwise naked top half but, more particularly, of the ripped, comfortable jeans that more closely enwrapped her nether regions. Faintly ridiculous bunny-rabbit slippers completed her ensemble. 'I can show you my top rings.' Her mouth refused to form the necessary syllables to encompass the word 'nipple' while those stern, grey eyes were upon her. 'There are the others, though. You know. Those other ones. I can't be expected to show you those, surely?'

Miss Doyle rose abruptly. 'I told you my time was valuable. There are a great many women on the waiting list who are eager for my visit. I think we can consider your application and contract to be null and void. Please fetch my coat.'

'No, wait!' Ella was in a fever of indecision. She must not let this opportunity pass simply for the sake of a little modesty. After all, what would it cost to lift her sweater and ease her jeans down over her hips just far enough to demonstrate that she had obeyed her instructions? She made up her mind. 'I'll show you.' She grasped the hem of her sweater and raised it so as to expose her breasts with their nipple ring ornaments. 'OK?'

Miss Doyle was still in the doorway. She had not come back into the room. 'Insufficient!'

'I know. It'll just take me a minute to wriggle my jeans down a bit.'

'You misunderstand me. You are now contracted to deliver your body and mind to me. That means that you obey all my orders instantly and without question. In the early stages, some slackness may be present, of course. What you have to understand is that any slight show of reluctance on your part calls for a penalty to be exacted. Had you done as I asked first time, without hesitation, it would have been sufficient for you simply to expose the necessary areas. However, you *did* hesitate. Because of that, it is now necessary that you remove all your clothes.'

Ella blinked. 'You mean you want me to strip right off? All my clothes?'

'Yes. As you so elegantly put it, I want you to strip.

51

That, on this occasion, is the price of disobedience. Later on, you will find that the cost rises considerably.' Miss Doyle looked pointedly at her watch. 'I do have other appointments.'

'Of course. I'm sorry, Miss Doyle.' Much chastened, Ella prepared for her ordeal. The sweater was easy to dispose of and she shucked it off over her head and dropped it on a chair. The jeans were more difficult and she cursed her choice of clothing as she struggled to heave the skin-tight denim down her thighs, very conscious of the fact that Miss Doyle's grey eyes were watching every move. As always, she had to sit down and wave her legs in the air to get the jeans right off and she found being watched while she did that to be particularly humiliating.

'I disapprove of women wearing trousers,' Miss Doyle said sharply. 'Please remember that in future and don't let me see you in such unfeminine garments again.'

'No, Miss Doyle.' Red-faced and a little breathless, Ella stood to remove her skimpy panties, her only remaining garment, then stood naked, awaiting the next trial.

Miss Doyle put down her briefcase and came over to stand close in front of Ella, stooping a little to inspect the gold nipple rings more closely. She glanced up sharply into Ella's face. 'They have been properly closed, I hope. They are not split so that they can be easily removed?'

'No.'

'Rotate them, so that I can see. I take nothing on trust.'

Dutifully, Ella rotated the rings through a full revolution to show that no joins were hidden by the brown, springy flesh of her nipples. The sensation of the cold metal sliding through its pierced pathway provided the same stimulus she had become accustomed to and she was annoyed to find her nipples reacting by erecting themselves.

Miss Doyle stooped lower. 'Now those,' she demanded, pointing. 'Stand with your legs wide apart and pull yourself open with your fingers so that I can see.'

Blushing furiously, Ella complied. She straddled her legs and pushed her pubes forward, pressing with her spread fingers on either side of her outer labia to open herself for inspection.

'Can you see to rotate them, or shall I do it for you?'

'No, please. I can manage.' Hastily, Ella felt for the rings which now ornamented the pink, crinkly lips of her inner labia and rotated them. That was something she usually did only when masturbating, and the association of ideas, added to the strange sensation of being closely observed while she fiddled with them, caused her to lubricate.

Miss Doyle straightened and nodded, apparently satisfied. 'Very well. You will leave your membership fee in locker seventeen. After that has been received, you will hear from me. Now hold out your hands.'

It was on the tip of Ella's tongue to ask why, but she refrained, remembering this woman's reaction to her previous disobedience. She put out both hands. From her briefcase, Miss Doyle took a large steel ring. From it, attached by metal eyes, hung a score of smaller rings, a little too large to be the jeweller's ring-sizers with which Ella was familiar. One after another, Miss Doyle fitted rings onto each of Ella's thumbs until she was satisfied with the fit, jotting down the number stamped onto the appropriate ring.

Ella could not restrain her curiosity. 'Will you tell me what that's for?'

'No. Sit down and hold up your right foot.' Ella obeyed and watched as Miss Doyle went through exactly the same procedure with both her big toes. When she had finished, she put the rings back into her briefcase and closed it. 'You may show me out.'

Ella reached for her discarded clothes, but Miss Doyle stopped her with a gesture. 'No. I don't have time for that. You will remain naked until I have left.'

'Yes, Miss Doyle.' Ella fetched the white raincoat and escorted her guest to the door.

She was about to close it behind her when Miss Doyle turned back. 'You understand that you will receive certain instructions from me?'

Ella hid herself behind the half-closed door, only her head showing. 'I see.'

'It is very rude to stand like that. Open the door properly at once!'

Reluctantly, Ella opened the door wide, very conscious of her naked state and that at any moment some other resident of the flats might appear on the landing. She was also very aware that Miss Doyle was deliberately detaining her at the door so as to increase her embarrassment.

'When you receive those instructions, you will carry them out to the letter.'

Ella was almost jigging now, in her anxiety to end the conversation and close the door. 'Of course.'

Miss Doyle looked at her keenly. 'You're sure you understand?'

'Yes, yes – instructions – I understand completely!'

'Now let me see, was there something else?' For long, long seconds that seemed like hours Ella's tormentor kept her standing naked at the door while she fingered her chin and pretended to be in deep thought. 'No, nothing else.' She turned on her heel and went away down the landing, her steps necessarily short and quick because of the hobbling effect of the pencil skirt, while her high heels clicked on the polished parquet surface.

With a huge sigh of relief, Ella closed the door, forcing herself to do so gently, rather than with the slam she would have preferred. Safely concealed inside again, she leaned her back against the protective wood and thought deeply about what she had just let herself in for. It was several minutes before she realised that her hand had strayed down between her legs. She had been fingering her sex, playing with the gold rings and feeling her wetness. She knew all too well what that meant. She had been excited by her encounter with Miss Doyle and that inner tension would have to be relieved by masturbation. She went into her bedroom and lay down on the bed, sifting through her more recent fantasies in search of the one that would suit the circumstances. It would have to be bondage, she decided. She had once seen a bondage video and been deeply unimpressed. There were too much artificiality in it. The girl involved had been a rotten actress, to start with. Her silicone-pumped breasts had seemed more like hard plastic than human flesh. More importantly, it had been obvious that she could, had she wished, escape easily from the ropes that had been wound carelessly around her body.

With a writer's imagination, Ella had embellished what she had seen with her own improvements. Now she had become the girl in the video. The ropes that bound her were tight and secure. There could be no possibility of escape. Sometimes the person holding her captive was a man, sometimes a woman. This time, she decided, it should be Paula. Paula had tied her down with her knees tucked up, as she had in reality. Paula was masturbating her, teasing the gold rings in her labia, pulling her open and thrusting urgent fingers inside her vagina. Ella inserted her own fingers and manipulated them. With her other hand, she reached out to the bedside drawer and took out her little dildo. She imagined herself helpless. Paula was going to plunge the dildo into her bottom while continuing to masturbate her. She was tied down. There was nothing she could do about it. Ella switched on the dildo and reached around with the buzzing instrument until she could stroke it across her sphincter, shuddering with pleasure as she did so. She pushed on it, delighting in the stretching ache it caused as it penetrated her. She teased herself with it, easing the tip in and out while her masturbatory movements increased in pace and she began to breathe deeply.

She felt herself close to orgasm. She was ready for the final stage of her fantasy. Here it was, now. The bedroom door was opening. A naked man, his massive penis fully erect, was watching what Paula was doing to her and there was no way she could cover herself. He would be able to see everything: the masturbation and the dildo in her bottom. Climax was almost upon her. The man was pushing Paula away from her; Ella knew exactly what he wanted. He was kneeling on the bed beneath her upturned buttocks. He was lunging forward, thrusting his enormous organ, hot and hard, into her anus. Ella pushed the little dildo as far in as it would go and masturbated frantically, grunting with the impact of her peak. The fantasy faded and she relaxed, allowing the plastic instrument to slide out of her, little by little.

She sighed. Masturbation was all very well, but it did not exactly hit the spot. At one time it would have been more satisfactory, but she had developed new tastes and moved on. Doing things to herself was not nearly as moving as having them done to her. Her mind drifted back to Miss Doyle's stimulating visit. Perhaps, at Interplay, she would find true sexual gratification.

Four

In the back of the limousine, between her two silent captors, Ella struggled to keep her wits about her. That was not an easy thing to do with her mind in the turmoil created by her naked, exposed state. The sensation communicated to her body by the cold steel of the handcuffs which trapped her wrists firmly behind her was sending confusing signals to her brain. She knew that she ought to have been terrified and could identify some element of fear within her. Overwhelming that fear, however, was a definite surge of sexual excitement which had begun the moment she put on the handcuffs, thus signalling her surrender to whatever strangers might choose to do with her. The way she had been bundled into the car and then efficiently stripped had caused that excitement to mount as the journey progressed. The blindfold was just as much of a restraint as the handcuffs, and just as much of a stimulation for her sex-drive. Total darkness prevented visual input from interfering with the perverse images which were filling her mind. Her experiences with Paula had taught her only too well about her own nature. To be dominated by another, to be forced to orgasm while being watched, to be shamed, tormented and humiliated were no longer subtly spicy frills to be enjoyed as a pleasurable part of a sexual act. So much did she now crave these things that, without them, it was impossible to achieve full gratification. Part of her mind considered that to be bizarre. Another larger part found it deliciously wicked and she revelled in that wickedness now, moving her bare bottom uneasily against the upholstery, suddenly conscious of a dampness beneath her.

Ella tried to sense whether her guards were male or female. Without the sound of a voice as a clue, she had only the texture of the clothing that brushed her skin on either side to go by and that was not conclusive. She found lewd ideas occurring to her. Surely, her naked vulnerability was a temptation to them, whatever their sex. If they would only interfere with her body, caress her breasts, the feel of their touch would tell her what she wanted to know. In particular, she discovered herself wishing that one of them would push their hand between her thighs. She knew herself to be close to orgasm. She would struggle and protest, but contrive to permit a questing finger to seek out the place that so badly needed touching. She opened her legs a trifle in invitation of assault, but if either of her companions noticed, they did nothing about it.

With a guilty start, she recalled that the primary objective of this ride and all that had gone before was not her own sexual gratification but in order to secure sufficient detail for a newspaper headline. Too late, she tried to work out the route the limousine had taken. She remembered the first few turns but, after that, it was all a blur. Certainly, the journey had gone on for long enough to carry her many miles from her flat, even assuming that the car was travelling as slowly as the smoothness of the ride seemed to indicate. She began to listen for external noises, but there were none that were significant. Left turns seemed to predominate, which made it likely that the route was a circuit designed to prevent her from guessing the distance travelled.

The first sign that they had arrived at their destination was a substantial slowing of the limousine, followed by a very sharp right turn and the crunching of tyres on gravel. From the length of time that passed, she deduced that the road or drive they were now on was a long one. The car stopped; she heard the door on her right open, then the person on her right moved away, pulling on her right arm. Ella understood that she was meant to get out and did so, stumbling awkwardly and needing support on either side. She could feel cold gravel beneath her bare feet and shivered a little in the night breeze, her nipples hardening into erection. Then she was being propelled forward and up a shallow flight of steps which felt like stone. A sudden change in temperature and wooden flooring told her that she was now inside a building and that was confirmed by a totally unexpected burst of laughter and applause.

Oh God – this was awful! Somehow, it had never occurred to her that she would be on public display. From the sound of the voices, Ella could tell that the room she was in was large and that there were many people, male and female, staring at her body. She was shamingly conscious of the fact that absolutely nothing would be hidden from them. Her breasts with their erect nipples and gold rings were necessarily thrust forward. The handcuffs behind her back saw to that and also prevented her from using her hands to cover her pubic area, something she felt an overwhelming urge to do. Instinctively, she bent forward, cowering over her nudity in an attempt to hide it. She was thwarted even in this futile gesture. A hand grasped her hair and forced her head back so that her chin pointed upwards. One of her captors was holding her firmly in that more revealing pose and they were both pushing her forward at the same time. Face aflame, Ella could only go where they thrust her. Stumbling again, she felt carpeted stairs beneath her feet and was propelled up them. A pause while a door opened; another forward movement, then she was abruptly released. She thought she heard the door close again, but could not be sure.

Ella stood irresolute, straining to hear any sound which might indicate that she was not alone. 'Hello! Is anybody there?' Cautiously, she extended one foot a little way, then further, sidling slowly in order to reach a wall or piece of furniture against which she might rub the blindfold and thus remove it.

'Welcome to Interplay.'

The shock of hearing a voice so close in front of her caused Ella to start mightily and give a little shriek of alarm. 'Who's that?'

'You mean you don't recognise my voice?'

'No . . . Wait a minute. Yes, I do. It's Miss Doyle, isn't it? Won't you take off the blindfold, please?'

'All in good time, if you behave. First I have to know that you have remembered the terms of your contract.'

'I have.'

'Kneel down.'

'What?'

Ella felt harsh fingers on her left arm, followed almost immediately by a stinging pain on the back of one calf. She yelped and jumped, only to be rewarded by another stroke on the other calf. She danced around in a circle, quite unable to defend herself and careless of what parts of herself she must be revealing by these undignified movements. She was having the backs of her legs smacked, something that was done to naughty children. That hadn't happened to her for more years than she could remember. It was humiliating but, at the same time, strangely arousing.

The beating stopped as suddenly as it had begun and the grip on her arm disappeared. Without waiting to be told again, Ella fell clumsily to her knees.

'That's better. Now I can take off your blindfold.'

After such a prolonged period in total darkness, the sudden burst of light was too much for Ella's eyes, causing her to squint and blink for a while until they became accustomed to it and she was able to look around her. She was in a panelled room which appeared to be some kind of office, to judge by the large desk which seemed at first to loom over everything else. Even the desk faded into insignificance when Ella focused on Miss Doyle. From her high collar to the heels of her boots, she was clad in a tight, sprayed-on garment which seemed to be made of thin patent leather or shiny plastic. It was cut away in a heart-shape at the groin so as to reveal a light fluff of black pubic hair and several inches of bare stomach above. In one black-gloved hand she held a tawse, a short leather strap divided at the end into three separate strands.

'You must remember, Ella, that hesitation or disobedience brings instant punishment. Last time, it was sufficient that you stripped. This time, you were already naked, so the punishment had to be different. Do you understand?'

'Yes.'

'Yes, Miss Doyle.'

Ella gulped. 'Yes, Miss Doyle.'

Miss Doyle smacked the tawse into the palm of her other hand. 'I'm glad we understand one another. It would be a pity if I had to go beyond the mild reminder I have just given. Think what it would feel like if laid across your pretty little pink bottom.'

Ella did think, and shivered.

'Or your breasts, perhaps? There are other places, too.'

'Other places?'

Miss Doyle smiled, but there was nothing comforting in that grimace. 'I see you don't understand. Open your legs. Wider. Wider still! Now do you understand?'

Ella paled, already feeling, in her imagination, the sting of that strap on her tender vulva. She swallowed and nodded. 'I understand, but please don't, Miss Doyle. Not there, I beg you.'

'Complete obedience, then?'

'Yes, Oh, yes!'

To Ella's intense relief, Miss Doyle put the tawse down on the desk. Coming back with a key, she reached behind Ella and unlocked the handcuffs. 'Get up!'

Thankfully, Ella rose, rubbing her wrists in an effort to restore the circulation which had been for so long slowed.

'Come over to the desk and sign the copy of your contract.'

As Ella complied, she was very aware that her stooped posture offered the tawse ready access to her bare backside, but Miss Doyle made no move to pick it up and the moment passed. Ella was puzzled to find that she did not know whether to be glad or sorry about that.

Miss Doyle settled herself into a chair behind the desk and gestured towards another chair in front of it. 'Sit down.' Ella sat and Miss Doyle went on, 'I will explain to you what happens here at Interplay. As the name implies, it is a club for sexual activities between consenting adults. These games call for dominant and submissive partners. Some people have a predilection for one or the other. Others feel in a dominant mood

62

one day and in a submissive mood the next. I try to cater for all tastes, but I am also fair. It would be unfair if someone overwhelmingly dominant were to be allowed that privilege all the time. Consequently, like it or not, they have to take their turn as a submissive. I keep a mental note of what goes on and my decision in the matter is final. Because you are new, your role will, at first, be submissive. Sooner or later, like it or not, you will have to act the part of a dominant partner. Everyone does what I tell them because, otherwise, they are excluded. No one, yet, has volunteered for exclusion.'

Ella nodded, many things now becoming clearer.

'Discretion and confidentiality are essential, which is why you were brought here blindfolded. You will go home the same way. You will not get to know the location of the club until I think you can be trusted. You will always be referred to simply as "Ella". You will never reveal your surname, nor will you make any effort to discover that of another member. All wear masks. This is yours.' Miss Doyle opened a drawer and took out a silver object, handing it across the desk to Ella who took it in her hands and examined it.

It was made of some light material which was not metal, but felt rather like it, except that it was more flexible. It was obviously intended to conceal the top part of her face and head completely, designed to be secured with an elastic strap, as her blindfold had been. It rather resembled Venetian masks Ella had seen and was not unattractive. She was unable to make up her mind if its appearance or its intended use was the source of the erotic stimulation she felt when handling it. She slipped the elastic over her head and settled the mask into place. It felt comfortable and in no way obstructed her vision.

'Good!' Miss Doyle took something else from the drawer and came around the desk. 'You will never remove your mask while in the company of other members and, of course, you will never attempt to remove theirs. Now hold out your hands and spread your fingers.'

Ella did so and Miss Doyle placed an object around the thumb of one hand. It was a broad, silver ring, hinged in the middle like half of a pair of miniature handcuffs. Ella understood at last why her thumbs had been so carefully sized. When Miss Doyle clicked it shut, the tiny thumb-manacle gripped her so closely that it would be impossible for it to be slid off, yet not so closely that there was any hint of interruption to circulation. While Miss Doyle busied herself with the other thumb, Ella examined the ring that was already in place. It seemed likely that the spring-lock could be released only by the insertion of a tiny, shaped key into a small hole. Where there would normally be a stone or a set of initials, there was a small, silver ring.

Miss Doyle was kneeling now, placing similar rings around both Ella's big toes. When she had finished, she got up, dusting her hands. 'I'll tell you what they're for to save you the need to ask,' she said. 'Members wear these when it is their night to be a submissive. They serve two purposes: they identify the wearer as being available as a submissive partner and they serve as restraints. Ah! I see you looking doubtful. Trust me; great clumsy cuffs and leather straps are not only inelegant, but quite unnecessary. You'll find these little things quite adequate for their purpose.'

Ella's mind raced. There were a great many implications in Miss Doyle's last statement that needed to be absorbed. The rings were the mark of someone destined to be submissive that night! They had been put on her which meant . . . She experienced a sudden rush of excited anticipation. The diminutive decorations on her thumbs and toes would be used to restrain her from free movement of arms and legs, making her naked body available to anyone who cared to use it. Her excitement was definitely sexual in nature now and she moved uneasily in her chair, feeling herself lubricating just as she had in the limousine.

Miss Doyle smiled slightly and Ella blushed. Were her feelings so apparent? She watched Miss Doyle move away to her desk drawer again, observing the extraordinarily erotic effect of her slender buttocks and thighs encased in shiny black. When she came back, she was carrying something very small between finger and thumb. She knelt in front of Ella's chair and held up the object for inspection. It was a tiny gold padlock, most perfectly fashioned, like a piece of jewellery or a locket.

'Open your legs.'

Ella obeyed instantly, fearing to do otherwise. She was unable to restrain her curiosity. 'What's that for?'

'To keep you safe. Open your legs wider.'

Miss Doyle reached forward and Ella suddenly realised the purpose of the padlock. She tensed, gripping the arms of the chair tightly and gasped as she felt gloved fingers rasping against her inner thighs and then groping in her pubic hair. She could not resist looking down her own body, in time to see Miss Doyle grasp each of her labial rings between fingers and thumbs and pull on them, stretching them apart. This so closely resembled her own actions when masturbating that Ella could not resist twitching violently, her body jumping with the contractions of her gluteal muscles on the seat.

'Keep still!'

Fascinated, Ella saw Miss Doyle pass the hasp of the tiny padlock through both rings, then click it shut. It was quite unnecessary to tug on the lock and twist it in order to verify its security, but Miss Doyle did so just the same, causing more twitching and jumping.

Miss Doyle got up from her kneeling position. 'All right. You can close your legs again now.'

Ella did so, feeling the strangeness of the ornament against her warm sex. 'Why have you done that?'

'I told you. To keep you safe. Now your sex is my possession. I have the only key. You will not be able to take anything inside you until I decide that it is time for you to be penetrated. When I make that decision, I will also decide to whom I shall give the key. That makes you a rather attractive gift, don't you think? Have you ever been given away as a present before?'

Ella shook her head, quite unable to speak because of the pent-up forces inside her. She had been hoping that Interplay would appeal to her newly found liking for submissive sex. This was beyond all her dreams. The mental processes involved in knowing, beforehand, what was in store for her, were a new experience and exciting in the extreme. In a sudden flash of comprehension, she understood that Miss Doyle knew very well what she was thinking and feeling and had acted deliberately to maximise the erotic stimuli that were now inflaming her.

'Get up and come over here.' Miss Doyle turned away and walked across the room without a backward glance, knowing that Ella would follow. Ella knew it too, and dutifully rose. Miss Doyle led the way to a padded leather bench against one wall and pulled it out, revealing that it was on large castors. It was only about four feet long and, at one end, it was tilted up to form a support for head and shoulders. Against the black of the leather headrest, a short, slender chain and miniature padlock glinted with the gleam of silver. Ella instantly divined the purpose of that chain and shivered, in spite of herself.

'Sit here.' Miss Doyle patted the lower end of the bench, which was at about hip-height.

'Lie back.'

Ella allowed her body to relax backwards until her head and shoulders rested on the headpad, her body in a backwards arch as her lower half draped, unsupported.

'Put your hands above your head.' Ella had been anticipating and, in a perverse way, looking forward to that order. She reached back with her hands, stretching and lifting her breasts in order to do so. Without needing to see, she knew that Miss Doyle had passed the padlock through the small rings on her thumb-manacles and that her hands were now fixed to the top of the bench. Miss Doyle went to the foot of the bench and fiddled with something there. Ella had been expecting that her feet would now be secured, but Miss Doyle evidently had other ideas.

'Lift your knees up.' As Ella obeyed, Miss Doyle extended a metal tube upwards and outwards from alongside Ella's hips. At the top of the tube was a padded, U-shaped bracket. Miss Doyle pulled Ella's raised right knee outwards, settled it in the bracket, adjusted it for height, then inserted a pin into one of the holes in the tube to keep it in place. She pulled Ella's foot down, passed a short chain around the tube and padlocked the ends of it to her big toe. When Miss Doyle went around and did the same thing with the other leg, Ella found that she was locked in a position usually adopted only on a gynaecologist's couch. Her thighs were stretched wide apart, supported by her knees in the brackets. However much she wriggled and struggled, she would be unable to kick or to get her knees out of the brackets. The device was cunningly designed, she realised, both for efficient restraint and maximum exposure. She found shame in the fact that Miss Doyle was now standing beside her, looking down at her. Ella blushed, realising what the woman must be able to see.

'Oh my! You are even more beautiful than I thought. I'm almost tempted to keep you all to myself. I mustn't be greedy, though. There are the others to think about. Perhaps I could allow myself one kiss, though.' Miss Doyle stooped over Ella, slowly bringing her face nearer and nearer. For a split second, Ella thought of turning her head away, but didn't. She tried to tell herself that her compliance was because of her fear of punishment, but recognised that as a lie. It occurred to her that she had never been kissed by a woman. Paula had never done that and she was intensely curious to see what it would be like. That kiss, from Miss Doyle's thin lips, was quite unlike a man's. It was warm and sweet. In contrast to the dominant costume, it supplicated, rather than demanded. Just the tiniest flicker of tongue hinted at the sexual content of it, yet it set Ella's body in an even greater ferment. Suddenly, she wanted to be touched. She wanted those leather gloves to feel her all over, to maul and pinch her breasts, to delve between her parted thighs and explore her sex. She sighed deeply and tensed, before relaxing, her juices making her warm and wet.

Miss Doyle stood up abruptly, breaking contact as though by a mighty effort of will. 'Time to go,' she said.

'Go? Go where? What are you doing?'

Miss Doyle had gone to the head of the bench and begun to push it towards the door. 'It's time to meet the other members.'

Ella began to struggle. 'No, please! I didn't realise you were going to take me out of the room like this. Not where other people can see me.'

Her words had as little effect as her struggles. What Miss Doyle had claimed for the efficiency of the little rings was true. Ella was as firmly held as by the thickest cuffs. As for her tormentor, she took not the slightest notice of Ella's protests as she wheeled her along a short landing to a large lift. During their short journey to the ground floor, Ella continued to beg and plead to be taken back to the office, or at least covered in some way.

The lift stopped and Miss Doyle paused before opening the door, her finger to her lips. 'Time to stop talking now. I want you to make a good impression. Are you going to be good, or do I have to take my tawse to you again?'

Ella realised the inevitability of what was to come. She nodded, resigned. 'I'll be good.'

'Excellent. Let's go and meet your new friends.'

The lift doors opened directly onto a very large, panelled room. As Ella was wheeled out, she gazed anxiously down between her raised and parted knees to see what was ahead. The room seemed to be filled with people. To her fevered eyes, they seemed to number hundreds but there were, as she discovered later, only about thirty. They were of both sexes, about equally divided. That was easy to see because, apart from the masks they all wore, they were completely naked. The same sort of noise of laughter and applause that had greeted Ella on her arrival arose again. They came forward and crowded around as the bench was pushed towards the centre of the room. Ella's face was redder than it had ever been with the shame of being stared at so closely and by so many. They would be able clearly to see her pierced and ringed labia, now joined by the little gold padlock nestling against the pink petals in their secret nest of golden hair between her strained thighs. They would know the significance of that lock which barred the way into her sex. They would understand that she was now an owned object, no longer a person, but a sex-machine, a possession to be given away at Miss Doyle's whim. That was humiliating and hard to bear. Now the crowd was pressing closer to the bench and Ella became acutely aware that her head was at the level of their groins. In spite of herself, she was fascinated by the sight of so much variety in the pubic hair of the women. None of them made any attempt to conceal that part of themselves and exhibited a complexity of colour, shape and quantity that was quite bewildering. One or two had none at all and Ella caught herself wondering if their pubic shave had been voluntary or enforced.

The penises of the men were just as varied and Ella found her eyes drawn to them, one after the other, particularly when they were so close that she could have touched them, had her hands been free. In different states of erection, long and thin, short and fat, circumcised and uncircumcised – the choice seemed infinite. The sight of so many at once was doing things to Ella. Her nipples were rock-hard, her clitoris was bulging and her vagina seemed to have a mind of its own. She closed her eyes in order to reduce the sensory input that was raising her temperature.

Her eyes opened with a jerk the instant she felt hands on her body. No longer content with looking, the crowd around her touched, felt and stroked. So many people, so many hands. Hands that knew exactly where to go and what to do in order to excite her. Ella tried to maximise the sensation by watching what was happening as well as feeling it, but there were just too many hands. No sooner did she concentrate on what was being done to her nipples than the tickling sensation on the soft skin of her inner thighs demanded that she transfer her gaze there. Suddenly she tensed, clenching the muscles of her bottom. Someone she could not see was at the foot of the bench. He or she was running their finger up and down the open cleft between her buttocks, brushing the fine hairs there and sliding to and fro across her exposed sphincter. The finger paused and she waited, her mind forming a soundless scream: 'Yes, go on, do it! Push! Please push!' Infuriatingly, the finger moved on, continuing its brushing motion.

At that moment, Ella's attention was diverted to a new sensation in her nipples. To judge by her body, the woman who now held her nipple-rings would not see forty again. She was a little overweight, with cellulite dimples on her thighs and buttocks. Her breasts were large, white and pendulous. She pulled and twisted, elongating the brown nipples.

Ella gasped and grimaced, moving uneasily. 'Please, not so hard. That hurts.'

The woman's answering grin was disturbing. Instead of lessening the strain, she increased it, at the same time twisting even more. She laughed. 'You enjoy it really.'

Ella looked down again at her nipples. The brown flesh was not only stretched, now, but twisted into a corkscrew shape. She struggled to bring her hands down to protect herself, but they were firmly locked by the thumbs to the little chain. She drew in her breath, sharply, between clenched teeth. If only that finger near her bottom would plunge into her, that might convert pain to pleasure, something she was used to which would enable her to endure what was being done to her top half.

'Now, now, Belle! We all know your tastes. You must wait until I give her to you before you do that. You know the rules.'

Belle released the rings and stepped back at once. 'Sorry, Miss Doyle. I thought she'd like it.'

'I know what you thought, Belle. Well, maybe you'll be the lucky one tonight, who knows?'

Another voice chipped in. 'Come on, Miss Doyle. Tell us who you're going to give her key to.'

Miss Doyle looked around at the sea of faces. 'Is that what you all want? Have you done enough looking and feeling?'

There was a loud murmur of approval and Miss Doyle gave in. 'Very well. I'll take her to the playroom.'

Ella found herself being propelled across the room towards a door on the far side. She twisted her head to look up at Miss Doyle behind her head. 'Where are we going now?'

'To the playroom.'

'But you haven't decided. I mean I don't know who it's going to be.'

'Nor will you, for a while. You'll wait in the playroom while I make my decision. It's by way of being a surprise for you. You won't know whose present you are until they come to you.'

There it was again. That element of the unknown that enabled her to build whatever fantasy she liked around that undeclared core. It was frightening, but intensely arousing at the same time.

'What will they do to me?'

'With you fixed like that, just about anything that takes their fancy, I should think.'

Ella shivered. 'It won't be Belle, will it? Please tell me you won't give me to Belle?'

Miss Doyle pretended to think hard. 'Let me see. Belle? Yes, I would say that Belle is definitely on the short list for consideration.'

'Oh God, no!'

They passed through the door into a smaller room. Miss Doyle pushed Ella into the centre of the room, then left, closing the door behind her without so much as a backward glance. Ella tried to calm her beating heart and looked around her. The room was panelled, as were the others she had seen. The furniture and decorations did not make for quiet thoughts. On boards and racks around the room, there were instruments of torment and restraint. Handcuffs, leg-irons, whips, straps and canes. Elsewhere, there were large upright chairs, a broad, scrubbed table and, incongruously enough, a vaulting horse. The seeming innocence of these items was belied by the presence of straps and buckles attached to places which made it clear that they were for the purpose of securing a human body in place. Her body! Those things, with the more obvious pillory and stocks, set Ella's heart racing all over again as she pictured herself as the defenceless victim.

If Ella thought that her heart could go no faster, she found out that she was wrong when she heard the door open. It was behind her head and, strain as she might, she could not twist around far enough to get a look at whoever was entering. Was it Belle? When a figure appeared beside the bench and she could see that it was a man, her relief was so great that she forgot her predicament to such an extent as to heave a great sigh of relief and flash him a beaming smile.

He smiled back. 'Hello, Ella. I'm Ralph.'

It was difficult to guess people's ages when part of

their face was masked, Ella decided. From what she could see, he must be in his thirties. Maybe even older, judging by a scattering of grey hairs among the darker ones on his chest. His build was sturdy, solid and muscular, fully matching the rampant erection of his penis, which jutted fiercely from his groin above the dangling testicles. Ella found herself lubricating fiercely, imagining what it would feel like to have that magnificent instrument rammed into her bottom. She flushed, suddenly aware that the direction of her gaze must be apparent.

'Hello, Ralph. Sorry I can't shake hands.'

He smiled again, but there was something odd about his manner. A sudden flash of intuition swept over Ella. The man was embarrassed! Here she was, naked, exposed and tied down. It was she who was supposed to feel embarrassed, not he. A little of her nervousness left her and she smiled back.

He rubbed his hand through the brown hair at the back of his head, the only part of it not covered by his mask. 'Look,' he said abruptly, 'this really isn't my thing at all.'

'I don't understand. Do you mean you don't want me?'

'Christ, no, don't think that. I've wanted you ever since you arrived and I first saw you.' He gestured downwards towards his erection, still as full and stiff as before. 'You caused that then, and it hasn't gone away for a second since. No, I mean you being tied down and all. It's not the way I like to do it, but Miss Doyle only gave me one key for . . .' he jerked his head sideways, not looking down her body '. . . for . . . you know.'

Ella giggled. 'You mean for my pussy padlock.'

He laughed, his tension easing a little. 'Yes. For that. I'd rather you were free to move about and . . .

you know . . . sort of say "No" if you didn't fancy me.'

'We'll just have to make the best of it, then,' she said.

'I'm not sure what you mean.'

Ella was not voluntarily going to give up the pleasure she knew she would find in submitting to the will of another while tied down and helpless. Saying, in so many words, that she was in a highly lubricated state of sexual expectancy and agitation, desperately needing that delicious-looking penis of his, would spoil the illusion. She attacked the problem boldly, head on. 'Well, I'm stuck like this and there's nothing you or I can do about it. After all, I've been given to you as a present. Are you going to open it, or are you going to take it back and ask for an exchange?'

'You mean . . .'

'I don't mean anything,' Ella said decisively, 'except that here I am and there you are and you have to make up your mind what you're going to do about it.'

It did not take Ralph long to make up his mind. He moved around to the foot of the bench and stood between her parted thighs. Ella threw back her head and gasped as she felt his fingers on her padlock, then there was the tiniest click as he removed it and laid it carefully on the bench alongside her. He leant forward and she gasped again as his lips brushed her flat, white stomach. She felt the warm skin at his waist on the inner surfaces of her thighs and wriggled impatiently, trying to bring them together to clamp his body between them. The fact that she was quite unable to do so was irritating and, at the same time, an exciting reminder of her helplessness.

'You are gorgeous. Good enough to eat. God, how I want you.' His kisses moved downwards and he nuzzled at her pubic hair for a moment before moving even lower. The tip of his tongue probed at her clitoris, pushing back the hood to expose the sensitive morsel within. That drove Ella to arch her back, thrusting up her breasts as though to receive invisible caresses, while her bottom bumped wildly on the black leather. His kisses travelled back up her body to her breasts, while his hands and arms came through her parted legs to rest on the bench alongside her waist. He licked the tips of her nipples, then took each gold ring in turn between his teeth and tugged very gently. Ella could feel the tip of his engorged organ between her bottom cheeks. She tried to open them even further, delighting in the feel of the hot, hard flesh passing across her sphincter. She longed for anal sex, that trapped, helpless, delicious sex she had experienced with Paula's probing finger. This would be different. His penis was so large that she would be severely stretched and hurt. Her teeth chattered with sexual tension and she waited breathlessly for his first, penetrating thrust into her bottom.

He put his hand down between her legs and grasped his penis, guiding the tip of it so that it wiped hard all the way up her vaginal cleft between the labia. His lips tantalised her nipples again as the underside of his penis sawed back and forth across her clitoris. Hot liquid spurted from the inner recesses of Ella's vagina, bathing the entrance with slippery readiness. She forgot for a moment about her anal fantasies. Now she knew very well where that penis truly belonged and it was all she could do to prevent herself from screaming aloud, 'Do it now – ram it up inside me!'

That deep need seemed to communicate itself to Ralph, or perhaps he could not wait any longer either. His hand went down again and he steadied his penis, dragging it down hard across her over-sensitive clitoris. That was the final straw. Ella had been itching for an orgasm all evening and this stimulation was too much to bear. Her head shot back, her teeth grinding, as she bucked into splendid, writhing climax, groaning loudly with the force of it. Before she could recover, he was in her, the tip of his penis forcing its way up past that most sensitive of internal places just inside her pubic bone. She moved with him as much as she was able, sucking greedily at his massive erection with her strong, young vaginal muscles, massaging him up and down in just the same way as his body massaged her. Ella had never been loud in her climaxes, but then she had never experienced such a glorious fusion as this one was proving to be. She screamed and groaned, open-mouthed, as she tugged madly at her thumb-manacles and kicked with her legs to reassure herself that there was no escape. She was trapped, upended, naked and open. There was nothing she could do to prevent this man from forcing his penis repeatedly into her gaping, wet vagina or from mauling her breasts with his strong hands. She had been captured and packaged as a gift, just for his sexual gratification. He was taking that gift, slaking his lust with urgent thrusting and there was nothing she could do about it. He was abusing her body, driving her mad, making her come against her will.

Her screams became one long, agonised wail as she surrendered to a second orgasm, her thighs and stomach twitching out of control as her peak bit and gripped at her brain and entrails. She felt his penis begin pumping spasms, then he suddenly withdrew from her with a force that made her cry out anew. The underside of his penis rasped again and again across her raw clitoris as he worked himself to climax against her pubic hair. With a loud groan, he shot his sperm far up her body and she felt the heat of it spattering on her breasts and even on her face. Instinctively, she jerked her head aside, then straightened it again, opening her mouth eagerly just in time to receive a few drops of his second mighty spasm. She drew them into her mouth, savouring the salty flavour, then extended her tongue as far as it would go in an effort to collect that which had missed her mouth and was decorating her cheek.

She opened her eyes to see him still between her legs. 'Come here!' she whispered urgently. 'I want to taste you.'

He moved up to stand alongside her head and she strained sideways until she could take the tip of his penis in her mouth, sucking hard to extract the last dregs from him. She thought she could taste herself on him, too, redolent of all that had gone before and that was very, very good. Perhaps there was one tiny tinge of regret in the midst of her satisfaction. She had still not experienced what she was certain would be the joy of anal penetration. Well, no matter. In this house, surely it was only a matter of time before that happened. She would just have to be patient.

Five

Ella had a problem. Her experiences at Interplay had been very much to her taste. She knew now, and accepted, that she was hooked on submissive sex. What Paula had taught her about herself had been only the tip of a very large iceberg, she discovered. She understood only too well why the members of Interplay were willing to pay well for the privilege, to remain loyal to their contractual agreements on confidentiality and to suffer any indignity in preference to dismissal from the club. Perhaps that caused them no problems. Ella's situation was a little different. The only reason she had contemplated joining in the first place was in order to secure a story for Paula and *The Globe* and she owed a debt of loyalty to the newspaper that provided her livelihood. Tugging against that loyalty was the knowledge that the moment she fulfilled her obligation to publish a piece about Interplay, her membership must cease and never be renewed. Probably, the club would be unable to survive after being publicly exposed for what it was. There would be no more exciting, bizarre possibilities to be explored. She would never find out just how many more stimulating sexual pleasures were available to her.

For the time being, she could ease her conscience by remembering that she had nothing concrete to go on yet. She did not even know the location of the club. She knew Miss Doyle's name and face, but nothing else about her. The name might not be her real one. As for the activities and other members, she had no photographs; just some first names without faces. It would be her unsupported word. Just in case, though, it would be better not to tell Paula absolutely everything that had happened to her. Plenty of time for that after she had made a lot more visits. Ella almost convinced herself that those visits were simply in order to gather more evidence and to worm her way further into Miss Doyle's confidence.

Thus it was that she introduced the subject to Paula next day at the office in a most casual and off-hand way. 'By the way, I went to that club last night.'

Paula put down the copy she was reading and stared. She came over to stand beside Ella at her keyboard. 'Do you mean Interplay? I thought they hadn't accepted you and the story had blown out.'

'Mm. So did I, but then they called for me last night.'

'Wow! So tell me all about it. Where is this place?'

'I don't know that yet. They asked me to wear a blindfold on the way there and back.'

'Kinky! Well? I'm all agog. What goes on there? Names? Details?'

'Well, it was all a bit tame, really. Just a lot of people walking about with no clothes on.'

'Recognise any of them? The mayor? Our local MP? Anyone really juicy?'

'I can't even tell you that. We all had to wear masks. Never mind. I expect it'll warm up a bit if I keep going.'

'Not much point if it's as dull as you say.'

'Oh, no,' Ella said a shade too quickly, as she realised that she had been a trifle too laid-back and casual. 'I'm sure there were things going on that I wasn't allowed to see on my first visit. I really think it's worth sticking at it for a while.'

'When are you going again?'

'I don't know. It doesn't work like that. They tell me when I'm to go, not the other way round.'

Paula stared at her thoughtfully. 'Hmm. You may be right. Perhaps you'd better stay with it for a while longer and see what develops. Keep me posted.'

'Oh, yes,' Ella lied. 'As soon as anything important happens, I'll tell you about it.'

Her next trip to Interplay was not nearly as traumatic or exciting as her first. She was not handcuffed, neither was she naked, although there was the same obligation to be blindfolded before she was collected. She chose to wear a sweatshirt and a loose, short skirt, reasoning that these would be easy to shuck off when the time came, as she was sure it would. This time, there was only one person to guide her and the blindfold was removed as soon as she was inside the house so that she was able to mount the stairs to Miss Doyle's office unaided.

Miss Doyle was sitting at her desk, studying a sheaf of papers. She was dressed in the same outfit she had worn for Ella's last visit. She looked up as Ella came into the room, tapped her papers into order and put them down, nodding a greeting. 'Put your clothes on that chair by the wall, then come and sit down here.'

Ella went over to the chair and stripped quickly. She had been right in her assessment of what to wear. It was interesting, she thought, to notice what happened to her outlook as she undressed. She wore only two garments, but they might as well have been a heavy suit of armour which protected her from the world. Wearing them, she had felt confident of her ability to deal with any situation that cropped up.

Without them, that confidence drained away, to be replaced by timid uncertainty. Shyly, with her hands shielding her pubic hair and breasts, she came to the desk and sat down in the chair in front of it.

Miss Doyle held up the tiny silver rings. 'You know what these mean?'

Ella felt her vagina twinge. 'I am to be a submissive again tonight.'

'Yes. Except that this time you have a fuller understanding of what that means. What did you think of your last visit?'

Ella's vagina jumped again and she felt her nipples begin to harden. She didn't know what she was expected to say. 'I didn't mind it,' she hazarded finally.

Miss Doyle tilted her head to one side and stared so hard that Ella blushed, wondering if the woman could read the images coursing through her mind. The silence continued as Miss Doyle came around the desk and fitted the rings to her thumbs and toes as before.

'I really don't know what to make of you, Ella,' Miss Doyle said at last. She got up off her knees and hitched her bottom onto the edge of the desk, one elegant and shiny black leg swinging. 'Sometimes I think one thing and sometimes another. Perhaps what we do with you tonight will resolve that.'

'What . . .? I mean, who . . .?'

'Now, now! You know better than to ask that, don't you?'

Ella nodded.

Miss Doyle leaned back across the desk and reached into her drawer. 'Put on your mask, then, and come on. We'll go and meet the others.' She got up and made for the door.

Ella followed her, adjusting the elastic strap of her mask. 'Does that mean that you're not going to fix me to the bench this time?'

Miss Doyle turned, her hand on the knob of the half-open door. 'Of course not. Any reason why I should?'

Ella flushed again. To her mind, there was a most excellent reason. There was a world of difference between being thrust, naked and exposed, into the midst of a crowd of near-strangers when it would be clear to them that it was happening against her will. To walk among them just as naked, yet apparently free to run or hide, was much more difficult. 'No,' she said. 'No reason.'

'Very well. Come along then.'

That journey, though short, was just as much of an ordeal as Ella had thought it would be. This time, they did not use the lift, but went down the broad staircase. Just how, Ella wondered, did one make a grand and impressive entrance when one was stark naked. The fact that all the other people in the room below were just as naked was a little help, but not much. Trying to keep her legs together and look elegant, yet manage the stairs at the same time was tricky. This time, there was no laughter or applause, just a murmur, as though there were nothing remarkable about her arrival in a state of undress.

Miss Doyle clapped her hands to command attention. 'You see that Ella is with us again tonight and wearing her rings. You all know what that means. Who is going to be the lucky one, I wonder? No, not you, Ralph. You had your share last time. You mustn't be greedy.' She stared around the circle of eager masks. 'Tonight, I think it must be . . . Belle!'

The plump, middle-aged woman was already making her way forward. Ella's jaw dropped in surprise and horror. She turned to Miss Doyle. 'But . . . but . . .'

'You wanted to say something, Ella?' Miss Doyle's

voice was deceptively sweet. The leather tawse in her hand moved fractionally, its three tails stirring with the movement.

'I . . . No, Miss Doyle. Nothing.'

Belle's eyes were glittering with wicked pleasure. 'Give her to me. I'll take her into the playroom myself.'

'Patience, Belle. You can take her in later. Think of the others. They have to have a little display first. Show them what you can do. You can fetch anything you need from the playroom.'

As Belle pushed her way through the crowd and disappeared towards the door of the playroom, Ella turned appealing eyes to Miss Doyle, hoping to see some sign of compassion. She was disappointed. If anything, Miss Doyle seemed just as lustfully eager as Belle. Ella sighed. She knew better than to voice a protest. She steeled herself for what was to come.

When Belle came back, she was carrying a cardboard box which she set down in front of Ella. When she straightened, Ella could see that she was breathing heavily with excitement, as though she had just been running. Her lips trembled and her tongue flickered over them repeatedly as if she could physically taste her anticipation.

'Kneel down.'

Ella had taken a violent dislike to Belle. In the circumstances, that was understandable, but it meant, nevertheless, that she hated obeying her. Staring at Miss Doyle, hoping for some last-minute reprieve, she obeyed, sinking slowly to her knees.

'Kiss my feet.'

Ella's face flushed crimson. It would be hateful enough to be obliged to make such a public demonstration of submission to this woman. Apart from that, to obey would oblige her to bend far forward, her face almost on the floor. She would be presenting her bare hindquarters in a most unbecoming pose to the interested gaze of many eyes. But Miss Doyle was watching and she still had her tawse in her hand. Ella bent forward. Belle pushed one foot forward and Ella kissed it. The act revolted her. There was nothing sexy in it for her at all. Belle's feet were not even beautiful, being blotchy and covered with raised blue veins just under the skin. One after the other, she kissed the proffered feet then straightened up, grateful that her ordeal was over. She soon found that it was only just beginning.

Belle grinned and thrust her lower body forward, her bushy patch of pubic hair prominent. She put both hands between her legs and separated her labia so that a large, almost flat patch of bright red inner surface showed between her labia.

'Now you can pleasure me with your lips and tongue.'

'What? No – I can't do that!'

Belle's laugh was triumphant. 'I was hoping you'd say that.' She removed her hands from her groin and stooped to rummage in the box. She held out a pair of objects and Ella stared at them uncomprehendingly. They were pyramidal in shape and looked like lead clock weights. Belle held them out to Ella, who took them from her, still without understanding.

'Hook one on each of your nipple rings!'

Ella stared at the weights, seeing for the first time the small hooks at the top of each. She looked down at her own breasts, then at the weights in her hands unable to believe what she had heard. She turned her head to look at Miss Doyle. 'Must I?'

Miss Doyle nodded firmly. 'Of course you must.'

Ella gulped. She raised one of the weights and, after a little fiddling, passed its hook through the ring in her right nipple. Supporting its weight in her right hand, she did the same thing with the weight in her left hand, then knelt there, supporting one weight in each hand.

Belle posed as before, her labia spread in invitation. 'Now do you think you can do it?'

Ella closed her eyes and shook her head miserably. 'No.'

'Good!' Belle stooped to the box again, coming up with two identical weights. She held them out. 'Take one in each hand.'

This was fiendish cruelty. To obey, Ella would have to let go of the weights on her nipple-rings so that they would be supported only by her own tender brown flesh. Slowly and carefully, she lowered the weights. As the downward pull came onto her nipples, she opened her mouth and groaned with the discomfort. If she were careful not to move, the sensation was just bearable. With infinite care, keeping her upper body perfectly still, she reached out and took the second pair of weights, even though she knew that she could not possibly bear to add them to the first.

'Open your legs. Really wide!'

This time, comprehension came more quickly and, with it, horror. Belle was going to make her hang these weights on the rings in her labia. Getting her legs apart was traumatic because it caused the weights on her nipples to move about, greatly increasing her discomfort.

'Well? Get on with it!' Belle's sadistic grin was infuriating.

Wincing and grimacing, Ella fumbled beneath herself until, with some difficulty, she contrived to hook the weights onto the rings. That done, she was able to support both in her left hand, leaving her right free to hold up her left nipple weight in such a way that the right rested on her forearm.

This relief was short-lived. 'Arms out to the sides!'

'Oh, no! Please . . .'

'Arms out, I said!'

Slowly and carefully, Ella lowered her hands until her nipples and labia were taking all the weight, then placed her arms in the required position, biting her lip in an effort to produce a counter-irritant which would make her discomfort easier to bear.

'You'll stay like that until you obey. Once your tongue's at work, you can hold up the weights again.'

Ella knelt, her head bowed. From time to time, a little hiss of pain escaped her as some tiny movement increased her anguish. Looking down at her breasts she could see that, despite the fact that they were young and firm, the downward force on her nipples was causing V-shaped wrinkles in the flesh. She could not see her labia, but knew them to be intolerably stretched downwards. The muscles in her arms quivered and her hands fluttered, only her will preventing them from moving to ease her suffering. This was not the jolly, sexy romp she had eagerly anticipated. Perhaps, had her tormentor been Paula or someone else, she might have been able to derive some perverse pleasure from what she was being forced to do. Not with Belle, though. Ella found herself hating her with a passion. It was mortifying to have to beg that bloated, self-satisfied face for leniency.

'Please . . .'

'Not until you lick me.'

Ella knew that she could stand no more. She capitulated. 'All right,' she whispered, moving her hands towards the weights.

'No, keep your arms out. Straight. Straighter! That's right. You can move them in when your tongue touches me, not before.' Belle held herself open again.

Ella stared at the exposed redness at the level of her eyes, feeling all this woman's evil sadism shrinking down until it was encapsulated within that black-haired groin. To kiss it, she would have to shuffle forward on her knees, causing the weights to move. Groaning with the effort, but still keeping her arms out, she inched forward. and reached out with her head. Belle took a short pace backwards and waited.

'Faster! Head up!'

Ella gulped. To go faster would be to increase the joggling of the weights. Belle knew that very well. Ella stiffened her resolve. She shuffled forward as fast as she could, groaning loudly at what that did to her nipples and labia. She leaned far forward, put out her tongue and placed it decisively in the centre of Belle's warm, pink wetness. To be allowed to support the weights again was a bliss that enabled Ella to forget, for a moment, that she was being forced to provide such a disgustingly intimate service for someone she so heartily detested. As her aches subsided and the reality of what she was doing was borne in on her, she closed her eyes and her mind to it, getting on with the task while trying to think of other, more pleasant things.

Miss Doyle's voice startled Ella. 'Very well. Enough. A most amusing and convincing demonstration of your tastes, Belle. You may take her to the playroom now.'

Belle beamed. 'Oh, thank you, Miss Doyle! All right, you, get going. Crawl on hands and knees!'

'No, please . . .' To be forced to move in that fashion would mean that the weights would be completely free again. Those on her nipples would hang straight down, swinging with her movements. She would not even have the tiny relief of the steadying friction of them against her breast flesh. Those on her labia would knock and bump against her thighs. Ella shuddered to think what that would feel like. She cast one last, imploring glance at Miss Doyle and Belle, but found no mercy in those eyes. She closed her eyes tightly in an effort to prevent tears of despair and frustration escaping from them before she slowly and carefully adopted the required position and began to crawl painfully towards the playroom. To ease her discomfort, she crawled with her legs as far apart as possible, shamed by the knowledge that in this most revealing position every detail of her vagina and anus could be scrutinised by the audience. She put the thought from her mind and crawled on doggedly, intent only on holding out until she was out of their sight. Belle followed her, prodding at the exposed backside with her bare foot every time Ella slowed a little, causing the weights to swing violently.

Ella stopped in the centre of the playroom and got up onto her knees again so that she could support the weights. Breathing heavily from her recent stress, she looked around the room and was immediately cast down. There were so many instruments there that this terrible woman could use on her. This had to stop, even if it meant dismissal from the club and loss of her story, she could not go on with this.

She was about to say as much when she heard Miss Doyle's voice behind her. 'Very good, Ella. You can take off the weights and get up now.'

With a huge sigh of relief, Ella fumbled to obey, careless now of the momentary increase in discomfort that this occasioned. She threw the hated objects on the floor and stood up, stretching stiff muscles.

Belle protested. 'But the fun's not over. I was going to do other things!'

89

'It's all right, Belle, you still are going to do other things and the fun certainly isn't over. Here, put these on.'

Belle stared at the tiny silver objects in Miss Doyle's gloved palm. 'Rings? My rings? You want me to put on my rings?'

'I do.'

'But why?'

'Because your turn at domination is over. It's time for you to be a submissive. I'm going to give you away as a present.'

Belle pouted and for a moment looked as though she would protest. She thought better of it, took the rings and went sulkily to sit in one of the high-backed chairs while she clicked them onto her thumbs. Looking up as she stooped to fasten her toe-rings, she said, 'Who are you going to give me to?'

For answer, Miss Doyle produced a tiny key and proceeded to unlock Ella's rings.

Belle stopped what she was doing, what could be seen of her face beneath her mask paling. 'Not her! You can't give me to her! This is only her second visit. She's not allowed to be a dominant yet.'

'She's allowed to be anything I say she can be,' Miss Doyle said calmly. 'I like to find out everything about my members. I've seen how Ella behaves as a submissive. Now I want to see how she does as a dominant. To bring out the best in her, it was necessary that she be well motivated, which is why I gave her to you, knowing your habits. Remember that I make the rules here. If you don't like them, it is always open to you to leave. The balance of your membership fee will be repaid. If you choose not to leave, you will do as you're told and get on with putting on your rings. Don't be all day about it.'

The two women locked eyes in a battle of wills,

which Belle lost. Bowing to the inevitable, she stooped to her task again.

Miss Doyle turned to Ella. 'Do you understand what's happened? Belle now belongs to you, to do with entirely as you wish. Like you, she has contracted to obey your every command, willingly suffer any punishment or torment you choose to inflict upon her. Normally the two of you would be alone and private. On this occasion, I shall stay to watch. I shall be looking to see how you take to the situation, how creative and imaginative you are, for instance. Understand?'

Ella did understand. Her stomach was turning cartwheels at the prospect. She had always thought of herself as a meek and obedient personality, having no wish to inflict harm on anyone. Why, then, did she find within herself a fierce joy in the prospect of owning Belle as a sex-slave? She stared at the naked fatness of her enemy, knowing just how badly she wanted to see her writhe in shame and humiliation, just as she had made her do. It was Ella's first taste of the pleasures of dominance, and it was heady stuff. The conviction grew in her that she knew exactly what she wanted her first demonstration of that power to be.

'May I borrow your tawse, please, Miss Doyle?'

'With pleasure.' Miss Doyle handed it over. 'If there are any other bits and pieces you need, just ask. I know where everything is kept.'

'Thank you. I know I'll need other things.' Ella took the tawse in her right hand and tested it by smacking it into her left palm. It stung every bit as badly as she remembered it had when applied to the backs of her own legs. Good! She stalked over to the chair where Belle was still sitting, cowering a little.

'Get up!' The speed with which that order was

obeyed pleased Ella mightily. 'Bend over! Touch your toes! Legs straight!' This was glorious! Belle was bent in half, puffing a little with the strain. Her breasts hung straight down, unsupported, swaying slightly, narrower near her body, like water-filled balloons. Ella hated those breasts. They would have to be tormented, but all in good time. First there was that vast expanse of pink and white bottom to be dealt with. Ella felt a twinge within her like the first signs of orgasm as she gazed at the Rubenesque fleshiness of it. It belonged to her now. She could do with it as she wished. Somehow, that was not enough. She searched her mind for the missing ingredient and found it. Shame. Humiliation. Mere discomfort was not suffering enough for this Belle bitch who had so tormented her.

'Say after me, "I've been a very bad girl." '

'What?'

'You heard me – say it.' Ella was pleased to see the red flush of embarrassment added to the colour occasioned by Belle's undignified stoop.

There was a long pause, then Belle's voice mumbled, 'I've been a very bad girl.'

'Do you know what happens to very bad girls, Belle?'

A long pause. 'Yes.'

'So tell me what's going to happen to you, Belle.'

An even longer pause. 'I'm going to be spanked.'

'Wrong, Belle! You're going to have your bottom thrashed. Say that.'

'I'm going . . .' Belle's voice cracked and trailed off. 'I can't!'

'Yes, you can. I insist.'

'I'm going . . . to have my . . . bottom thrashed.'

Ella could delay no longer. She raised the tawse high and swiped it with all the power of her arm and weight of her body at the unmissable target. For a split second, the pink flesh yielded, indenting deeply in the shape of the tawse before springing back and communicating rippling wobbles to the whole expanse of Belle's naked posterior. Forgetful of her orders, she sprang upright, leaping into the air with a loud shriek and rubbing her stung bottom.

'Down! Down, I say! Who told you to move?' Ella pushed at Belle's shoulders until she bent again, touching her toes with knees straight, gasping and sniffling. Ella gazed at her bottom. The mark of the tawse was plain to see, fiery red against the pinky-whiteness, its three little tails separately delineated. Ella felt a surge of lust and was surprised to find that, without knowing it, she had been fingering her clitoris. She pulled her hand away from herself. Intuitively, she knew that coming to climax would shorten the time during which she would enjoy what she was doing. She raised the tawse again. This time, if anything, the stroke was even harder than the first. It fell on the other cheek of Belle's bottom and provoked an even more gratifying response. Belle's leap was higher, her shriek louder and her rubbing more frantic. Ella considered administering more, but rejected the idea. If she did, she might come to spontaneous orgasm and that would never do. Time to move on.

'Kneel down. Hands on head.'

'What are you going to do?' Belle asked fearfully.

'Never you mind. Just do as I say.'

Belle fell to her knees and put her hands on her head. Ella walked around her, relishing her submission and noting the deepening redness of the two tawse marks. She stooped and lifted Belle's right breast in her left hand. It was very soft and curiously heavy. She held it out so that the upper surface was extended and almost horizontal, then raised the tawse high in her right hand.

Belle dropped her hands to clutch protectively at herself. 'No – oh, God, no!'

'You don't want me to think you're a bad girl again, do you, Belle? You know what happens to bad girls. Get those hands back on your head at once!'

Belle hastily replaced her hands on her head, screwing her eyes tightly shut in anticipation of the stroke to come. Ella lowered her arm and slapped the breast she held. It was a light stroke, but, in that exquisitely tender place, it was still enough to sting so that Belle could not resist dropping her forearms to hug herself, covering her breasts.

'Hands on head, Belle. We don't want the other one to feel neglected, do we?' Ella picked up the other breast and gripped it firmly while she administered another stroke. Belle's reaction to it was as before but it was vaguely unsatisfying. That magic ingredient of shame was missing. Ella searched her mind. She recalled the way her hatred had condensed and homed in to be directed at one particular part of Belle's anatomy, then remembered other things she had seen on that first evening at the club.

She turned to Miss Doyle who had been in her favourite pose on the edge of a table, one leg swinging. 'Am I allowed to shave her?'

Miss Doyle beamed. 'Creative and imaginative! Excellent! Of course you are allowed. Is that something you've done before?'

'No, never.'

'Then you'll need a little guidance. I'll stand by and watch, shall I?'

'Please.'

Miss Doyle moved away to collect the necessary equipment and Belle sidled closer to Ella. 'Please,' she whispered. 'Please don't do it. I'm sorry for what I made you do. Can't you let me off?'

'Why should I?'

'It will be so awkward for me. My husband . . . he doesn't know. How will I explain?'

For a second, Ella felt a twinge of sympathy, then hardened her heart. 'You could always leave the club. If it's going to be awkward for you to explain, I'm even more glad I thought of it. Now get up on the table and lie on your back with your legs open.'

'No! Look, I'll give you money. How much . . .?'

Miss Doyle was coming back with the equipment. It was too late for further protests and Belle knew it. She sat on the edge of the table, then shuffled back until she could lie down, her lower legs hanging over the end.

Miss Doyle put her things down on the table. 'Let me see. I don't think you've been shaved before, have you, Belle?'

'No, Miss Doyle.'

'Well, it will be a new experience for both of you.' She handed Ella a pair of scissors. 'A common mistake is to start shaving straight away. That just clogs the razor. You have to get all the long stuff off first. Come on, Belle, you can open your legs wider than that!'

Belle spread her plump thighs a little further until her labia opened like the petals of a flower, revealing the pinkness within. She shuddered, hiding her face in her hands.

'That's right,' Miss Doyle directed briskly. 'Start at the top. My, she has got a lot, hasn't she? Good! Now snip down on either side of her slit, where it's thickest. Careful just there, you'll have to grab hold of those lips, one by one, and pull them out straight. Use the rings. Stop twitching, Belle, anyone would think you were getting excited!'

Belle was not the only one. What Ella was doing and the intimate way she had to handle Belle to do it was stirring her in a most enjoyable way. The fact that Belle was obviously getting sexual pleasure, in spite of her previous protests, was another ingredient in Ella's learning process which she would have to remember for future reference.

What had been a thicket of black curly hair was now reduced to a short, irregular stubble. Miss Doyle held out a can of shaving foam. 'Give her a good dose of this, now. Start at the top again, on her belly. No! Don't be mean with it. Use plenty. More than that. Let's have a big pile of it. You can stop squirming, Belle. I know it's cold. Now smear it all over. Not with your fingers. Use your whole palm. Slap it on and smear it down between her legs. There, see? She likes it really, don't you, Belle?'

The scratchy feel of the cut pubic hair and the way individual tufts stuck up through the thick foam which Ella was systematically slathering all around Belle's crotch was causing Ella to lubricate again. That sensation increased when Miss Doyle passed over a disposable razor and indicated that shaving should begin. There was now an exultant quality to Ella's enjoyment. To be standing between those widely parted legs, staring at that exposed and besmeared body and to know that she owned Belle to do with as she liked was wonderful in itself, making her feel powerful. Added to that was a clear understanding of how humiliating it must be for Belle to be shaved against her will, knowing that every detail of the process was being closely observed. And, as the final icing on the cake of satisfaction, Belle's movements and her sighs proved that she was getting worked up by this treatment.

'Start at the top again. One long, clean stroke right

across. See how that removes all the hair, leaving her belly completely smooth. Now another, a little lower. Keep going. You've got it. More carefully now, between her legs. Belle, keep those legs wide apart. Pull on the rings again now, and change direction. Down strokes. You missed a bit – nibble away at it. Oh, I see the razor's clogged already. Here's another. Try again.'

Ella was fascinated. What was emerging from the foam was a full-grown woman's genitalia, something she had never seen without a covering, however slight, of pubic hair. Every crease and detail was clear and sharp. The bulging *mons veneris* and vulva, the soft pinkness of the wrinkled labia. They stood out starkly, vulnerable in their total baldness.

Miss Doyle said, 'Now for the rest of it. You didn't think we were going to leave all that underneath, did you, Belle? Roll over. Now get up on your knees. Knees wide apart, please. That's right. Stick it out! Offer it up for sacrifice!'

Ella took up the scissors again and snipped busily at this fresh supply of rich and thick hair. It was particularly interesting to see the puckered brown dimple of Belle's sphincter as the protective hair was removed from around it. When the time came to apply the foam, Ella had great difficulty in resisting temptation, but contented herself with sliding a soapy finger up and down across it, rejoicing in the squirming protests this produced. She stored that away in her memory too.

The shaving over, Ella wiped away the last traces of foam with a damp cloth and contemplated her handiwork. The completeness of the shave both pleased and excited her. She knew exactly what would come next. 'I think she should stay on the table like that and work herself off with her fingers while we watch to see that she makes a thorough job of it. What do you think, Miss Doyle?'

Miss Doyle laughed. 'I think you're learning fast.'

Ella said, 'Go on then, Belle. Get started.'

'I can't!' Belle wailed. 'Not with you both watching.'

'Would you prefer the weights?'

'No, please! I'll do it. Look, I'm doing it.' Belle extended her right hand backwards between her parted thighs and felt urgently at her sex while Ella and Miss Doyle watched her technique with interest.

Ella climbed onto the table, stood up, then straddled Belle's plump body, facing her bottom. She sat down in the small of her back, clamping her with her strong, young thighs as she would have done a pony she intended to ride. The bare skin that pressed against Ella's spread sex felt good and she rubbed herself against it. She slapped at the jiggling buttocks. 'Faster! Do it properly!' The wobbling plumpness of that bottom against her palm was thrilling. Ella slapped again and again, watching the parts that had not been reddened by the tawse deepen to pink, then red.

To Miss Doyle, she said, 'Have you got one of those little condom things that goes on your finger?'

Miss Doyle was amused. 'Oh, yes. Plenty of those.'

'May I have one? I have a use for it.'

Beneath her, she heard Belle emit a muffled groan. Miss Doyle brought her the condom and a tube of gel. Ella fitted the rubber over her right middle finger and smeared it with gel. She was close to climax herself, overcome by the knowledge of what she was about to do. She put the covered finger squarely on Belle's brown sphincter and pressed. Belle bucked forward mightily with a little scream. Ella held her firmly between her thighs and rewarded her with an extra slap or two. She pressed again and her finger disappeared into Belle's intimate orifice. Ella knew very well what that would feel like and rotated it with teasing, wriggling movements, feeling the body beneath her quiver and shudder in response, communicating its excitement to her own exposed vagina. Ella slapped again at Belle's bottom. 'You've stopped masturbating. Get on with it! Put three fingers right up there and do it properly!'

As Belle obeyed, Ella thrust her finger in as far as it would go and held it there. Belle screamed loudly and began to buck and jump in the beginnings of a climax. Ella clung on, using those movements to provoke her own orgasm, helping them along by vigorously rubbing her clitoris on Belle's bare back. They came to a peak together, Ella still slapping and Belle pounding the table with her fists and drumming her feet in time with the intensity of her spasms.

When it was over, Miss Doyle helped Ella down from the table. 'We'll leave Belle here to recover a bit. You can come back to the office with me.'

Back in the office, Miss Doyle invited Ella to sit, then surprised her by going across the room to a cocktail cabinet. 'You can take off the mask. Drink?'

'Oh! Yes, please. I think I'd like a gin.'

'By itself?'

'With Italian, please.'

Miss Doyle made drinks, then handed the gin to Ella before going around the desk and sitting in her chair, setting her own glass in front of her. 'You did well tonight, Ella. You took your punishment well and dished it out imaginatively. You actually stirred me, and not many things do.'

Ella blushed. 'I was just getting by as best I could and doing whatever came into my head.'

'Maybe so. All the same, I am inclined to trust you already; much more quickly than I have ever trusted any member before. You will not be blindfolded when you go home and can make your own way here in future.'

'Thank you.'

'Nevertheless, you are still very new and there are some things you will have to get used to. I noticed that you weren't keen on using your lips and tongue on Belle. It's something you'll have to learn to do, however much you dislike it.'

Ella thought about this. 'I'm not sure it was the tongue thing. I've never even thought about it before, let alone done it. I think it was more that I didn't like Belle than anything else.'

'You mean that with someone else it might be pleasurable?'

Ella blushed. 'I don't know. Maybe.'

'With me, perhaps?'

Ella did not know what to say, suspecting some malevolent trap, so she said nothing.

Miss Doyle went on, 'You've got to learn with someone. Why not with me?'

Ella took a big gulp of her gin. 'I suppose so.' She shrugged. 'Why not?'

Miss Doyle twisted her thin red lips into a smile. 'Finish your drink. Take your time, then we'll talk about it some more.' She put down her own drink and rose. Reaching behind her body, she found the zip at the back of her costume and pulled it down. She wiggled it down over her hips, revealing that she wore nothing beneath. Peeping covertly, Ella saw that her body was thin, almost gaunt. Her hip bones and ribs were clearly visible beneath the pale skin. The outfit she wore must have been subtly padded at the front, because her breasts were so small as to be hardly discernible. Slack and flat, only a wrinkle in the skin below each nipple showed that they were there at all. There was, however, no doubt at all about the femininity of her nipples. At least an inch long and deepest brown in colour, they projected aggressively from large aureolae that were only slightly less brown in colour. When Miss Doyle was naked, she sat down again and picked up her drink. 'There! Now we're equal. That should make you feel better.'

In fact, it did. To have Miss Doyle as nude as she was herself was the equivalent, for Ella, of putting her own clothes back on. She felt a certain amount of confidence returning and, with it, great curiosity about what was going to happen between them. When she had finished her drink, Ella put it down on the desk and met Miss Doyle's eyes boldly, challenging her to make the first move. Miss Doyle responded by getting up and coming round to the front of the desk, where she perched with one leg swinging. Ella found that movement and that pose oddly erotic and supposed it must be because she had always associated the woman's dominance with the clothing she wore. Now that she was naked, she seemed suddenly to be more approachable and available for sex.

'I think we should start by finding out just how much you already know,' Miss Doyle said. 'You've told me that you've never used your mouth on a woman. Have you any experience of what it feels like to be kissed and licked like that?'

Ella nodded, a little embarrassed by the question. 'Once,' she said. 'But it was a man, not a woman.'

'Did you like it?'

Ella experienced a tiny squirt of fluid high up in her vagina as she recalled Ralph's delicious treatment of her clitoris and she moved a fraction in her chair. 'It was all right,' she admitted.

Miss Doyle nodded. 'Some men are quite good at it, but there's nothing like another woman. She knows exactly where and how to do it for maximum effect.'

Another spasm and another spurt of liquid – lower down this time as Ella realised exactly where this conversation was leading. She nodded slowly. 'I can see that,' she said.

'So, if you are going to gratify a woman in that way, it's only sensible to know exactly what she will feel when you do certain things to her. I suggest that I show you what's possible.'

Ella moved uneasily again, very conscious of the fact that the outer entrance of her vagina was as wet and slippery as the rest. 'What do you want me to do?'

'You?' Miss Doyle smiled. 'You do nothing, except to lean back in your chair and spread your legs. I'll do the rest.'

Ella willingly obeyed, shuffling her bare bottom forward on the leather seat and opening her thighs to make her sex more available. Miss Doyle got off the desk and came forward, dropping to her knees between the parted legs. She put both hands flat on the tops of Ella's thighs and slid them forward until both hands could dive into Ella's crotch. Grasping a gold ring in each hand, she pulled them apart, then leaned forward to inspect the result.

She looked up, smiling. 'You have a very pretty pussy, Ella. Also a very wet one. Do you know what it tastes like?'

Ella licked her lips. 'Maybe. I'm not sure.'

Miss Doyle inserted two fingers of her right hand into Ella's vagina with a twisting, turning, scraping motion. Ella jumped and gasped aloud, her gluteal muscles tensing violently. Miss Doyle withdrew the fingers and reached up to offer them to Ella.

'Take them into your mouth and suck on them.'

Amazed at herself for doing so, Ella opened her mouth and accepted the fingers that were thrust into it. She ran her tongue around them, sucking at the wetness. The taste was vaguely familiar, faintly musky with a hint of salt. It could not be only the taste, though, that was so exciting her. It was the knowledge of where those fingers had been and how they had felt, as if the thrill she had experienced through her sense of touch were now being added to by its transfer to her sense of taste. She could tell that Miss Doyle was getting some sort of charge out of having her fingers sucked and she tried to increase that by moving her tongue faster and sucking harder. Her vagina was now so wet that she could feel some of her fluid oozing out.

Miss Doyle removed her fingers from Ella's mouth. 'It would be greedy to keep that all to yourself. Are you going to let me taste you now?'

'Yes! Oh, yes!' Ella breathed. She was close to boiling point already, although her 'treatment' had hardly begun. Almost without her conscious volition, her hips were rotating in large circles, endeavouring to thrust her vagina forward even more towards what she knew would be a certain source of pleasure.

Miss Doyle pulled on the rings again to open the pink flower of Ella's sex. She leaned forward and used the tip of her tongue to flip back the hood of Ella's clitoris. When it was fully exposed, she allowed her tongue to flicker over it with the lightest of light touches. Ella felt herself being driven crazy. She moaned and clutched at her own breasts, pulling and twisting at her gold rings to maximise her stimulation.

'Harder! Do it harder!'

Miss Doyle pulled her head back. 'No, that's the trick of it. I bring you up to a certain level, then I hold you there for as long as possible, not letting you finish. Build up a head of steam so that, when it lets go, it is perfect and glorious.'

What followed was bliss for Ella. Miss Doyle licked up and down at the entrance to her vagina, carefully avoiding her clitoris. She had an extraordinarily long and strong tongue which, from time to time, she plunged deep into Ella, using it as a man uses his penis. This was like no penis Ella had ever felt, though. It was infinitely flexible. It could change shape, curving, licking and lapping inside her until she could feel her brain bursting with desire for climax. Withdrawal of the tongue was followed immediately by more flickering on her clitoris then, just as Ella thought she must come, Miss Doyle's tongue went back to licking and probing and the whole process began all over again. Time and again, Ella approached her peak, only to be held there and not finished. Each time, her hands scrabbled down over her bare belly, clawing for her clitoris in an agony of frustration, but each time Miss Doyle knocked them away, not allowing her to touch herself.

Ella felt herself being reduced to a quivering jelly of pure lust. She had never been so worked up. Great waves of pre-orgasmic pulsing engulfed the lower part of her body. Her nipples were standing out as never before from grossly swollen aureolae. Her teeth chattered uncontrollably, lending a curious sound to the breath that hissed out between them with every gasp. Every now and then, her hands would cease their churning of her nipple-rings and pause in mid-air, the fingers opening and closing convulsively in her frustration at not being able to fulfil her overwhelming desire to use them to masturbate frantically. She could feel her senses leaving her.

At the last possible moment, Miss Doyle clamped

her lips firmly around Ella's jutting, yearning clitoris, sucking vigorously and nibbling at the same time. Ella screamed loud and long, her head jerking back and her legs clamping together to grip the head that was doing such amazing things to her. Her orgasm ripped through her whole body, devouring her brain as well. Her stomach muscles griped and tensed, bending her far forward, her head forced down in paroxysmal jerks towards the centre of her rapture as though to drive an imaginary penis far up inside her.

When Miss Doyle stopped and got up, Ella remained slumped forward, her breasts pressed against her thighs, panting for breath. It was a long while before she recovered sufficiently to look up. When she did, she saw Miss Doyle in her familiar place on the desk.

Miss Doyle raised her eyebrows in interrogation. 'Well? Was I right?'

Ella sat up wearily, her mouth still hanging open. It was a few seconds before she regained sufficient control of it to be able to speak. 'Yes. Oh, yes ... That was ... It was ...' There were no adequate words. 'Thank you! I feel I ought to repay you in some way.'

'So you shall and now you know exactly how to do it. But not right now. Just remember that you owe me one.'

Funny, Ella thought. That was exactly what Paula had said.

Six

'You mean you've been there twice and you still don't know where it is?'

Paula's question was one Ella had prepared herself for, but that made it no easier. She bent forward over her keyboard, pretending to be intent on correcting a mistake, thus allowing her long, blonde hair to fall forwards to conceal any slight blush. 'It takes time, Paula. They're very suspicious of newcomers. I'm sure I'll find out soon.'

'I hope so,' Paula grumbled. 'Old Flatt is already nagging at me to know when he's going to see a story for all that money. Well, what happened this time?'

'Oh, nothing much. It was all a bit dull, really.'

Paula raised her eyebrows. 'Oh, come on! You're not going to tell me you sat about knitting all evening?'

Ella realised the improbability of a really dull evening. She would have to give Paula some small titbit. 'There was a little instruction. Sort of a class, if you know what I mean.'

'What did you learn?'

'Just the usual things. You know.'

'No, I don't know. That's why I'm asking. You're not holding back on me, are you?'

Ella's typing error became even more interesting. 'Of course not. It's a bit embarrassing to talk about it, that's all.'

107

'So be embarrassed. It won't be the first time. Tell me all.'

Ella took a deep breath. 'Well, I learned how a woman can please another woman. Kissing, and that sort of thing.'

Paula was relentless in her pursuit of detail. 'Surely you knew how to kiss?'

'No, not that sort of kissing. Not mouth to mouth. Sort of mouth to . . . down there. You know.'

'Ah! I see! So how, precisely, did you learn this mystic art? A text book? A film?'

'No, a sort of demonstration. You know.'

Paula snorted. 'If you tell me I know just once more, I shall slap you. Details! Who demonstrated?'

'Miss Doyle.'

'On you?'

'Yes.'

'While the rest of the class watched?'

For a second, Ella considered inventing a room full of students. That would be a difficult fib to maintain and she rejected the notion. 'Er . . . There wasn't any rest of the class.'

'Just you and Miss Doyle?'

'Yes. It was better that way.'

'I'll just bet it was.' Paula took out a cigarette and tapped it on her thumbnail. There was something odd about the way she looked at Ella, as if staring through her to the office wall behind. She lit the cigarette and exhaled slowly, her head tilted back to blow the smoke towards the ceiling. 'Is she good at it?'

'Oh, yes!' Ella bit her tongue and winced. The close questioning had revived her memories of that gorgeous, totally fantastic, wriggling, ecstatic, tongue-induced orgasm and her blurted affirmation had carried far too much enthusiasm. She could tell by Paula's change of expression.

'Come into my office. I want to talk to you private-ly.' Paula turned away and stalked off. Ella was a little shocked. Clearly, she had done something wrong. Did Paula suspect that she had been lied to? Feeling rather like a schoolgirl ordered to report to the headmistress's study, Ella got up from her keyboard and followed her editor into her office.

'Shut the door behind you and sit down.'

Ella closed the door that separated Paula's office from the press-room and took her seat in front of a desk no less large and impressive than Miss Doyle's. Paula put her elbows on the desk, clasped her hands and supported her chin on her thumbs while she gazed fixedly at Ella. The smoke from the cigarette between her fingers rose in an absolutely straight line and Ella followed it intently, anxious not to meet that stare, lest it should be able to detect the uncertainty in her head. The ticking of the office clock on the wall was deafeningly loud. Surely the Factories Act did not allow so many decibels?

At last, Paula moved. She took a final drag on her cigarette, then stubbed it out in the ashtray. She drew a piece of paper towards her and began to write. Ella tilted her head to try to see what she was writing, but she had never been very good at reading upside-down. It seemed to be some sort of list.

Paula turned the paper and pushed it across the desk. 'You will report to my flat at eight-thirty sharp tonight. That is what you will wear. No more and no less. Do you have all those things?'

Ella ran her eye down the list. 'Yes, of course, but why? What have I done, Paula?'

'You owe me, remember? I said I would collect one day and this is the day.'

Ella could not shake off her anxiety. 'That's all it is, then? No other reason?'

'You'll find out tonight.'

That didn't sound good at all and did nothing to calm Ella's churning stomach. 'But suppose Interplay send for me?' she prevaricated.

'You'll just have to politely decline, owing to a previous engagement, won't you? Don't be late.'

'No, Paula.' Ella left the office with her mind in a whirl. Paula's attitude was so strange. Ella was as certain as she could be that her lies and omissions had gone undetected. What, then, could it be? She was back at her desk before a possible answer struck her. Paula was jealous!

Ella's previous approach to Paula's apartment had been intimidating enough. It was doubly so, this time. In the privacy of her own flat, it had been rather wicked and exciting to dress exactly as Paula had ordered. The sheer black nylons had caressed her long, shapely legs as she drew them on, while the flimsy, lacy strands of her smallest black garter belt accentuated the rounded whiteness of her thighs. Although the knickers Paula had specified were also black they concealed very little, being so light and thin as to be almost transparent. They brushed the tops of her thighs like thistledown and dimpled revealingly into every crease and cranny of her lower anatomy. Shiny black, high-heeled shoes came next. So far, sexy but fairly routine. The shock had been to find that there was only one more item on the list – a light, unlined raincoat. The lightest she had was also fairly short. It was that particular shade of grey that accentuated shadows and, when Ella inspected her reflection in her full-length mirror, she was certain that her nipple erection and rings would be obvious to anyone. She would have liked to cover her breasts with a brassière, however gauzy, but did not dare disobey Paula's explicit command.

Leaving her flat and walking down the communal stairway had been an ordeal, but faded into insignificance as soon as she hit the street outside. At once, the drop in temperature and the chilly wind informed her, as if she did not already know, that she was most improperly dressed for an excursion into the outside world. The cool air which seeped immediately through the unlined coat hardened her nipples into erection all over again, so that she felt obliged to cover them by pretending to clutch at her coat collar. The lower half of the coat kept flapping open so that she not only had a constant reminder of the naked state of her thighs and the sparseness of the covering on her bottom, but had to grab at the fluttering material with her other hand, lest she should inadvertently be showing her suspenders and knickers to the world.

She had subsided gratefully into her car and cowered there, safe for a moment from prying eyes. That respite was short-lived. It was not far to Paula's apartment block and the journey was over far too soon. Knowing in advance how it would feel made it much more difficult to get out of the car than it had been to leave her flat. Ella became convinced that the doorman would know very well exactly what she was wearing, or not wearing, under her coat. He had smiled at her as he held the door open. What had that meant? Anything? Nothing? Was Paula cruel enough to have briefed him in advance?

She had managed to shrug off a little of her paranoia in the lift, but it returned on the long trudge down the corridor, any residual confidence oozing out of her with every step. And now, here she was at that door again, her heart pounding even more loudly than before. She knocked.

Paula was wearing the same dark green robe. This

time, there was no cheerful greeting. Paula simply jerked her thumb in the direction of the living room and Ella went there, feeling like a convicted felon passing through the prison gates. Paula closed the door and followed her. No invitation to sit down; no offer of a sociable drink. Paula regarded her, hands on hips, for a while then pointed.

'Off!'

Ella crossed her arms, pulling the lapels of her coat protectively across her body. 'Wait! Wait a minute, Paula. What's this about?'

Paula pointed again, her finger a penetrating sword. 'Off!'

Ella shivered. Meekly, she unbuttoned the coat, took it off and looked about her for somewhere to put it.

'Drop it on the floor; you won't need it for a long while.'

Ella obeyed, then stood uncertainly, protecting her breasts with her arms.

'Clasp your hands behind your head! Do it! Push your elbows back! More! Now stay like that.'

Ella's vagina watered and twinged almost painfully. In this position, her breasts were lifted and thrust forward provocatively, the nipples long and hard, the gold rings dangling. Paula stepped forward and grasped the rings firmly, pulling on them so as to oblige Ella to turn to face the light streaming from the standard lamp in one corner.

'That's better. I want to see what I'm getting.' Paula's face was only inches away from Ella's own, her eyes daring her victim to look away. With a start, Ella felt Paula's hands at the waistband of her knickers, easing them away from her body and pulling them inexorably downwards.

It was very difficult to maintain her strained pose,

but Ella managed it. 'What are you doing?' she whispered hoarsely.

'Pulling your knickers down, of course. Do you know why I'm doing that?'

Ella quivered with suppressed lust, her longing for a demonstration of Paula's dominance overwhelming her. A sudden image of Paula fingering her sex, massaging her clitoris, sprang into her mind. 'No.'

'Let me help you to guess.' Paula transferred her attention to the nipple-rings again, pulling on them until Ella had turned right round and had her back to the light. Paula tugged again on her knickers, pulling them down to mid-thigh, exposing her creamy white buttocks to the glare of the lamp.

'Any idea now?'

'No.' A black lie! Ella knew exactly what Paula intended. She was going to poke her long, wriggling finger into her bottom again while she masturbated her into a frenzy. Ella could feel her sphincter making little, expectant, gripping movements, while her vagina leaked slippery fluid.

'All right. Take your knickers right off and give them to me.' Ella stooped to obey, taking first one leg, then the other, out of her black undergarment, then handing it over.

'Open your mouth.'

'What?'

'You heard me. I said, "open your mouth." I don't want a lot of screaming and shouting to disturb the neighbours.'

'I don't understand, Paula. Why ... Mff! Mm!' Ella was cut off in mid-protest as Paula stuffed her knickers into her open mouth, stabbing at them with her forefinger to ensure that they filled it completely.

'Now shut your mouth and keep it shut!' Paula pointed at the carpet. 'Kneel down! Down!'

Ella knelt, alarm mingling with sexual excitement.

'Put your forehead on the carpet. Knees wide apart. Stick your backside right out. Further. Now stay like that.'

Out of the corner of her eye, Ella saw Paula go to the sofa and shuck off her green robe. She was naked beneath it. She picked up a thin, black leather glove from a side table and fitted it carefully onto her right hand, pushing between the fingers to ensure that it was skin-tight.

'Do you know why I've put this on?'

As best she could while still obeying the order to keep her forehead on the carpet, Ella shook her head.

'Because I don't want to hurt my hand when I give you a thorough, knickers-off spanking on your bare bum.'

In spite of her resolve, Ella raised her head. 'Mff! Mm!'

'Get your head back on the carpet. That'll show what a low piece of vermin you are.' Paula was pacing back and forth, working herself up into a rage. 'Slut! Trollop! It was on that very carpet that you swore to me that your body was mine and no one else's. I give you a little leeway and this is the thanks I get. I expected you to indulge in sex games. I did not expect that you would be so treacherous as to enjoy them with some strange woman.'

Paula fell to her knees on Ella's left side and turned to face her feet. She stretched her left arm far across Ella's naked waist, curling it underneath her until her fingers dug into the soft flesh of her belly, holding her firmly in a grip from which there could be no escape. She raised her gloved right hand high and began to beat the exposed, defenceless white buttocks. She smacked steadily and mercilessly with all her strength, the reports of the blows loud in the still room, while Ella wriggled and struggled to buck forward in an effort to avoid them.

This was a most efficient demonstration of Paula's jealousy, Ella thought. And she deserved this humiliating pain. She had been a very bad girl. She ought not to have enjoyed the episode with Miss Doyle. She ought to have considered Paula's feelings. She deserved to be punished on another account. Had she not, herself, thoroughly enjoyed spanking Belle? This was just retribution and she must endure it without complaint. Her bottom was a mass of stinging fire and still the smacks came with undiminished force, first on one cheek, then on the other. She could feel the heat of them. There was another heat, too. Her vagina was sucking and twitching at nothing, as if at the approach of orgasm. This was what Belle must have felt; what had driven her crazy.

Ella reached back with her right hand, feeling for her clitoris. It was only a small movement, but Paula saw it. 'Stop that! This is for my pleasure, not yours. Get both hands out in front of you where I can see them. Stretch them right out. Don't you dare to touch yourself again.'

As she struggled to obey, stretching far forward, Ella's knees slipped backwards and she fell flat on her stomach, her pubis grinding into the roughness of the carpet. Paula fell with her, her weight across her, holding her down while the terrible, relentless spanking went on. Ella screamed into her gag, large tears of frustration, pain and shame rolling down her cheeks, her legs kicking fruitlessly while her fists pounded the floor in front of her.

Just as Ella thought that she could not possibly stand any more without fainting, the smacking stopped and Paula rolled away from her. Ella lay where she was, hands and feet stretched out, sobbing quietly while her bright red bottom throbbed and smarted.

Paula got up a little breathlessly, went to the couch and flung herself down on it, legs splayed wide. 'Now take those things out of your mouth, come here and show me everything that bitch taught you. No! Don't stand up. Crawl to me. It's all you deserve.'

Ella rolled on her side, wincing and grimacing as the hairy carpet grated at the edge of her spanked area. She spat out the knickers, got up onto hands and knees and crawled to the sofa until she was positioned between Paula's spread legs. That dense, frizzy pubic hair was so unlike Miss Doyle's thin covering. She had not seen it since they had been in the Jacuzzi together and had forgotten how much of it there was. Ella knew herself to be worked up and hungry for orgasm. The pain of her spanking ought to have had the opposite effect. In fact, it had reawakened the thrill of being Paula's sex-toy and her kneeling position, coupled with what she was now obliged to do, reinforced that thrill.

She put her hands on the tops of Paula's thighs, feeling the taut, hard musculature beneath the brown skin – so unlike Miss Doyle's body. Paula's thighs epitomised her dominant character: hard, yet infinitely desirable. Ella wanted very badly to taste Paula, to lick and to please. She leaned forward, then hesitated, allowing part of her mind to drift to her spanked bottom, relishing the stinging heat of it. There was something that would make her service to Paula even more enjoyable.

'Must I?' she pleaded, looking up into Paula's stern face with wide and innocent eyes.

Paula grabbed Ella's hair with her left hand, cruelly dragging her head up and back. Holding it there, she slapped Ella's face twice, back and forth, with her right. 'Do you want me to smack your bottom again?'

'No, Paula.'

'Tell me who owns you, then.'

'You do, Paula.'

'Are you my sex-slave, or someone else's?'

'Yours! Only yours, Paula.'

'Then get on with it!'

'Yes, Paula.' That was better! Delicious quakes of apprehension and arousal were again coursing up and down Ella's spine at this confirmation of her abased and possessed status. She was less than nothing; a non-person; a dusty mat beneath Paula's feet, existing only to obey. She must do as she was told, whether she liked it or not. She leaned forward again and pulled on Paula's gold rings to open the way to her vagina. It was already very wet. Extending her tongue as far as it would go, Ella poked it into the gap thus created, lapping at the interior to collect as much of the wetness within as she could. She took her tongue back into her mouth and moved it against her palate, snuffing and tasting at the musky flavour. Her lips shone with Paula's juices and that was good. That was how the lips of a degraded slave should be. She lunged forward again, stretching Paula wider and wiping her face, nose, forehead and chin against her moist surfaces. Ella's sense of degradation escalated and she felt her own vagina twitch into renewed response at the knowledge than anyone could now plainly see the extent of her subservience.

Paula sighed and moved uneasily, the first sign she had given that what Ella was doing for her was in any way pleasurable. Ella heard and saw. She determined to move Paula as she had never been moved before; to do more than the minimum demanded of a sex-toy. Thanks to Miss Doyle's demonstration, she knew exactly how to set about it. With subtle kisses and licks, skilfully directed at labia, vagina and clitoris, she took her Mistress up the ladder of lust to the point of orgasm; held her there for long seconds, then brought her down a rung or two before beginning again.

Paula's hips began to grind and she sighed heavily. At first, she was over-eager for climax, grabbing Ella by the hair and forcing her face into her groin in an attempt to make her continue past that magic point of peak pleasure. Ella refused to take the hint, knowing just how much extra pleasure that refusal would cause. After a while, Paula began dimly to realise what might be in store if she accepted Ella's tribute in the way it was being offered. She stopped trying to achieve orgasm by force and allowed her body to acquiesce in the treatment.

That small change in power differential communicated itself as though psychically to Ella. There was now an ambivalence about her status. She was still the slave, ministering to her Mistress, yet she had subtly taken charge of Paula's orgasm, controlling and directing the moment of its occurrence and its intensity. That was good, too, because she felt able to slip one hand down between her own legs and finger her clitoris, saving the other to slap Paula's hand away with authority every time it attempted to interfere.

Paula was moaning in earnest now, just as much a jelly of lust as Ella had been when subjected to the same ordeal. Close on either side of Ella's face, her gorgeous brown legs twitched and jerked, while her flat stomach writhed. She was pulling and twisting at her nipple-rings and her voice was no longer one of command, but husky with desire and love.

'Yes, oh, yes! Like that! Mm! Now! Oh, I can't bear it! Oh, Ella, my little love, what are you doing to me?' Now Paula's hands no longer gripped. They stroked Ella's hair gently, accompanied by whispered endearments.

When Ella judged that the moment was exactly right, she deliberately gave Paula notice of that fact. Detaching her mouth for an instant, she murmured, 'It's now, Paula darling! You're going up and over the top!'

Paula's neck muscles tightened and her whole body tautened in anticipation of what was in store. 'Yes!' she screamed. 'Now! Take me there!' As Ella sank her teeth into Paula's straining clitoris, she had the greatest difficulty in holding her down and had to throw her full weight onto the thighs under her armpits in order to finish the job. Paula was wriggling and shouting, her hands clawing at her breasts, as she toppled over into glorious climax. That brought on Ella's own peak, making it a joyous union of spirit.

When it was over, Ella lay with her breasts against Paula's pubic hair, her cheek on her flat stomach, listening to the mad pounding of her heart as it slowly returned to normal.

Paula reached down and pulled Ella up towards her. 'Come and kiss me, golden girl.'

Ella responded gladly kissing a woman for only the second time in her life. She was happy. The slave had served her Mistress well and was now being rewarded by the emancipation of a return to a loving friendship.

Ella, wearing nothing but her mask, completed the ceremony of re-signing her contract. She had been a little concerned about the length of time she had been obliged to wait to receive her next summons to Interplay, but was glad that the period had been sufficient to allow all traces of Paula's spanking to disappear. Those marks might have been a little difficult to explain.

She turned away from the desk. 'You will want me to wear my rings, I expect.'

Miss Doyle shook her head. 'Not tonight. I have been particularly pleased with your progress. So much so that I have decided that you shall dominate again. You dealt pleasantly enough with a woman. I want to see how you handle a man.'

'A man!' That was a startling notion and one that Ella had not anticipated. The idea of such a thing took a little getting used to and Ella thought about it. The way her body was responding told her that the notion was not entirely unpleasing to her.

'Do you think I'm ready for that?'

Miss Doyle shrugged. 'I believe so, but time will tell.'

'What man? Do I know him? I mean, will I recognise his body?' An image of Ralph had flashed across her mind. She knew exactly what she would like to do with Ralph's penis, given the opportunity.

'No, you don't know him. In fact, no one does. He's new. He's young and has lots of stamina too.'

'What should I do to him?'

Miss Doyle smiled slightly. 'You know the answer to that one only too well. He'll be tied down for you, so . . .'

Ella grinned. 'I know. Anything I like.'

'Exactly! This is as much a test for you as it is for him. Just be imaginative and different. That's what we like to see.'

'All right, I'll do my best.'

Miss Doyle leaned forward and planted a small kiss on Ella's cheek. 'I know that will be good enough. Now run along and join the others. I have to go and get Gunter ready for his entrance.'

'Gunter? That's his name?'

'Yes, but don't tell anyone that you know. And don't tell anyone, particularly the women, that you know he is going to be your present tonight.'

'I won't.' Ella went out of the office and down the stairs. She had grown so used to being naked in public that, even if her mind had not been distracted by thoughts of Gunter and her good fortune, she would still not have bothered with elaborate precautions to keep her legs together, something which made the stairs easier. In the panelled communal room, she mingled easily with other members. She was getting to recognise them and associate a name with their bodies. Ralph, with his gorgeous penis, was easy to spot. She was amused to see that it twitched into semi-erection, apparently motivated only by the fact that she paused to say good evening to him.

Ella had no trouble in recognising Belle when she bore down on her out of the throng. Ella hesitated for a moment before acknowledging her, not quite certain of her ground. She was relieved when Belle seemed to harbour no ill-will over their previous encounter. Her greeting was cordial and Ella responded in kind, smiling and taking the proffered hand.

'I'm glad you don't feel too badly about what happened.'

Belle smiled widely. 'Oh, no! Quite the reverse. I wasn't happy at the time, I admit, but then I thought about it and I found the more I thought about it, the more fun I could have with the idea. You know what I mean. On the bed for a solitary afternoon nap sort of fun.'

Ella found that the image of Belle masturbating and fantasising about what had been done to her was quite appealing. It was something she would do herself and not a little flattering. 'I'm glad it worked out all right.'

'Oh, it did. I discovered that I like a girl with spirit. Maybe we could get together some time and try some new things?'

'Maybe,' Ella allowed cautiously. 'But what about your shave? Wasn't there a problem about that at home?'

'Oh, you mean my husband? He seldom takes an interest in what's between my legs. That's why I come here. It could all have grown back before he saw it. Just in case, though, I bought myself an outrageously skimpy bikini, put it on at breakfast time, wiggled about in it and told him I'd had to shave off just for him because of it.'

'Did he believe you?'

'Didn't really care, the sod. Didn't even look up from the *Financial Times*. Just said I hadn't got the figure for it, finished his toast and marmalade and buggered off to the office, as usual.'

Ella suddenly had more of an insight into the demons inside Belle that expressed themselves in sadism. 'I'm sorry,' she said, and meant it.

'Never mind. At least I don't go to waste here. I say, have you heard the rumour that we're getting a new young man to play with tonight?'

'No. Are we?'

'Apparently.' Belle held up her hands. 'Look! No rings. That means I might get him all to myself. '

'Oh, Belle. I hope you do. That would be lovely for you.' This time Ella didn't mean it. She had never met this Gunter, whoever he was, but suddenly felt an affinity with him. At least she would be saving him from Belle's clutches. Whatever she did to him would be infinitely preferable, she believed. That made the erotic fantasies that had already begun to skip about in her head much more acceptable to her.

At that moment, there was a burst of laughter and applause that made both women turn to see the cause. Miss Doyle was emerging from the lift, pushing her wheeled bench. Immovably strapped to it was

122

a naked man. He was fixed by his thumb-rings exactly as Ella had been, except that his legs were not in the air. Instead, they were bent at the knees over the end of the bench and kept there by chains fastening his toe-rings to the front legs. Ella could tell by his physique that he was young. He had an all-over tan and his stomach was washboard flat. He was pleasantly, though not excessively muscled. The hair under his arms and at his crotch was so fair as to be almost white. His penis fascinated Ella because it was not erect. What had been done to him and what he was now experiencing must have been at least a little arousing. She guessed that he was exercising supreme self-control as an act of denial. As long as he did not allow his feelings to become apparent, there was some small part of himself that did not belong to his captors.

Ella joined the forward movement of the spectators to get closer to him. Beside her, Belle murmured, 'Excuse me. I've been waiting for one of these. I must fetch something.'

It was not easy to get close to the bench because of the other members who wanted to touch and feel. Ella, knowing that she would see plenty later, was content to remain on the outskirts of the crowd, catching only an occasional glimpse. Even that, though, was sufficient to show her that Gunter was maintaining his stoicism and remaining resolutely unmoved by what was happening to him.

There was a sudden jostle and sway in the crowd as Belle pushed her way to the front. Triumphantly, she set a small box down on the bench alongside him, then said, 'Hello, Gunter. I'm Belle. I'm hoping to see more of you later, but just in case, I bought you a present.'

Gunter said nothing but regarded her with some suspicion.

123

Belle delved into her box and held up what looked like a large crayon. 'Look,' she said. 'It's greasepaint. I'm sure it must be embarrassing for you to be showing your penis like that. Wouldn't you like me to cover it for you?'

That broke Gunter's silence. 'With that? No, thank you.'

Belle turned to the crowd. 'I'm sure you'd all like to see it, though, wouldn't you?'

Their murmurs and laughter being taken for assent, Belle turned back to Gunter. 'See,' she said. 'I'm afraid you've been outvoted.' She reached out and took his flaccid penis in her left hand, expertly pulling back the foreskin to reveal his pink, shiny glans. The stick of greasepaint in her right hand was bright red and she smeared it liberally all over the pinkness while he squirmed in a fruitless attempt to snatch his penis from her hand. She held on tightly and did not relax her grip until she was satisfied with the quantity she had applied. By the time she did release him, there was no longer any need to hold back his foreskin. Under her attention, his penis had erected itself sufficiently to prevent retraction.

Belle selected a black stick next and, pinching his glans delicately between the finger and thumb of her left hand, she stretched his penis upwards, making it clear that the shaft was about to be maltreated.

'No, please! Not more!' Gunter wriggled again but Belle was not in the least put off. She was clearly deriving considerable sadistic satisfaction from having this naked young man at her mercy and was making the most of it. Soon the shaft of Gunter's penis was very black indeed. 'Now I must massage it in for you,' Belle said and, suiting actions to words, she grasped his shaft in the encircling finger and thumb of her right hand, masturbating briskly.

Gunter's penis was, by now, fiercely erect. His eyes were closed and he bit his lip in concentration as he fought for control over his feelings. He sighed with relief when the masturbation stopped, only to open his eyes in disbelief as he felt Belle make a start on blackening his scrotum.

At that point, Miss Doyle laid her hand on Belle's arm. 'Enough, Belle. You've had your fun. Someone else's turn.' She pushed Gunter away to the playroom, then came back to make the necessary announcement. Belle's disappointment at not being selected as the recipient of that night's gift was evident, but her new-found rapport with Ella was sufficient to allow congratulations on her good fortune.

Ella had been revising her plans in the light of what Belle had done and, on the way to the playroom, she stopped off at the kitchen to collect a few things. When she went into the playroom, she was carrying a bucket of hot water, towels and such other things as she deemed necessary to restore Gunter's penis to a state in which it would be fit for the purpose she intended. As she closed the door behind her, the reality of the situation was borne in upon her. She was alone with this young man who had been stripped and prepared for her pleasure. He was completely helpless and at the mercy of her slightest whim. The sensation of power and control swept over her and she delighted in it.

'Hello, Gunter. I'm Ella.'

He turned his head as she came alongside him and the apprehension in his glance made her stomach muscles pulse.

His eyes behind the mask were imbued with pleading. 'What are you going to do to me?'

Ella smiled encouragingly. 'Don't worry, Gunter.

I'm not cruel, like Belle. Who knows, if you're a good boy and don't upset me, you might even enjoy it.'

'Enjoy what?' he asked, suspiciously.

'Well, first of all, we've got to get all that nasty stuff off you,' Ella replied brightly. She picked up a jar of cold cream and dipped into it, smearing it onto his testicles and penis before working it well in to dissolve the make-up. His hips bucked at the sensation and she stopped, turning to regard him with mock severity. 'I won't be able to do it if you wriggle about so,' she said, then pretended to think. 'I know what will keep you still.' She wiped her hands on a tissue and went to a side-table, returning with a pair of tiny clamps like miniature vices.

'What are you going to do with those?'

'Why, put them on your nipples, of course.'

'What?'

Ella explained patiently. 'I'll just tighten them a little bit, so that you can see how they work. Then every time you jump about and interfere with what I'm doing, I'll tighten them a little bit more. That sounds fair, doesn't it?'

She teased his nipples into a better state of erection then spent some time getting the clamps on. It wasn't easy, because his nipples were small and she was intent on not including any of the aureole around them – something which might have decreased the discomfort he felt. She tightened them carefully, watching his face to see the first grimace of pain. When she was sure that he was feeling sufficient but by no means all the pain they could cause, she resumed her massage with the cold cream, noticing that he kept perfectly still and allowed her to do so. That job completed, she dipped her hands into her bucket, then worked up a lather. He gasped and could not avoid a sudden movement as she began to wash his penis and testicles.

Ella shook her head. 'Naughty!' she said. She moved up beside the top part of his body and he knew what was coming.

'No, please! I won't move again, I promise. I . . . Ah! Agh!'

Ella stood watching him for a moment, enjoying his expression of pain as his breath hissed in and out in his efforts to avoid crying out at the cruel pinching to which his nipples were now being subjected. His hands moved constantly as he tried to bring them down to remove the hated objects, while his pectoral muscles jerked and jumped in sympathy.

Satisfied, Ella returned to her bucket. She had selected her next implement of torture with care. It was a perfectly ordinary washing-up sponge, intended for dishes; on one surface, it had an abrasive nylon pad. She dipped it into the bucket and wrung most of the water from it. Gunter watched with widened, horrified eyes as she pointedly held it where he could see its intended use. When she wiped the nylon pad around the head of his penis, he trembled violently and groaned.

'You moved,' she accused.

'No! I swear I didn't!'

'You moved.' Shaking her head sadly, as though with the deepest regret at what she was obliged to do, Ella tightened his clamps again. This time, there could be no doubt about what he felt. His mouth opened in a long, sighing shout of pain that continued as Ella completed her washing operation. She did not use the nylon side of the sponge again. Had she done that, she was sure he would have moved and she was equally sure that he could stand no more nipple-torture. She dried him carefully with a towel, then stood looking at him, drinking in his pain and helplessness.

'Would you like me to take them off?'

'Please! Oh, please!'

'I might be tempted to do that if you kiss me nicely enough.' She moved to his head and leaned over. He brought his head up to meet hers and she kissed him on the mouth.

'Now?' he begged.

'No. I don't think you meant that kiss. Make it a really passionate one.' She stooped over him again, offering her lips. This time he put his heart, soul and tongue into the effort to relieve himself of pain. Ella allowed her left hand to stray down his body and play with the nipple-clamps, moving them and tugging on them just a little, simply for the pleasure of feeling his efforts to be passionate in the midst of agony. Her domination of him was complete and her vagina was dripping with desire for fulfilment.

When she took off the clamps, his relief was evident. 'Thank you! Oh, thank you!' he gasped.

Ella went away to the side-table again. She came back, unwrapping the condom she had selected. It was thick enough to absorb sufficient sensation so that the wearer would take longer than usual to come to the boil. Better than that, it had rows of little protrusions that would, she was sure, prove to be a most satisfactory source of stimulation. As she unrolled the thing onto his rigidly erect shaft, she was pleased to see that he turned his head away, as though embarrassed at his inability to prevent her from doing what she wanted. That was good. It made him an object to be used for her gratification. She frowned suddenly. Something was less than completely satisfactory and she puzzled over what it could be. Then she knew. He was not totally naked; not completely hers. As long as part of his face was hidden from her, she felt that she could not fully own all his personality. She hesitated only for a second. Miss Doyle had told her to be creative and imaginative.

On an impulse, she reached for the elastic strap that held his mask in place and ripped it off his face. His expression almost made her laugh aloud. She had been right! He had been protecting some part of himself with that mask. Its removal was equivalent to ripping the shorts off a fully clothed man. He was humiliated and now completely owned by his Mistress. Compared to that, the fact that he was handsome and that his head-hair matched that on his body was insignificant.

Unreasonably aroused, she put her face close to his. 'Have you ever fucked a girl's bum, Gunter?' She chose the crude words deliberately to shock and his reaction excited her even more.

He flushed. 'No.'

'Ever wanted to?'

He shook his head vigorously. 'No, I don't like it like that.'

'How do you know if you've never tried?' she reasoned. 'Anyway, you're going to today.'

'No, please! Not like that. The other way I would like.'

'But it's not about what you'd like, is it, Gunter? It's about what I'd like.' She squeezed a large gobbet of gel from a tube into her palm and smeared it all over the knobbly condom before she climbed onto the bench and straddled him, facing his head, her knees on either side of his waist. She reached behind her with her left hand and groped for his straining pole, at the same time easing back onto her heels and guiding the tip of his penis into the crack between her bottom cheeks. She worked herself up and down the tip, feeling the heat of it through the rubber before centring it on her sphincter.

Ella's heart was singing. This was the culmination of all her recent fantasies. She had only to let her weight fall back and his magnificent organ would be rammed right up inside her. Her right hand was already manipulating her clitoris in joyous expectation of the rapture to come.

'Stop!' Miss Doyle was striding into the room, her face as black as thunder, the door swinging back against the wall with a crash from the force with which she had flung it open.

'Wha ... what is it?' Ella gasped, startled out of her wits at this sudden intrusion.

'Get off! Get off him at once! Go to my office this minute. Run there! While you wait for me to come, you will not wander about or sit down. You will prostrate yourself face down on the carpet with your arms and legs spread right out. Whether I come at once, or in several hours' time, you will remain in that position. If you don't, I can assure you that you will wish most heartily that you had.'

'But ... but ...'

'Don't argue! Get out and do as I say at once!'

'Yes, Miss Doyle.'

It seemed to Ella that she had been lying face down on Miss Doyle's carpet for ever. When she first ran into the office and cast herself down in that position, her heart had been thudding as much with apprehension as with her recent exertion. Her pulse had returned to normal in a very short time, but her apprehension was as great as ever. So great, in fact, that it never occurred to her to change her position or to move so much as a finger, lest she incur the unspecified but frightening penalty with which Miss Doyle had threatened her. She had long ago sifted through her mind to determine what she had done which had brought about such a stern reaction. She blamed herself and her perverse appetite. She had known in her heart that anal sex was wicked, yet she had persisted in spite of that knowledge. She was a thoroughly sinful person who had earned whatever punishment she was about to receive. Such a wanton as she was deserved no better than to be spread-eagled, face down, in this lowly position, as firmly fixed there by fear as she would have been by ropes and chains.

The fact that she had been ordered to lie with her bottom exposed gave her a fair indication of the form her punishment might take. She had been able to deal with a spanking, but surely Miss Doyle's black anger would not be assuaged by such mild correction? There had been whips and canes in the playroom. Ella's skin crawled at the prospect of a whipping, yet, even as she wondered if she could stand the pain, the sensations inside her stomach and vagina reminded her forcibly of the depths of depravity to which she had sunk. To be ill-used in such a way would fuel the fire of her lust, not dampen it.

The sound of the door behind her opening set Ella's heart racing all over again and she froze into obedient stillness, feeling Miss Doyle's eyes on her bare skin. Then the high-heeled black boots were alongside her face. Ella did not turn her head, but could see them with her peripheral vision.

'How dare you?' Miss Doyle's voice was a low hiss of suppressed anger, as deadly as a spitting cobra's venom. 'How dare you do that?'

Ella turned her head towards the boots. 'Miss Doyle, I'm sorry. I . . .'

'Silence! You will not say one single word!' The boots moved a few feet away, then patrolled up and down, a few paces in each direction. 'You cannot possibly claim to have misunderstood. My instructions with regard to the removal of masks were explicit. They always are.'

Masks? Masks! Of course! That was it. This wasn't about anal sex at all.

Miss Doyle was continuing to pace. 'In an establishment such as Interplay, discretion and confidentiality are everything. We cannot survive without them. There is only one punishment for such a flagrant breach of my rules and that is to be banned for ever from future attendance.'

In spite of her fear of reprisals, Ella could not resist protesting. 'No! Not that, Miss Doyle. Don't send me away. Whip me, cane me, torture me, but don't stop me from coming here. I need it so.'

When Ella began that impassioned plea, she had not thought it to be anything other than a device to be able to continue her investigation for *The Globe*. By the time she got to the end of it, she realised that she was speaking the truth. It was something she had never fully acknowledged before; an unpalatable truth that she had turned her mind away from. She could no longer envisage a sex-life which did not include the ups and downs of submission and dominance such as she could obtain by continued contact with Miss Doyle and her club.

Miss Doyle did not immediately order Ella to silence. 'So, you would accept a whipping, would you?'

'Yes! Oh, yes! Please don't send me away.'

'Hm!' Miss Doyle's long pause was indicative of deep thought. 'It is lucky for you that I controlled myself. I did not leave you here alone for such a long time simply to punish you. I did it in order to be able to calm myself. Had that not been the case, you would already be outside the gates with no hope of ever returning.' Another long, pacing pause, then, 'No ordinary punishment is adequate for what you have done. Suppose it were something far, far worse than a whipping? What then?'

'Anything! I'll take anything!'

Miss Doyle snorted. 'You answered far too quickly to have thought about it. Only an idiot volunteers for something unpleasant without having even some slight idea how unpleasant that will be. Get up and sit in the chair in front of the desk.'

Ella scrambled quickly to her feet, her head spinning slightly after such a long time lying flat. She took her seat and waited until Miss Doyle had settled herself into her own chair. 'Does this mean you won't send me away?' she asked hopefully.

Miss Doyle stared at her. 'After what I tell you, you may wish to absent yourself permanently from these premises. However, this is the chance I have decided to give you. I will summon you to the club just once more. You must make up your mind whether or not to come.'

Ella opened her mouth to speak, but Miss Doyle held up a commanding hand for silence. 'You must understand that the degree of punishment you deserve is beyond my skill to administer. Therefore, if you return, I will deliver you into the hands of the Master.'

'The Master?'

'It is a name you may come to know well. One which will fill you with awe and dread whenever you hear it. I worship at his feet. He is a god. One of the Immortals. His power is infinite. There is no refinement of the art of torture which is unknown to him. He will use and possess your mind as he uses and possesses your body. One single encounter with him is more than most people can tolerate. What you must do now is to get dressed and go home. There, you will think about what I have said and arrive at your decision. Think carefully and long because, whatever your decision may be, there will be no going back on it once it is made.'

'But . . .'

Miss Doyle gestured again for silence. 'Say no more! My patience and generosity are exhausted for this evening. Go!'

Ella went, with much to think about.

Seven

Paula drew her notepad across the desk towards her. 'At last! I thought you were never going to find out. So where is this Interplay?'

'I'm sorry it's taken me such a long time, Paula, but this was the first time I've been allowed to see where I was going.' Ella was developing a remarkable facility for lying to Paula. 'You know the Fernham Road? Well, about three miles out of town, there's this big house with a high, stone wall.'

'Big iron gates and a long gravel drive?'

Ella nodded. 'That's the one.'

Paula scribbled. 'That's the old Rodley place. Everyone wondered who had bought it.' She sucked her pencil. 'Too soon for the Voters' Register. Maybe Land Registry will give us a name or two? You've still not been able to recognise any faces, then?'

'No. Except Miss Doyle, of course.' Ella was not quite sure why she was holding back on Gunter, the one person whose face she had seen. She told herself that it was a matter of pride. A good reporter should have been able to find out more about the young German and she was ashamed to admit that she had not done so. She knew that was another lie. To tell Paula any more than she had would, she felt, represent some sort of disloyalty to Miss Doyle and Interplay and she recognised her deep need for both. At the same time, thoughts of Gunter had reminded her of the incident of the mask. She shivered at the recollection of the only condition on which she would be allowed to revisit Interplay.

'What's the matter? You catching a cold?'

'No. Not really.'

'Wouldn't be surprised,' Paula said unsympathetically. 'All that running about with no clothes on. Well? Come on. Suggestions. How do we tackle this one? Sneak a reporter and a photographer in?'

'Oh, no!' Ella said, hastily. 'I'm sure that wouldn't work. There are security people all over the grounds and around the house. Dogs and everything.'

Paula sighed. 'I suppose it will have to be you then. You'll just have to keep going back until you get something. Just don't get too friendly with that Doyle woman.'

'Er . . . I'm not sure about that.'

'Oh? Why's that?'

Ella gnawed her lip. How much should she tell Paula? 'I sort of got myself into trouble. I sort of broke one of the rules.'

Paula clicked her tongue in exasperation. 'Really! Your job was to gather information, not to make yourself conspicuous.'

Ella blushed. 'Oh, well, it wasn't anything very serious. It's just that if I go back I have to accept their punishment.'

'So? What's your point? You've had your bottom spanked before.'

Ella's blush deepened. 'I know. Only they say it's going to be a man who does it.'

'What man?'

'Oh, they didn't give a name. Just a man.'

Paula snorted. 'I reckon I spank just as hard as any

man. Anyway, you said you didn't do anything serious, didn't you?'

'Yes. I mean, no. I didn't, Paula, honestly.'

'Won't be much of a spanking then, I shouldn't
think. Look, Ella, you're getting to be a bit of a
wimp, you know. A reporter is supposed to be able
to put up with a bit of hardship for the sake of her
career. Now just pull yourself together and get back
there as soon as they invite you again. And this time,
pull a few masks off or do something that gets me
faces and names!'

'Yes, Paula,' Ella said, miserably.

Recently, the Fernham Road had been a place of delight for Ella. Driving out of town along it gave her
time to indulge in pleasurable fantasies about the
things she might experience at Interplay. Today,
though, she drove her little red Fiesta more slowly,
realising that she did so in order deliberately to delay
her arrival. The security guard at the gate recognised
her, opened it and nodded her through. Her progress
up the drive was even slower and, when she parked
the car, she lingered over getting out of it for as long
as possible, reluctant to leave the reassuring comfort
of its familiarity. Eventually, though, there was
nothing for it but to go into the house and up the
long staircase to Miss Doyle's office. Ella knocked
timidly on the door and was bidden to enter.

Miss Doyle was sitting at her desk in her usual shiny
outfit. 'Close the door and stand there.' She pointed at
a spot on the carpet some way from the desk.

Ella took up the required position and waited. Miss
Doyle put her elbows on the desk and pressed her
long, bony fingertips together, staring hard. 'Do you
clearly understand the terms on which you have been
allowed to return?'

'Yes, Miss Doyle.'

'And you will accept without complaint anything that is done to you from now on?'

'Yes, Miss Doyle.'

'What are you wearing?'

The unexpectedness of the question startled Ella. 'What?' She gestured at her clothing. 'You can see. Jacket, blouse, skirt.'

Miss Doyle sighed impatiently. 'Yes, but underneath, girl. Underneath!'

'Oh!' Ella blushed. 'Black panty-hose, black knickers, black bra. That's all.'

'Hm! Well, at least you heeded my warning about those awful denim trousers. Anyway, those things won't do.'

'Do you want me to take them off?'

'Yes.' As Ella began to unbutton her jacket, Miss Doyle held up her hand to stop her. 'Not here. Go into the next room. You'll find a bed in there. On the bed is the clothing you are to wear to meet the Master. Put it all on, but nothing else. The Master is very particular about the way offerings are presented to him.'

Ella went obediently into the next room. She didn't like the sound of that word 'offerings'. It sounded ominous and she felt her heart beginning to accelerate in pace. She examined the clothing laid out on the bed. She had expected some bizarre collection of leather and metal, but this stuff was reassuringly normal. She slipped out of her own clothes and put them on the far side of the bed. Naked, she began to put on the new clothes. There were no shoes or stockings. She stepped into a pair of white panties and pulled them up. They felt very light and gauzy and they were cut high on the side, but not outrageously so. She owned more sexy garments. There was no brassière.

In its place was a sort of bodice with thin shoulder straps. It seemed to be made of the same material as the panties. She pulled it on over her head and settled it down over her breasts. It came only as far as her navel and clearly revealed her nipple erection. She shrugged. What did that matter? She had been too often naked in that house to care about such details.

The only other items appeared to be a jacket and skirt of a grey, two-piece suit. That, too, was curiously light in weight. She slipped into the skirt and zipped it up, then completed her ensemble with the jacket. Woman-like, she could not resist inspecting her reflection in the full-length mirror. Apart from bare legs and feet, she looked quite smart. The suit was well-cut, if a little old-fashioned, she decided. With one final glance at herself, she turned away and padded back into the office.

Miss Doyle looked her up and down. 'Very well. You'll do. Now come over here; put on your rings and sign your contract.'

Of course! That was the reason for the absence of shoes and stockings. Ella would not have been able to put on her rings over panty-hose. As for the reason for the rest of her outfit, she could not guess. It seemed to her to be not particularly sexy or appropriate for what might be coming next. Ella put on her bondage rings, completed her signing and pushed the contract back towards Miss Doyle, straightening as she did so.

'No, don't get up. Stay where you were, leaning over the front of the desk.'

As Ella resumed her stooped position, Miss Doyle took tiny padlocks from her drawer. 'Give me your right hand!'

Ella watched as Miss Doyle pulled her hand to one side and towards the centre of the desk. For the first time, she noticed three small staples evenly spaced in a row along the length of the desk top. The outer ones were about three feet apart. Miss Doyle padlocked Ella's right thumb-ring to the right staple, then drew her left hand out to the side and locked that to the left staple. Ella was now locked in her stooped position, hands spread and fixed to the centre of the desk.

Miss Doyle came around to the front of the desk and knelt. She tapped the inside of Ella's right ankle. 'Spread!'

Ella moved her foot sideways and felt her toe-ring being locked to what she assumed must be another staple at the base of the desk, although she could not see it.

Another tap, this time on the left ankle. 'Spread!'

Ella tried. 'I can't,' she complained. 'It's the skirt.' The width of it was insufficient to allow the straddle Miss Doyle was demanding.

Miss Doyle stood up and hitched Ella's skirt up a little way, allowing the necessary leg separation, then knelt and attached her left toe-ring. Ella moved experimentally. It felt strange, but not uncomfortable, to be secured in this way. Apart from the fact that her skirt was pulled up far enough to reveal a good part of the backs of her thighs, she was fully dressed and trying hard to work out why that should be so.

Miss Doyle went around the desk again and stood where Ella could see her. 'You have now been secured in the position and the clothing appropriate for the commencement of the ceremony of the Rites of Correction, as devised and administered by the Master. There now follows a period of quiet reflection, during which you should think about your reason for being here and the extent to which you regret the error of your ways. I earnestly advise you to do that. It will make a difference to what happens to you.'

Miss Doyle passed out of Ella's sight again and the sound of the door closing made it likely that she had left the room. Ella was baffled. This was all so weird – nothing like what she had been imagining. What on earth was the point in thinking about the episode of the mask? Who would be able to tell what she had or had not been thinking about while she was alone? It seemed like a lot of spooky mumbo-jumbo, designed to scare her. Perhaps this ordeal was not going to be as bad as she had thought. She wished, now, that she had told Paula more. Next time, she would report all she had seen and heard.

The sound of the door opening startled Ella, then she heard Miss Doyle's voice. 'Here is the offering I make to you, Master. I make it in the hope that you will look upon it with favour and grace this house with your presence again in the future.'

Ella continued to listen, expecting some acknowledgement, some reply. There was none and that was faintly alarming. Ella became very conscious of the fact that her lifted skirt was revealing an undignified amount of thigh to the man who must be standing behind her, staring. She could almost feel his eyes on her skin. Suddenly a figure appeared on her right, passing round the desk to stand facing her. She had heard no sound of his approach and she jumped violently.

Ella looked up at the stranger and gasped. He was of average height and build and was wearing a cream-coloured, open-necked silk shirt with loose, wide sleeves. Below the shirt, a black cummerbund separated the shirt from his trousers which were cut tight so as to cling to his muscular legs. He had jet-black hair smoothed back without a parting. His eyebrows were also black and turned up at the inner ends in a way that was slightly Mephistophelian. He had a thin, black moustache and a very small, triangular black beard adorned the tip of his chin.

All these things were a little strange, but none of them was the reason for Ella's gasp. That was due entirely to his eyes. They were wide open, yet even so, the light grey irises were so large that they seemed completely to fill the space between upper and lower lids. His pupils were proportionately large: black and yet, somehow, not black. Ella found that it was like looking into two deep caves. There was darkness yet she knew, somehow, that there would be something to be seen inside if only the interior could be illuminated in some way. He was staring at her and suddenly Ella experienced a very strange sensation, as though her own eyes had become caves that matched his, except that her caves were well lit and this man could see everything within.

The feeling was disturbing and she tried to look away, but found that she could not. The darkness of his pupils fascinated her, luring her on with an unspoken promise of some momentous revelation and she had to keep looking. He reached out with both hands towards her face. Ella's natural reaction was to shy away from his touch, but she remained perfectly still, held in the grip of his eyes. The tips of his forefingers touched either side of her head at the temples. It was a touch so light and gentle that she could hardly feel it, but it seemed that at the moment of contact, a force transferred itself from his body to hers, instantly converted to a flow in the opposite direction. She felt her youth and energy run out into his fingers.

He drew a deep breath and let it out in a long, sighing exhalation, his breath carrying with it a scent of sandalwood and cinnamon. Ella felt her outward flow stop.

The Master spoke for the first time. His voice was

soft, deep and resonant. 'I am pleased, Sister Martha. you have made a good choice and done your work well.' His eyes never left Ella's.

'I am happy to serve the Master,' Miss Doyle said.

The pressure of the Master's fingers increased just a fraction. 'Don't be alarmed. I am merely exploring. Ella? Your name is Ella?'

'Yes.'

'The proper form of address is, "Yes, Master".'

'Yes, Master.'

'March . . .? Mast . . .? No . . . Mask! I see a mask. Why is that?'

Miss Doyle made a small noise like the beginning of a word, but the Master interrupted her. 'No! She will tell me.'

Ella's head was spinning. This was obviously some theatrical performance just to impress her. Clearly Miss Doyle had told the man the reason for her predicament. Even though she suspected that, Ella still could not tear her eyes away from his, or prevent herself from speaking. 'I broke the rules by taking off someone's mask, Master.'

The Master nodded. 'Ah yes! I see that clearly now.' He paused for a moment, frowning. 'I do not see contrition, Sister Martha. You told her of the need for quiet contemplation and repentance?'

'Yes, Master. I made that quite clear.'

'Ella, why did you not use your period of atonement correctly?'

'I did, Master. I did think about what I had done.'

He hissed softly and dropped his fingers from her temples, rubbing the tips together as though he had received a small electric shock. 'A lie is a bad thing, Ella. It is black and poisonous.' He placed the palms of both hands flat on the desk. 'See how the small black lie falls from the lips of a liar.' He raised his

143

hands suddenly, spreading them apart. Released from beneath them, a tiny black snake writhed, coiling and wriggling.

Ella hardly had time to react by jerking back away from the convulsing horror of the small creature before he snatched it up, grabbing it behind the head so swiftly that it had no time to strike at his hand. With a contemptuous gesture, he threw it onto the floor out of sight behind the desk and trod on it heavily, grinding it under his heel. He leaned over the desk again and replaced his fingertips at her temples. 'And now the truth, Ella.'

Ella opened her mouth to reinforce her previous story, but suddenly could not do so. His demonstration prevented it. Maybe a score of tiny, black lie-snakes were ready to slide out over her tongue and fall onto the desk if she told another untruth. 'I'm sorry, Master. You are right. I didn't think . . .' Her eyes prickled with tears.

'Ah! The truth! How soft and white is the dove of truth, Ella; it's warm wings fluttering, bathing you with an inner glow of satisfaction.'

It was remarkable! He was absolutely right! That was a comforting image. How simple it was to tell the truth and not have to lie. How pleasant was the reward for honesty. She smiled at the Master, realising at that moment just how handsome he was.

The pressure of his fingers increased again. 'And now I must search for other things.'

It seemed to Ella that all she thought and felt had passed out of her through his fingertips and were now in his possession. She was embarrassed, thinking of her desire for anal sex and her need for domination and humiliation.

'I see!' he said.

Ella stared into the deep caves of his pupils. Was

144

that some tiny image flickering there, bright blue, but indistinct? 'You see, Master?'

'Everything!'

'Everything, Master? Even . . . Even . . .' She could not bring herself to put her anal sex fantasies into words.

'Yes, even that, Ella. But that is good. Every human is flawed. Only we, the Immortals who have detached from humanity, are free of defect. Fortunately for you, I can start to remove your flaws by means of the Rites of Correction. By chastisement of the body and by frequent satiation with the perversions that afflict you, you may be cleansed. When you are so cleansed, Ella, your whole body will be a temple; a comforting shrine to your easy conscience. Would you like me to do that for you, Ella? To help you? To cleanse you by chastisement and satiation?'

Ella felt the familiar thrill of submission to a will stronger than her own. His words were as exciting as his charisma. 'Yes, Master. Help me, please. I need you to help me.'

He dropped his hands to his sides and stood erect. 'Very well. I will prepare you for what must come. Sister Martha. I know that this procedure interests you. I offer you my permission to stay and watch.'

Miss Doyle placed the palms of her hands together in an attitude of prayer and bowed her head over them. 'My Master is gracious, as always. I am very conscious of the privilege.'

Ella's nipples tingled. Whatever was going to happen to her was going to be watched! That added an extra dimension of humiliation to the proceedings and she was conscious of a thrill of sexual expectancy at the prospect of having her appetite for degraded submission fed. She felt the Master behind her, the front of his body pressing against her buttocks. His

145

hands came around her body and she looked down at them. They were very masculine hands, strong, clean and brown. As she watched, each hand gripped one lapel of her jacket and with a swift, outward wrench, ripped it open, buttons showering onto the desk in front of her. That action was an affirmation of his power. He could do with her what he liked and she could not prevent it. She drew in her breath sharply and tugged at her thumb-rings to confirm her helplessness. The tiny restraints were just as effective as huge handcuffs. There was something very definitely sexy about that. To a casual observer, she would appear to be posed voluntarily. In fact, there was no way she could protect her breasts, but was forced to stand with her hands spread apart on the desk.

She looked down at herself. Beneath the thin bodice, the tingling in her nipples had become full erection, forcing her rings against the material so that the shape of them showed through clearly. She sucked in her chest in an attempt to remedy this display of arousal, but even the protection of the bodice was to be denied her. The Master's strong hands gripped and ripped again, tearing the light cloth away from her soft, white breasts and allowing them full exposure. Freed from even such a flimsy support, the weight of the twin orbs drew them down towards the desk below, wobbling slightly in the aftermath of the force of his action. She saw him grip her nipple rings between fingers and thumbs, then felt a steady pull as he pushed his hands forward, extending the tender brown flesh. She moaned softly and moved with him to relieve the tension on her nipples, her breasts following his hands out and down until she was bent far forward.

'Sister Martha?'

In front of Ella, Miss Doyle took a pair of slender

silver chains from her drawer and Ella comprehended instantly what was going to be done to her. The import of that centre staple became obvious. She was going to be chained to it by her nipples, forced to remain bent over. Each chain had a clip at one end and, one by one, Miss Doyle fastened them to each nipple ring as it was held out to her by the Master. She passed the other end of both chains through the staple and held them, looking to the Master for instructions.

He released his hold on the rings. 'A little lower.'

Miss Doyle pulled on the ends of the chains she held, drawing them through the staple and forcing Ella to stoop slightly more.

'Good! There!'

Miss Doyle brought the ends of the chains back up to meet the parts above the staple and passed a tiny padlock through four links at once. When she clicked it shut, Ella was fixed where she was. She could bend further down, but would not be able to straighten up any more without stretching her nipples unbearably.

The Master came back to stand in front of Ella and she saw his eyes on her captive breasts. For some reason, knowing that he was looking at her and seeing this enforced genuflection was arousing.

When he spoke again, the sound of his voice thrilled her as much as the words he used. 'The Path to the Light is through the Portal of Pain. You will have to tread that path – feel that pain.'

'Yes, Master.'

'I can see that you are impatient to begin your journey to enlightenment. You wonder how that may be done. Think, Ella! Think! The answer lies within you.'

Ella knew that what he said was true. All her thoughts, for days, had been about the prospect of pain. She realised that all through the build-up of her preparation, she had been actively looking forward to the moment when that pain would begin. It had become more than a desire – it was an urgent need which must be satisfied right now. Experimentally, she straightened a little. The strain on her nipples increased. She tugged a little, moving her upper body with small, jerky, rocking motions. At each tug, a little jolt of unease passed from her nipples, through her breasts and into her soul, easing the craving she felt there. Joyfully, she strained upwards as hard as she could, elongating her nipples and stretching her breast flesh into long cones against the resistance of the taut chains. Her head went back, her eyes closed and she opened her mouth to let out a long shout of agony and elation.

The Master's warm hand between her shoulder blades pressed her down towards the desk-top, relaxing the tension on the chains. 'Enough.'

Disappointed, Ella relaxed, breathing hard.

'I understand your needs, Ella. I have seen deep inside you and know everything about you, remember.'

Now the Master's fingers were not touching her, but that was no longer necessary. The bond of his voice was all that was necessary to soothe her, calm all her fears, raise her hopes and expectations.

'Pain cleanses. Pain elevates the human spirit to a new and better plane.'

'Yes, Master.'

'Yet I forbid you to cause pain to yourself again. That is a puzzle, isn't it, Ella? A puzzle you must solve. How to obtain that inner peace you so desperately need?'

'You must give me the pain I need. Is that the answer to the puzzle, Master?'

'In a way, but you do not say "must" to me.'

'Please, then. Please give me the pain I need.'

'Gladly, but first you must give voice to your most earnest wish, apart from pain. I know what it is, because I have seen it in you, but you must announce it here, in the presence of witnesses. It is part of the Rites of Correction to do this. Only by externalising such things may you detach from them and be free. Speak!'

For a few seconds Ella rebelled, reluctant to make public her perverse craving to have her anus penetrated. Then desire swamped such thoughts out of existence. The Master knew every nook and cranny of her inner self. He knew all about her secret passion and was trying to help her. Her eyes filled with tears at the thought of such generosity. She knew that she loved him. He was kind and gentle. She could rely on him if only she put complete faith in him.

'I want you to ... to do it to my bottom.'

The Master's voice was gently chiding. 'That is an unclear statement, Ella. It does not reveal either the act or the way you feel about it. Use the words that you are storing in your most secret place. The words I have seen. The words you dare not use.'

'I want you to fuck me in the arse!' It was almost a defiant shout and Ella was appalled and amazed to hear herself say something she had hardly been able to express silently within her. Immediately, though, there followed an immense relief, as though some heavy burden had been lifted from her.

'Very well. All things in order. Your immediate need is for pain and I will attend to that first. Only when that appetite is sated will we proceed to the next hunger and deal with that as well.' He held out his hand towards Miss Doyle. She passed out of Ella's sight and there was the sound of a cupboard door opening and closing. When she came back, she was carrying a length of leather which she passed to the Master. He took it from her and laid it lengthways on the desk in front of Ella. 'Behold! The instrument of your salvation. Your key to the Portal of Pain that leads to the Path of Light.'

Ella looked at the fearsome thing. It was about thirty inches long and four inches wide, made of leather thick enough to render it a flexible arc when Miss Doyle had carried it. One end of it was shaped into a convenient handle. All the edges and the end, where she would have expected abrupt corners, were rounded off. The skin of her buttocks crawled suddenly, as her vivid imagination told her of the instrument's likely use and she shuddered without knowing whether that was a sign of apprehension or sexual expectancy.

'Are you ready to begin your journey, Ella?'

The Master's resonant voice startled Ella out of her fascinated reverie. With difficulty, she dragged her eyes away from the terrible implement and considered his question seriously. This was the point of decision to which her wanton ways had led her, then. She had allowed her base urges to get the better of her, swamping her finer feelings. She had not controlled her aberrant longing to be dominated and humiliated. Now it was entirely just and logical that she should be punished for that omission. It was the only way she could get over her strange lusts – by experiencing them to the point of satiation. She gulped and nodded, not trusting her voice.

The Master nodded in return, apparently satisfied. He passed out of Ella's sight behind her and she jumped as she felt his hands brush the backs of her thighs. He gripped the hem of her strained skirt in both hands and ripped outwards and upwards. The material tore almost as easily as tissue paper and Ella realised the reason for the odd lightness of the materials she wore. They had been specially woven with tearing in mind. His hands slid up under the back of her jacket and dug into the small of her back as he curled his fingers into the waistband of the skirt. It gave way with a slight popping sound and fell to the floor. That sound and the slight draught of air on her lower body were wildly exciting to Ella. She was being stripped in preparation for a beating and that knowledge drove a bolt of sexual lightning deep into her vagina and anus. The knickers she wore would tear in the same way as her other clothing and she waited in tense, glad expectation for his next move.

She felt his fingers in the waistband of her flimsy panties and braced herself. He did not tear them. Instead, he eased them down, little by little, gradually revealing more and more of her bare bottom until it was all exposed and the panties strained across the gap between her straddled thighs just below the two white moons that were her buttocks. At once, Ella realised what he was doing. Of course! He knew everything about her and her weird craving for humiliation. To leave her like that with her knickers pulled down like a naughty schoolgirl about to be caned for some prank was much more debasing than ripping them off. This man was, indeed, a master of torment!

He was in front of her again, picking up the leather strip. He held it out towards her face. 'Kiss the agency of your correction.'

Ella turned her face away and pulled back. The chains on her nipples stopped her with a jerk and she felt the supple leather brushing her cheek. She shuddered. Soon, that leather would slap across her carefully prepared bare bottom, that naughty part of her body in which most of her sinful desires were concentrated. Another electric thrill ran through her vagina. She submitted to his charismatic will and her own craving. Slowly, her head turned to the front. Her nose absorbed the animal scent of the leather as her lips touched the tough hide. Unable to stop herself, she opened her mouth and kissed it as she would have kissed an impatient lover, her tongue flickering and tasting as if it were not inanimate but had a libido of its own so that, by exciting it, she could encourage the thing in what it was about to do to her.

When the Master moved the strip away, she followed it, grovelling for one last caress until she was brought up short by her nipple restraint. She experienced the tense hiatus that comes between foreplay and penetration. She drew in her breath and waited in quivering expectation, the muscles under the skin of her buttocks twitching repeatedly as he moved out of her sight to her left.

Thwack!

The leather strip indented the springy flesh of her buttocks, its flexibility allowing it to encompass the whole curve of them to lay a full stripe right across, from side to side. A four-inch wide band of fire ignited it its wake, stinging and pulsating.

'Nng!' Ella's head jerked back as if pulled by a string. Her teeth clenched and her mouth became a thin line across her lower face, only the outer corners of it open in a rictus of agony to emit the strangulated sound of her pain and shock. She longed to move her hands backwards to massage the centre of her discomfort, but the thumb-rings held firm, no matter how much she struggled. Deep inside herself, she felt the warm gush of total arousal. She was demeaned, in a bondage that was as much mental as physical. The man who had enslaved her had placed his brand of fire on her backside, his mark of ownership and control. Even now, he was flaunting his power over her, looking at her nudity above the humiliating, lowered, schoolgirl panties. In her straddled pose, he would be able to see every detail of her sphincter in its lightly haired crevice between the cheeks of her bottom. Below that, her vagina was gaping and vulnerable. She could feel herself twitching and knew that he would see this sign of his dominance over her emotions as movement in her protruding labia.

There had been no second blow. Ella waited with as much fortitude as she could muster. Was this a cruel elaboration of her punishment? She thought she heard brief mutterings. What was happening? Miss Doyle appeared on her right. In her hand she was carrying a red plastic bowl – the kind from which dogs are fed. She put it down on the desk top between Ella's hands. Ella stared down at it. It was filled with a disgusting green slime. Had it not been green, she would have guessed that it was watery tapioca pudding. Whatever it was, it turned her stomach to look at it.

'Eat.' The Master's voice battered again at her will.

Ella looked down at the bowl again and bile bit at the back of her throat. 'Ugh! No, I can't!'

She felt his hands at the back of her jacket. A thudding rip and it came apart, tearing effortlessly up the back seam. A second rip parted the collar of the jacket and it fell down her arms onto the desk. A third assault tore apart the back of the flimsy bodice which was her only covering. One by one, he snapped the thin shoulder straps and threw the garment away. Now, from her neck to the mid-point of her thighs, she was naked and her quaking white flesh was completely available to the predations of the hungry, punishing leather.

'You have experienced one light stroke, in order to

show you what is in store. Now, stage one of the Rites of Correction begins in earnest. I have deliberately not gagged you. That way you may scream, protest and beg as much as you like. It is thus that you externalise your pain in order that you may eventually detach from it, as you must detach from all worldly things in order to find the Path to the Light. Your beating will continue until you eat. Eating symbolises bodily hungers of all kinds. When you eat, you will show that you acknowledge those hungers. Acknowledgement of their existence is the essential prerequisite of detachment from them.'

Ella understood instantly. The Master knew how to torment the mind as well as the body. He knew her deep need to be enslaved, knew that for her to beg and plead without hope of mercy would multiply all she felt. Yet he was placing in her own hands control over the extent of her pain. That was almost a loving thing to do. Yet subtle. He also knew of her need for degradation. To stop the pain, she would have to degrade herself further than ever before, to the level of a captive animal. She would have to eat that vile, green slop by dipping her face into a dog's feeding bowl. She felt the first internal rumblings of spontaneous orgasm.

Thwack!

The leather strip bit into her bare back at the bottom of her shoulder blades. The end of it curled down the right side of her body and slapped the side of her breast, causing it to judder violently.

Thwack!

The next blow was at the level of her hips, across the twin dimples above her buttocks.

Thwack! Thwack! Thwack!

Mercilessly, the leather marched up and down the full extent of her nakedness. The strokes were regularly spaced in time so as to be predictable. Not knowing where each one would fall increased the torture. Time and again, Ella drew in her buttocks, then was obliged to stick them out again as she arched her back downwards in response to a change in the target area.

'Agh! No more, Master, I beg you. Mercy! Please, no more!' Ella's face was wet with real tears of pain as her back, bottom and thighs were submerged in a sea of blazing heat. She knew that she could not stand much more without fainting. She did not want to faint. That would mean that she would not feel the pain she needed, the pain that she deserved, the pain that would purge her sins. The green slop in the bowl beckoned to her now, not because it would signal her release from agony, but because she longed for that final, climactic act of self-humiliation and debauchery that would mark her, irrevocably, as being completely subject to his authority.

Slowly, very slowly, she bowed her head until her lips touched the cold, slippery surface of the goo. Retching a little, she extended her tongue to lap at it. As if that contact had been a switch, the beating stopped. Ella didn't know whether to be glad or sorry about that. While she was still wondering, she felt the Master's strong fingers in the hair at the back of her head. Gripping, he plunged her face into the bowl, twisting his hand so as to press her nose against the curvature of the bottom and wipe it from side to side. The slime was up her nose, the tasteless ghastliness of it in her mouth. He let her go and she lifted her head, gasping, blinded and spluttering; gobbets of green slime trickling down her face.

It took a lot of head-shaking and blinking before Ella regained full use of her eyes. When she did, she saw the Master and Miss Doyle in front of her. A square flap at the front of his tight trousers was hanging down and his penis was exposed and erect. Miss Doyle was in the act of rolling onto it a condom of precisely the same type that Ella had put on Gunter. She stared at its black bumpiness, understanding very well the wordless message that was being transmitted. She had been tethered like an animal, beaten like an animal, forced to eat like an animal and now she was going to be used as a dog uses a stray bitch on heat in the street.

And she was on heat, she knew. As she stared at that long, curving, stiff penis, now sheathed in black rubber and being lubricated by Miss Doyle from a tube of gel, she knew that she had never wanted anything more in her life. The Master passed out of her sight to her left and she arched the small of her back down, thrusting her buttocks out lewdly in a pose of total subservience, lust and surrender, making little, mewing sounds of excitement and anticipation. He grabbed at her panties, tearing them from her. That was good and right. For what she was about to suffer, it was only proper that she should have no protection at all, however slight. She felt his thumbs on each of her bottom cheeks, pressing and stretching them apart to make her more accessible, then the tip of his penis was pushing at her anus, demanding admission. He knew her mood and what she wanted. He gave it to her in full measure, thrusting himself brutally into her depths, spearing and impaling.

Ella screamed with pain and delight. She had never taken anything so large and long into that cavity. He had a firm grip on her hips and was thrusting hard and fast, the rubber bumps of the condom doing their dreadful work while his dangling testicles slapped tantalisingly at the backs of her thighs. She fought to get a hand free, so that she could masturbate her aching clitoris. Being unable to do so identified her as a tethered bitch and excited her enormously. As though reading her mind, the Master slid his right hand round and under her body until he could grope through her pubic hair and find her special button of delight. She thought she could actually hear the sound of her hood being popped back, then his fingers were in, flesh to flesh, in direct contact with that most sensitive and yearning of all her places.

He co-ordinated his circling rubs with his urgent plunges, maximising the ecstasy. She screamed again as she came to orgasm, then flopped, relaxing. He did not slow for a second. Relentlessly, his penis continued to ream at her anus and his hand redoubled its masturbatory movements. Ella came to orgasm again, the spasms being forced from her by powerful stomach contractions. Still he did not stop and she knew that he was going to take her to a point of satiation beyond exhaustion. Panting, she submerged herself in the profound sensations of what he was doing to her. She reminded herself of her faults, telling herself that she deserved this punishment. The forbidden words welled up in her mind and she savoured them, allowing them to increase her perverse enjoyment. 'I am being fucked in the arse!'

By the time the Master stopped and withdrew from her, Ella was only semi-conscious. As far as she could tell, he had not ejaculated, while she had lost count of the number of explosive orgasms he had brought about in her. She lay across the desk panting, heedless of the fact that her breasts rested in the feeding bowl. Her sorely tried sphincter burned and stung and she could feel her juices trickling down the insides of her thighs. Sexual pleasure, she felt, could never possibly be the same again. Anything less than she had just experienced would pale into insignificance by comparison.

Eight

Ella woke gradually, coming to consciousness by stages from a deep and peaceful sleep. Stirring, she opened her eyes and did not, for a moment, know where she was. Then she identified the bedroom next to Miss Doyle's office and sat up with a start, grunting as the movement caused her sore back and bottom to smart. She sat on the edge of the bed, knuckling her eyes. She remembered Miss Doyle leading her into the bedroom and inviting her to shower and dress before going home. She remembered sitting down on the bed, then lying back to collect her thoughts for a moment. She must have fallen asleep and been there ever since. How long ago was that? She found her wristwatch with her discarded clothing and looked at it. Ten-thirty? That didn't make sense. It was still light outside. She put the watch to her ear before she remembered that quartz watches don't tick. Suddenly, the puzzle was solved. It wasn't ten-thirty at night. It was ten-thirty in the morning! She had slept for more than fourteen hours. She was late for work!

For a few seconds, she panicked, then relaxed. However much she rushed, there was nothing she could do which would now get her to the office on time, so she might as well take her time. She got off the bed and went over to the dressing table to inspect herself in the mirror. She looked like the wrath of God. Bits of dried green yuk were stuck to her face and her breasts. She teased out a lock of hair. There were green bits in that as well. She padded over to the small bathroom that Miss Doyle had pointed out to her the previous evening and turned on the shower. Gratefully, she stepped into the hissing heat of the falling water, holding up her face to its benison so as to remove all traces of her ordeal. Soaping in a leisurely fashion, she realised that there were some traces she would not be able to remove so easily. Craning over her shoulder, she could see the swathes of red weals on her bottom and had to assume that those on her back were just as apparent.

Her ablutions complete, she turned off the shower, stepped out and wrapped her hair in a towel, turban fashion. She picked up another and made her way back into the bedroom, patting herself dry as she went.

Miss Doyle was there waiting for her, sitting on the edge of the bed. 'Good morning. I thought I heard you moving about.'

Ella wrapped the towel around herself like a sarong, rolling the top above her breasts to keep it up. 'I'm sorry. I must have fallen asleep. Why didn't you wake me?'

'I didn't have the heart. You looked as though you needed it.'

Ella laughed. 'I did, but now I'm late for the office.'

'That's easy. Don't go in today.'

Ella considered this. 'I suppose I could call in sick,' she said.

'Of course you could. Not right at the moment, though. We've had trouble of some sort with the line. I'm expecting it to be repaired at any moment. They won't worry about you for a while, will they?'

No, Ella thought. Paula wouldn't worry. She'd assume that Ella had got somewhere with the story and was following it up. In a way, she had. She deserved a day off after what she'd been through. She made up her mind. 'No. No one will worry.'

'Good, because there has been a rather interesting development.'

'There has?'

'Yes. You have found favour with the Master and he has agreed that you should be allowed to visit his Temple of Pleasure, if you wish to do so.'

If she wished to do so! Ella's heart leapt at the prospect, although whether her excitement was due to the fact that she would be able to develop her story or whether it was at the prospect of seeing the Master again – perhaps being spoken to or even touched by him – she could not decide. She tried to conceal her enthusiasm. 'That sounds nice.'

Miss Doyle smiled. 'Nicer than being stuck in an office all day.' She got up. 'Dry your hair and brush it. When you're ready, come into the office.'

'What should I wear? My everyday clothes?'

Miss Doyle's keen eyes swept over Ella's body, noting the fresh, healthy glow of her skin. 'Leave the towels here. Otherwise, come as you are.'

'Oh! You mean . . .'

'Yes. Just wear whatever you've got on under the towels.'

When Ella walked naked into the office, Miss Doyle was sitting behind the desk. She gestured to the usual chair. 'Sit down. There are some things you have to understand before we go. You have looked into the Master's face. Does it appear in any way familiar to you?'

Ella frowned. 'It's funny you should say that. I couldn't place it then, and I still can't, but there was something about it.'

'Suppose I jog your memory. Have you seen many very old prints or woodcuts?'

'Yes, I suppose I have.'

'Like these?' Miss Doyle opened a heavy, calf-bound book and turned it so that Ella could see the rather poorly reproduced etching. It was of a semi-nude satyr, complete with horns, forked tail and cloven hooves.

Ella laughed. 'Oh! I see what you mean. It is a bit like him, isn't it? It's the eyebrows, I think.'

Miss Doyle flicked the pages over. 'And this ... and this ... and this ...?'

Ella looked at her a little strangely. 'You're not suggesting he's the Devil, are you?'

Miss Doyle smiled and closed the book. 'Of course not. But what is interesting is that all those pictures, like all depictions of supposedly non-existent legends, have their basis in one original. You have heard of the legend of Faust?'

'The magician who sold his soul to Lucifer in exchange for magic powers? I know of Marlowe's version. I'm a bit shaky on Goethe and Lessing. It was all a tall tale, anyway. There wasn't really any Faust.'

'Johann Faust was born nearly five hundred years ago. It was not until some two hundred years after his supposed death that Marlowe wrote the first account of his dealings with the Devil. It was based on some very old papers and drawings brought to him by someone claiming first-hand knowledge.'

Ella smiled. 'After two hundred years? Come on!'

Miss Doyle did not return her smile. 'The drawings purported to be likenesses of Johann himself and Lucifer. The stranger who brought them bore an un-canny resemblance to the supposedly dead Johann Faust. He would, he said, help Marlowe to complete

162

a work that would make his name world-famous, but on one rather unusual condition. He had to agree to transpose the two drawings so that Lucifer, who was a heavily bearded, rather undistinguished-looking man, despite his black powers, would become known as Faust, while Faust's image would become famous as the archetypal representation of Hell's ruler.'

'But why?'

'Suppose, for a moment, that this fantastic story could be true. If someone had actually traded with the Devil and won for himself eternal life, would he want the whole world to be able to identify him on sight? Would it not be better if he bore a passing resemblance to someone who was known not to exist?'

'I suppose so,' Ella said, wonderingly. 'But you're not saying . . . I mean you can't be suggesting . . . Five hundred years? I can't swallow that, I'm afraid.'

'Of course not. It defies logic and all the natural laws we know. I didn't insist that you believe. I only pointed out to you that Johann Faust was a real person and that Marlowe wrote about him with no logical way of acquiring his intimate knowledge of the facts. I have shown you some illustrations and you have made your own observations of a certain person now very much alive. Faith becomes necessary when complete knowledge fails us. It has to be built on an incomplete set of premises, otherwise it would not be faith.'

'Yes . . .' Ella said, slowly, 'I see that, but . . . Wait a minute! The deal Marlowe wrote about was that when Faust died, the Devil would grab his soul. He couldn't have become immortal, otherwise the deal would have been null and void.'

Miss Doyle nodded approvingly. 'Good! You are using your brain. But that was only the original bargain, of course. You are supposing that there were no subsequent meetings.'

'And there were?'

'Many of them. Faust tired quickly of worldly pleasures. Immortality was his one way of getting the better of Lucifer. To do that, he had to seek the path to enlightenment through the Portal of Pain. He had to pay many times over for his enjoyment of riches and success. He had to detach from wealth and hand back most of the powers he had obtained. In the end, perhaps through sheer admiration for his persistence, Lucifer gave in and granted his desire. As one might expect from the Devil, there was a fiendish condition. To retain his magical powers and his immortality, he has to continue to prove that his Path to the Light is a valid one, open to anyone. He has to bring three other mortals through the Portal of Pain to enlightenment and immortality every year.'

Ella shook her head. The concept was too amazing, too bizarre. 'You're saying that the Master is . . . that Faust is . . . Surely, such a thing couldn't have been kept secret for centuries. The world would know about people trying to becoming immortal.'

'It does know a little. However, it does not know about the successes. For obvious reasons, the immortals don't advertise the fact, so the world knows only the failures; the ones who tried for immortality through enlightenment, but failed and remained mortal. Does it not strike you as odd how many connected with the Faust legend have also sought what they called philosophical enlightenment eschewing conventional religion? Goethe, for instance; Pascal; Locke; Descartes?'

Ella didn't answer. Not only was she ashamed to admit that she was not that well read, her brain was reeling with the magnitude of what she had been told. Surely, this woman must be touched in the head to believe . . . But she clearly did believe and she did not appear to be at all irrational. The thing needed a lot of thought and that required much time alone in some quiet place.

Miss Doyle rose and held out her hand. 'Come now. I will take you to the Temple of Pleasure and once more into the presence of the Master.'

Ella got up automatically, then glanced down at her naked state. 'Like this? Is it far?'

Miss Doyle laughed. 'You won't need clothes. It's only a short journey.'

She led the way out of the office and along a corridor on the same floor. At intervals along the passage, uniformed security guards were standing as though on sentry duty. That was a little embarrassing for Ella. She had got used to being in the presence of others when they were naked too, but not while they were clothed. The guards did not attempt to interfere with Miss Doyle and her protégée. At the far end, a large oak door barred the way. As they approached, a guard outside knocked in a particular way and the door was swung open by another guard on the inside. Ahead of her, Ella saw a wide carpeted staircase, more fitting for a palace than for the old Rodley place, despite its impressive size.

At the top of the stairs, across a short landing, a door stood open and they went inside. The room in which Ella found herself was surprisingly large, about the size of a ballroom. It seemed to her that it must have occupied most of the top floor of the house. There were no windows and the walls were all draped with grey satin curtains gathered in decorative loops and festoons. What light there was came from rather dim chandeliers overhead. Even in that poor illumination, Ella could see that there were a dozen or so young women in the room. None were masked. They all wore identical clothing: long, white flowing gowns which covered them completely from neck to floor. Or perhaps, she corrected herself, the gowns would have covered them had they not been made of some diaphanous, gauzy material which was practically transparent so that almost every detail of their bodies could be seen through it.

It was a moment or two more before Ella realised that there was something odd about the women. They were not standing about in groups, chatting animatedly. They were completely silent and arranged in a double row which stretched towards the far end of the room, half turned inwards, facing away from her.

Miss Doyle called softly to the nearest. 'Sister Beatrice.'

The girl turned and came towards them, moving with an easy grace. She was about the same height as Ella, but with dark, short hair. Her figure was plumper than Ella's and her breasts, which could be clearly seen through her gown, were full and well rounded with very large, brown aureolae and nipples. Her pubic hair was a mist of darkness under the gauze. She was, perhaps, not conventionally beautiful, but there was a strange serenity about her, a sort of gentle peace, that lent her features dignity and composure.

'Sister Beatrice, this is Ella. You are to be her warden for this visit.'

'Of course, Sister Martha.' Beatrice smiled at Ella and unfastened the bow that kept her gown together at the neck. She pulled it open, exposing the front of her body, then lifted her left breast in her left hand, squeezing and pushing so that her long, brown nipple with its gold ring stood out, offering it to Miss Doyle.

Miss Doyle took hold of the ring in her right hand, then grasped the ring in Ella's right nipple with her left hand. She pulled, drawing the two women together until their nipples touched. She let go of

Beatrice's ring to feel in her pocket for a small, gold padlock. Looping the hasp through Ella's ring and Beatrice's, she clicked it shut, locking them together.

Ella said, 'What are you doing?' but Miss Doyle made no reply. Passing behind Ella she drew her left nipple ring close to Beatrice's right and locked those together as well.

Miss Doyle nodded, satisfied. 'There!' she said brightly. 'Beatrice will explain everything. Just ask.' She walked away, her shiny black posterior in its tight, cat-suit cover swaying as seductively as ever.

Ella found herself in a state of high embarrassment and confusion. She had read about the concept of 'personal space' but had never really appreciated it until now. Not only was Beatrice well inside the space Ella thought of as her own, she was also semi-naked and their nipples were locked together. Ella was acutely aware of her own nudity and blushed as she realised that she did not know what to do with her hands. She shuffled her feet a little, but that pulled on her own and Beatrice's nipples and that did not seem to be a polite thing to do to someone she had only just met. Ella decided to stand perfectly still, her head politely turned to one side so as not to breathe into Beatrice's face.

Beatrice said gently, 'It's quite all right, Ella. You mustn't be alarmed.'

Ella looked at her and returned her smile. 'I'm sorry,' she said. 'It's all so strange and ... and ... I don't know what to do with my hands.'

'Oh, that's all right, too. I should have told you. Put them on me, like this.' She reached around Ella and laid her warm hands flat on the top part of Ella's buttocks.

Ella fumbled for a moment.

'No, not over the gown. Under it, on my bare body. There! Isn't that better?'

Ella wasn't sure that it was. The feel of Beatrice's soft haunches under her hands was awakening what she thought best left asleep, in view of their present proximity. To distract herself from that line of thought, she said, 'What's going on? Who are these other girls?'

'We are the Sisters of Light, Disciples of the Master. Through his perfection, we seek immortality by means of detachment and enlightenment.'

The statement sounded to Ella like a set of lines being recited after having been learned by constant repetition. 'Why are they all standing like that?'

'This is the audience chamber. We await eagerly the moment when the Master will wake from his sleep and once more favour us with his glance.'

'I see, but why have my . . . Why have your . . . I mean, why are we locked together like this?'

'You are not a Sister. I will turn my mind to good thoughts on your behalf so that you may be granted that privilege but, until you are, you must be permitted to see no more than an outsider. The lights are not always as bright as this and it would be easy for you to slip away while we are blinded by the divine light from our Master's eyes. I have been chosen as your warden and my punishment would be severe if you intruded upon our ceremonies. Therefore, Sister Martha has thoughtfully removed all risk to me by making sure that you cannot go anywhere without taking me with you.'

That was true, Ella thought. It would be hard to find a more intimate connection. Her mind went back onto its previous course. Beatrice's skin seemed hot under her hands and Beatrice's lips were invitingly close.

A small sound like a collective sigh attracted Ella's attention to the end of the room. The wall curtains there were being drawn back as in a theatre and Ella was instantly reminded of the Master's eyes. The space beyond the grey curtains was black, yet not black. It had depth and lacked only light to illuminate whatever was there. As she watched, something began to appear in the blackness. About three or four feet up from the floor, a grey mistiness was condensing out of nothing. The mist grew more solid until it could be said to have a definite square shape. Still more detail emerged and it became obvious that the shape was a large grey throne. When finally it resolved itself without distortion, Ella could see the Master seated on the throne, his elbow on one arm, his hand supporting his head. He stirred, his head lifting away from his hand and becoming upright as he stared at his Disciples. He stretched high and wide, an action that opened his silk shirt to reveal his chest. The sighing noise was repeated.

'What happens now?' Ella whispered.

'Sh!' Beatrice whispered back. 'The Master now awaits the arrival of one of the Old Ones, those other immortals who are on a plane higher that this world.'

Another mist was forming to the right of the Master's throne. That, too, grew more distinct in shape until it was clear that it was a woman in a long, flowing robe. It grew no more vivid than that, remaining a misty wavering image. The Master spoke, his voice deep and resonant, each syllable clear. However, it was no language Ella had ever heard. The misty image replied in the same language, then faded slowly and disappeared.

The Master sighed heavily. 'Sister Belle!'

Ella's ears pricked up at the familiarity of the name and she looked to see who would respond to that call.

A woman near the stage threw off her gown, clasped her hands behind her head and sank to her knees, her legs spread wide, her breasts thrust forward. 'Master, I hear your call!' It was the same Belle with whom Ella had enjoyed such interesting encounters. She must have become a Disciple.

'The words of the Old One fill me with sadness, Sister Belle. They inform me that you have not completely detached from worldly things.'

Belle's voice had an unfamiliar, whining quality. 'I have, Master! I swear I have! I have left my house and my husband. No part of the house was mine to sell. I have sold my car and closed my bank account.'

'And the other account, Sister? What of the other account?'

'I . . . I . . .'

'Do you deny its existence?'

'No, Master. It was . . . It was the account I used for clothes. It was so hard to give it up. I wouldn't ever have used it again, I swear. It was just something familiar . . .'

The Master shook his head sadly. 'A relic of vanity as well as all the weight of Mammon. How can I help you to enlightenment when you deliberately shackle yourself to such a heavy burden. This means expulsion from the family. You must leave your Sisters of the Light and return to your mercenary, mortal ways.'

'No, Master! Have mercy! Please don't send me away!'

The Master thought deeply, his chin resting on his clenched fist. At last, he raised his head and looked around. 'Sisters, what say you? Can Sister Belle be saved?'

Twelve voices, Beatrice's included, answered in unison. 'We can save her, Master!'

'How can you save her?'

'By our love, Master!' Again, the reply was in unison.

'Do you, then, have so much love to give?'

'We are Sisters of the Light! The love of one Sister for another is as boundless as the ocean! The love of all Sisters for the Master is as great as Creation!'

Ella realised that she was again listening to a learned ritual chant. That appeared to be the end of it. She could tell by the tone of the Master's voice.

'Sister Belle, your Sisters have agreed to help you. You must begin again on the road to enlightenment by passing once more through the Portal of Pain.'

'Yes, Master!'

'Sister Verity?'

A tall girl in the centre of the double line took off her robe and knelt in exact imitation of Belle. 'Master, I hear your call.'

'Your latest task was to prepare Sister Joan and Sister Rebecca for just such an eventuality. Have you done so?'

'I have, Master.'

'You know that, for a second attempt at a passage, the threshold of the Portal must necessarily be much higher than before?'

'We do, Master.'

'Do you believe that what you have devised will guide Sister Belle to such a height?'

'That high, and higher, Master.'

'Very well, you may begin.'

Sister Verity turned and beckoned. Two other Sisters dropped their gowns on the floor and went with her to one side of the room. They drew aside a portion of the curtains and disappeared. When they came back, they were pushing and pulling at a wheeled truck. It consisted of a very low platform, about six feet square, at one end of which was mounted a sturdy, vertical frame, also six feet square. The legs of the frame rested on the corners of the platform, making the cross-piece about six feet high.

Belle saw this piece of apparatus coming and sank back on her heels in dismay, burying her face in her hands. The three Sisters positioned the device in the centre of the room so that the end with the frame faced Ella. They went to Belle and lifted her up, holding her, stroking her and talking to her in low tones, apparently trying to comfort and reassure her. Reluctantly, she allowed them to push her forward until she stood in front of the frame with her back to the platform. Still supporting and comforting, they encouraged her to sit on the front of the platform, then they gently lowered her upper body until she was lying on her back.

She wore no thumb-rings, but there were leather straps riveted to the platform in such positions that, when she spread her arms wide, the straps could be buckled around her wrists and upper arms, holding her firmly. Sister Verity stayed by Belle's head, kissing her and talking to her, while Sister Joan and Sister Rebecca went to her feet. They buckled wide leather straps around her ankles. There were already chains attached to these anklets and, when they were certain that they were secure and comfortable, the two women lifted the chains, heaving at them so that Belle's legs were pulled into the air. Belle was not slightly built and it was with some difficulty that they managed to haul the lower half of her body off the platform before clipping the ends of the chains to staples set in the side of the frame. That meant that Belle's upper body was flat on the platform, her widespread arms emphasising the complete exposure of her large breasts, while her lower half was curved upwards, her bottom well clear of support, her legs strained straight and very wide apart. Ella could see that there was still no trace of pubic hair around her vagina or on her pubes. Had it been allowed to grow back naturally, there should have been at least a light fluff after this length of time. It seemed, therefore, that Belle had continued to shave, for reasons best known to herself.

Sister Joan and Sister Rebecca armed themselves with lashes that they took from where they hung on hooks at the side of the upright frame. Those lashes consisted of a handle from which many leather tails protruded. The tails were quite short, perhaps nine inches in length. The lash that Sister Verity took had tails that were about twice as long. She took up a position alongside Belle and to her right, then calmly, without any great show of passion, began to stripe the lash across Belle's breasts. She did not appear to be striking with any great force, but the weight of the tails as they fell was sufficient to cause Belle's soft flesh to wobble and dance with each blow. She moaned softly and turned her head from side to side in distress as the white skin of her breasts slowly turned to red under the steady torment.

Sister Joan turned her attention to Belle's right foot, the sole of which was completely available and unprotected. She struck at the underside with her short lash. Again, the blow did not appear to Ella to be a very hard one, but Belle's reaction seemed to demonstrate that the resulting pain was severe. She screamed aloud and jerked her foot back, kicking as far as the length of the securing chain would permit. When Sister Rebecca started on the sole of her other foot, her screams became louder and her frantic movements made it very difficult for either Sister to find her target.

Sister Verity stopped her own beating and came to the foot of the platform, where she held a brief, whispered conversation with her two Sisters. It seemed to Ella that this was a complication for which the three had not allowed and they were having to make improvised plans to devise a means to overcome it. From the angle of Belle's head it appeared likely that she was straining to hear what was being discussed, but Ella guessed that she could not possibly have done so. When the conference broke up, their strategy became immediately clear. Sister Verity and Sister Rebecca positioned themselves on either side of Belle's outstretched right leg and grasped it firmly near the ankle, preventing her from kicking away from what was in store. Sister Joan raised her lash again and struck at the sole that was now conveniently placed. This time, the blow was true and the smack with which it landed echoed around the room.

Belle screamed even more loudly. The only part she could now move was her left leg and she did so, kicking wildly. That had the effect of revealing even more of her vagina and anus and, even at that distance, Ella could see that both were puckering and twitching constantly. She imagined what it must be like to be undergoing such torment. On those few occasions when her own feet had been tickled, she had become aware of the hysterical reaction that produced in her; the feeling that she must pull her feet away, or die. She could not imagine that tickling being completely inescapable, as well as being converted into painful smacks with a lash such as Sister Joan was using, but she tried. The result of that effort was that the soles of her own feet tingled, her vagina lurched and became very wet inside.

The Sisters changed places. Now Sister Joan and Sister Verity held Belle's left ankle while Sister Rebecca plied her lash. Ella could see the skin on the sole of Belle's left foot becoming as bright red as that on her right and her voice was hoarse with screeching.

Ella was so engrossed in what she was watching

that Sister Beatrice's voice startled her, soft though it was. 'How much they love her! They are determined to save her by using every scrap of their ingenuity!'

Ella thought about this. At first, it seemed to be a perverse distortion, a weird way of looking at what was happening. The more she thought about it, however, the more that seemed to be a right and proper perspective. She knew that Belle's home life was far from happy. Within this community, she had found love and contentment. Surely that could not be wrong? That stability was now threatened. Only by receiving this treatment from her loving Sisters could she continue to be with them. Beatrice was right! Ella flashed her a quick smile of understanding.

The punishment of Belle's feet seemed to be over for the time being. Sister Verity had gone back to the top end of the platform and was once more lashing Belle's breasts, while Sister Joan and Sister Verity had turned their attention to the tender skin on the insides of her spread legs. Belle's kicking and writhing was just as fierce, but the target area was larger and her movements did not unduly upset their aim.

Ella felt Sister Beatrice's hands move on her buttocks. They had been resting there quietly, but were now stroking back and forth. Ella glanced sharply into her face. Her lips were wet and shining, her dark brown eyes liquid with passion. Ella gulped, feeling the lesbian part of her responding. Tentatively, she moved her own hands across Sister Beatrice's bottom, relishing the soft resilience of her young flesh.

Sister Beatrice smiled at her. 'The love of one Sister for another is as boundless as the ocean!'

Ella nodded, completely unfamiliar thoughts welling up in her. She had no brothers or sisters and her relationship with her parents had not been particularly close. Only with Paula had there been anything that could be described as a familiar intimacy and even that had been based on Paula's desire to dominate her. Here, in this place, were twelve women and one quite extraordinary man who loved unselfishly, who gave unselfishly each to the other. It was a real family, such as she had never known. And now Beatrice was including her in that family, was welcoming her just as though she had been a true Sister, instead of an outsider. Ella's heart reached out towards such generosity. She leaned forward and kissed Beatrice full on the lips.

To her delight, the kiss was returned in full measure. Sister Beatrice's hands moved off her bottom and explored her pubic hair, feeling for her clitoris. Ella moved her own in imitation, finding that Sister Beatrice's vagina was just as moist and ready for penetration by fingers as her own. She, too, had pierced and ringed labia.

Sister Joan and Sister Verity had worked their way up the insides of Belle's thighs and their lashes now worked on the area directly between her legs. Alternately, the leather tails smacked onto Belle's vulva and pubes. Sister Verity had dropped her lash and was kneeling, now, fastening to Belle's nipples the same sort of clamps that Ella had used on Gunter. Soon, there would not be even the brief respite from pain occasioned by the need to swing the lash. The clamps would see to it that the torment was continuous. Sister Verity was trying to pull a large amount of aureole through the gap in the clamp before tightening it. When it was tightened, Belle's nipple, already long, would appear to be grossly elongated and would remain fully erect until the clamp was released.

Ella felt herself to be close to orgasm. Sister Beatrice was very skilled in the art of masturbation and Ella tried to match that skill with her own efforts to bring Sister Beatrice to climax.

Sister Beatrice kissed Ella again and murmured, 'We must share Sister Belle's pain, you and I.'

That was a wildly exciting suggestion. 'Do you want to slap me?'

Sister Beatrice smiled at Ella's enthusiasm. 'No need. Just lean back!'

Of course! If they both pulled away from each other, the fact that their nipple rings were joined would mean that each was torturing themselves and the other at the same time. Ella leaned back, still masturbating and being masturbated. This was an unbelievably sexy thing to do. She watched her brown nipple elongate and felt the pain begin. She could tell that Sister Beatrice must be undergoing the same torment. Ella stared at her, daring her. 'More?'

'More!' Sister Beatrice leaned far back. Now the aureolae of their nipples was forced into a sharp cone by the strain, the soft flesh behind it pulled into arrow-shaped creases which pointed at the centre of their discomfort.

Out of the corner of her eye, Ella saw that Belle's nipple clamping was complete. Inches of pinched flesh were sticking up out of each clamp, obscene, yet perfect. She was still jerking about under the impact of the thrashing her vagina was receiving, but now there was a difference in her movements and in the sound of her hoarse moans. She was coming to climax, unable to withstand the jolting vibration of the lashes as they fell repeatedly on the fleshy mound covering her clitoris. Ella was coming to orgasm too. She was sharing Belle's pain as well as Sister Beatrice's. They would all come at the same time, in loving harmony. The love of one Sister for another was as boundless as the ocean. They were as one family, moving towards the Light and at one with the Master. The love of all Sisters for the Master was as great as Creation! Love . . . Sisters . . . the Master!

Bucking, wriggling and rubbing her body lasciviously against that of Sister Beatrice, Ella came to the boil at the same time as the others, then relaxed, completely at peace with herself, her cheek pressed against that of her dear Sister.

It took Ella a few minutes to recover herself. When she did so, she turned to see what was happening to Belle. She was being released from her restraint and helped to her feet by the three Sisters who had helped her through the Portal of Pain. They were kissing her and comforting her, stroking her sore places before covering her with her gown. Ella looked towards the end of the room, into the blackness there. The Master was still sitting where she had last seen him, his throne apparently suspended in space. Only now his image was much less distinct; greyer and fuzzy.

'Oh!' There was a world of disappointment in Sister Beatrice's voice.

Ella looked at her. 'What is it?'

There were tears at the corners of Sister Beatrice's eyes. 'The Master is returning to his sleep. Sometimes he comes down among us. I had hoped . . .'

At that precise moment, as though a light had been switched off, the Master and his throne disappeared, leaving only blackness. Ella, too, felt a sense of loss and disappointment.

'Well, Ella? Has Sister Beatrice been looking after you?'

Ella leapt in surprise, her head jerking around. The Master was standing beside them, smiling a little.

Ella looked from him to the blackness, over which the curtains were now closing, then back to him again. 'Master! Where . . .? I mean, how . . .?'

He smiled. 'I was there, and now I am here. Is that what troubles you? It is very simple. You would see nothing odd about my arrival had it been, say, five minutes later. That has to do with your fixation with time. Mortals see time as though looking down through a narrow slot. Draw a meandering line on a long piece of paper and pass it beneath that slot and your unenlightened brain translates it as random movement from side to side. I, on the other hand, am free to move in the dimension of the paper – on the other side of the slot, as it were. I can move to any point I choose on the line. I am moving in space, but you see it as a movement in time. Consequently, it must appear to you that I can materialise in places separated from each other only by the single tick of a clock.' His smile broadened into a laugh at Ella's apparent bewilderment. 'Never mind, little one. Just don't be alarmed. What seems to you to be a miracle is really a very ordinary application of a rule of Nature not yet recognised by most of the world.'

Ella experienced a sensation of awe. Truly, this man was not as others were. She looked again at his face – so handsome, so wise, so infinitely kind. With a sudden buzz of rekindled appetite, she remembered the way he had dealt with her body: understanding its needs, dominating her, owning her, yet satisfying her completely. She very badly wanted to repeat that experience. Perhaps that is why he had transported himself to her side? Perhaps he would touch her? Caress her? She trembled a little at the thought.

Then Miss Doyle was also at her side, brisk and businesslike. 'We must not take up too much of the Master's time. He has much to meditate about in order to be able to teach today.' She was unlocking the little gold padlocks, freeing Ella's body from that of Sister Beatrice, her warden. 'Come, now! You are permitted to see a little more of the Temple of Pleasure. Did you hear, Ella? Come with me. It's all right. You will see the Master, and Sister Beatrice, again.'

Ella reluctantly allowed herself to be drawn away, keeping her eyes fixed on the Master until the last possible moment. Only when they were outside the audience chamber did she speak. 'Where are we going?'

'To see how the Sisters live.' They were walking down a long corridor with doors at regular intervals on either side. Miss Doyle stopped at one, turned the handle and went in without knocking. The room was quite small; clean, neat and well-lit by a large window. The furniture was spartan, consisting only of an iron-framed single bed, a chair and a chest of drawers. On the wall above the chest there was a photograph of the Master, showing only head and shoulders. Perhaps it was the emotions she had felt during her recent close contact with him that put the thought into Ella's head that the portrait had the quality of a religious icon.

'This is Sister Hazel. Sister Hazel, this is Ella.'

Ella spun round, startled. Because of the twin obstructions of Miss Doyle's body and the opened door, she had been completely unaware until that moment that the room was occupied. Now she saw that there was a handsome, young, red-haired woman standing facing the blank wall behind the door. She turned her head towards Ella with the same beatific, gentle smile that Beatrice had.

'Welcome, Ella.'

Hazel was naked. There was something unnaturally still about her pose. It was a few seconds before Ella perceived the reason why only Hazel's head had turned, not her body. From each of her nipple rings, fine strands about three feet long extended to the wall, where they were secured to little hooks.

Miss Doyle stepped aside a little, to afford Ella a better view. 'I wanted you to see this, because it is a perfect illustration of the way the Master's Disciples strive to follow his teachings, even when deprived of the glory of his personal presence. Hazel is subjecting herself to the pain of exhaustion. Observe that she is standing on a section of the floor that appears to be a rubber mat. Actually, it is a moving walkway – a sort of horizontal treadmill. At intervals, it will begin to move, either fast or slowly. She will then walk, trot or run until it stops again, impelled to do so by her attachment to the wall.'

Ella looked more closely. 'But she is not tied up or anything? Her hands are free. If she wanted to, she could unhook those strings and get off the treadmill.'

'Of course! That is the whole idea. Anyone can endure torment inflicted upon them when there is nothing they can do about it. It takes a special kind of self-discipline to inflict the torment on oneself. It is rather like the flagellation practised by nuns in a past, less civilised age and serves the same purpose. Through mortification of the body, they hoped to achieve enlightenment of the mind.'

At that moment, the treadmill started to move. After an initial lurch to recover her balance, Sister Hazel began to walk forward to maintain her position, striding with a regular, easy pace. The speed of the walkway increased and she began to jog, her breasts jouncing and her buttocks, trim though they were, joggling at every step. Faster still, and she was running in earnest, a look of intense concentration on her face. Now a light sheen of perspiration was breaking out all over her nude body and the room was filled with the sound of her laboured breathing.

Ella was concerned, well aware of the fragility of the tissue of those ringed nipples. 'But what if she trips or stumbles? Surely that would result in the most dreadful injury?'

'No. She has tied herself with a very light, wool yarn which would snap long before that could happen. That is why she has to be alert and vigilant all the time, even when the walkway is at rest. If she were not, the yarn could easily break. If that happened, she would feel obliged to report the fact and volunteer for another day of total exhaustion tomorrow. She will not sit or sleep for twenty-four hours. I remind you that this is self-discipline. The mild restraint of her nipples is symbolic. It joins her to the fabric of this Temple and thereby unites her in spirit with the Master while she strives to reach the path to enlightenment through the Portal of Pain.'

The treadmill slowed and stopped. Hazel stopped too, quite drained of breath and energy. She stooped, her hands resting on her knees, her lungs sucking in great gulps of air. Unable to speak, she turned her head to look at Ella and nodded her agreement with what Miss Doyle had said.

'And now there is a treat,' Miss Doyle said as she led Ella out of the room and closed the door. 'Today, we are to have a communal feeding.' She took Ella back to the audience chamber.

This time, the gowned women were arranged in a single line down the centre of the room. As Miss Doyle and Ella came in at one end, Sisters Verity, Joan and Rebecca came in at the other. Each was carrying a set of red feeding bowls stacked one on top of the other. Ella remembered using a bowl like that only too well and felt her insides squelch at the recollection. The Sisters passed down the line, setting one of the bowls on the floor in front of each woman, then put down bowls for themselves before taking their place in the line.

'What are they doing?' Ella whispered. There was no sensible reason why she should have whispered, but it seemed to her that it was the right thing to do in that place, such was the religious fervour manifest in the attitudes and expression of the assembled Sisters.

'Today, the Master is being most generous with his time and energy,' Miss Doyle explained. 'He knows how much the Sisters look forward to his personal presence and the slightest opportunity of contact with him. They will kneel, naked, to eat; not using their hands. The food is only symbolic – just a few crumbs of cereal. The importance of the gesture is to signify their humble acknowledgement of worldly, animal desires. Do you remember the teachings of the Master?'

Ella nodded. 'Yes, I remember.'

'As you did, the Sisters admit their sinful lust, thus externalising it. When it is sated, they can detach from it. Unfortunately, the Master cannot satiate so many appetites at once. Only one Sister will be chosen for that privilege. They all know that the position they are obliged to adopt in order to eat will display their hindquarters to best advantage. They use that part of themselves as best they can to further demonstrate their acknowledgement and externalisation of sin. The Master will decide who best exemplifies that mute confession and it is she who will receive the favour of his attention. In the spirit of love and generosity which typifies the Disciples of the Master, the Sisters who have not been so fortunate will not envy the chosen one. They will rejoice for her, watch her receive her reward and do all they can to make sure she is fully satisfied.'

Ella swallowed convulsively, wetting her lips. The image forming in her mind was both lewd and enticing. The notion of a row of nude women, heads down and bottoms high in the air, all presenting their genitalia simultaneously for the Master's inspection, was stimulating. To know what would be the result for one lucky one was devastating!

Miss Doyle was watching Ella closely, gauging her degree of arousal. 'Would you like to join the line?'

Ella restrained an impulse to plunge both hands into her groin and press hard in order to still the rampant surging she was experiencing in that area. 'Yes, oh, yes!'

'Very well.' Miss Doyle beckoned to Sister Beatrice. 'Another bowl for Ella, please.'

'Of course, Sister Martha.' Sister Beatrice smiled her Giaconda smile and moved away. Presently, she came back with a red bowl and placed it beside her own in the line. She took Ella's hand and led her to stand with the others before resuming her own place. 'Just do what we do,' she said. 'Don't worry about not having the habit of a Sister. We will all be taking them off presently, then we will be as bare as you are.'

Ella could feel her heart increasing in pace – a sure sign to her of her sexual anticipation. It scaled up as the Master entered the audience chamber from a door at the far end. He moved to a position at the front and centre of the line of waiting women.

'Sisters!'

'Master, I hear your call!' All twelve women cast off their robes simultaneously and sank to their knees. Ella, though mindful of Beatrice's recent admonition, was taken a little by surprise and was a fraction behind the others in echoing their response and in kneeling. Glancing sideways to see what they did, she copied their pose, clasping her hands behind her head, splaying her knees and sticking her chest out.

The Master looked up and down the row, then nodded, satisfied.

'Eat.'

Ella looked sideways again, to check on the correct procedure. Beatrice and the others had clasped their hands in the small of their backs and were now grovelling with their faces in their dishes. Ella did likewise and found it not an easy thing to do without the support of her hands. With her eyes below the level of the rim of the bowl, she had no peripheral vision as she sought the few scraps of cereal at the bottom with the tip of her extended tongue. She was breathless with sexual tension. She was once more an animal – a bitch on heat, degraded and humiliated beyond belief. This time, though, she was in competition with twelve other bitches, all equally highly sexed and motivated by the same lewd, unveiled, unbridled craving. Which of them would win the prize of repletion?

She could not see the Master, but knew that he must be walking up and down behind them. There would be acres of desirable flesh for him to choose from. There would be pubic hair of every conceivable shade in which nestled femininity of assorted sizes and contours. Would that be what attracted the Master's attention? Perhaps he preferred the total exposure offered by complete hairlessness? Ella shuffled her knees a little further apart and forced her back down so as to make her buttocks protrude as clearly and sharply as possible, moving them from side to side ever so slightly. Any more vigorous movement would, she felt, be less sexually attractive by virtue of its blatant vulgarity. She wondered if that were an error or not. Perhaps some of her competitors were, even now, gyrating wildly and receiving more attention because of it? She felt her labia part, exposing the entrance to her vagina, and was glad of it. Her clitoris was erect but, with its infuriating

185

propensity for remaining hooded, in spite of its tumescence, that would not be obvious to the Master. She longed to reach under herself and pop it free, but dared not move her hands from what seemed to be the required position. Perhaps that was as well. Had she been free to touch that area, she knew that she would have been incapable of refraining from masturbating furiously. She could, at least, employ her strong young muscles to manipulate her sphincter and she did so, causing it to pucker and relax in kissing movements and thus draw attention to itself.

'I select Sister Belle!'

Ella raised her head from her bowl, sick with disappointment. She looked down the line and saw all the Sisters, except Sister Belle, getting to their feet. She got up too. Why had the Master chosen Belle? She was definitely not as young or as comely as herself. Perhaps it was the fact of her pubic shave, the shave that Ella had given her? Irrationally, she experienced a pang of chagrin. Then she understood. The Master had selected Belle precisely because of her failure to obey the dictates of his teaching. He had set her on the Path to the Light again. He had given her a wonderful, second chance at the Portal of Pain and now he was physically expressing his complete forgiveness of her failing. What a marvellous man he was! Truly one of the Gods, deserving of his immortality! When Ella saw the expression on Belle's face, Ella could no longer find it in herself to feel jealous of her preferment. Although she had raised her head from her bowl, she was still kneeling with her buttocks thrust out in provocative invitation. Her expression was radiant with happiness and there were tears of relief and joy in her eyes. Poor Belle! Like Ella, she had not known what true love and family unity could be until she entered this conclave of Sisters. The recent threat of expulsion would have been like a death-knell. Her unexpected salvation, followed by this demonstration of renewed acceptance, must be traumatic.

The Master was beckoning to the other Sisters. Ella joined them as they gathered around him. Not until they reached out to him and began to remove his clothes did Ella realise that Belle's privilege was to be even greater than could be imagined. Belle was going to feel his naked body pressed against hers without even the slight barrier of clothing to separate her from his sacred person. That brought on another instant of jealousy. Ella had not been accorded that great joy. She overcame it. Perhaps, by diligent following of the Master's teaching, she too could reach the height of enlightenment necessary before she would be allowed such an intimate liaison.

He was nude, now, and his body was everything that Ella's fevered imagination had driven her to think it would be. Without quite knowing how it came about, she found herself on her knees in front of him. She stared at his erect penis, that instrument of wonder that had driven her to such heights of ecstasy. She reached out with both hands, then stopped, amazed at her own temerity.

She looked up into his face. 'May I, Master? Please?'

He smiled down at her, then nodded indulgently. 'Very well, then. Just for a moment or two.'

She took the treasured article in her hands, then leant forwards and engulfed it with her mouth, sucking it deep into the back of her throat. The whole force of him communicated itself to her brain through this close connection and made her feel dizzy. She began to suck and tongue the length of it, urgent and demanding.

She felt his hand on her forehead, forcing her away. 'Now, Ella. It is for Belle today, remember.'

She drew back, ashamed, but still relishing the taste of him. 'I'm sorry, Master.'

'It's all right,' he reassured her gently. 'Would you like me to allow you to help me to enter Belle?'

'Yes, please, Master!'

'Kneel down with me, behind her. Now you may take my penis and guide it to its appointed place.'

Ella, kneeling behind Belle on the Master's left, reached out again with her right hand and grasped the shaft of his penis low down, just above his testicles. Belle's thighs were wide apart and her vagina and anus yawned in invitation. Belle looked round and saw what Ella was doing. By her expression and her indrawn breath, Ella could tell that it was not just the imminence of penetration that was exciting her; it was the fact that the penetration was to be accomplished with Ella's assistance. Ella drew the hot shaft of living Godhood towards the soft, white buttocks in front of it and placed the tip squarely on Belle's puckered, pink sphincter, so clear and open in the absence of hairy covering.

The Master shook his head reprovingly. 'We are not indulging your tastes today, but Belle's.'

'I'm sorry, Master.' Chastened, Ella dragged his solid prepuce down to the entrance to Belle's love canal and placed it within. With the greatest possible satisfaction she watched in fascination as the Master slid the whole length of his shaft smoothly forward until it disappeared completely, his body and testicles preventing further ingress. Belle gave a mighty shout of pleasure and satisfaction, her neck muscles straining as she pushed her head far back to bay her joy at the ceiling.

The Master began to work himself back and forth,

little squelching, sucking noises indicating that Belle was already fully lubricated and thoroughly enjoying the process. At each inward thrust, Belle's swollen and inflamed labia indented and at each withdrawal they protruded, slavering wet kisses on his iron-hard rod in order to encourage its speedy return. Experimentally, Ella reached under Belle and felt for her clitoris with her left hand, at the same time delicately stroking the Master's hard, brown buttocks with her right.

'Yes! God, yes!' Belle jerked and wriggled in orgasm, then flopped lower, her elbows on the floor.

Ella looked questioningly at the Master, who nodded, understanding her unspoken question.

Ella used her right hand again, this time to slap sharply at Belle's right buttock cheek. 'Up, get up! You've got to go again!'

Belle straightened her arms, locking her elbows and the Master recommenced his plunging torment.

Ella slapped again. 'Go for it, Belle!' She groped again with her left hand.

'No, Ella, don't touch me there. I'll come again!'

Ella slapped harder. 'Yes, you will, won't you?' She found Belle's taut clitoris again and rubbed it remorselessly.

'No! Please! I . . . Agh!' Belle exploded into orgasm again.

This time, no exchange of glances was necessary. Ella knew exactly what the Master intended and she would do everything in her power to see that Belle got every ounce of satisfaction and exhaustion out of that intention. Slapping and rubbing, timing her movements as though the Master were some orchestral conductor and his penis a baton, she watched Belle climax three more times, each tiring her more than the last.

Ella's mind-bond with the Master was complete and intact. She knew again what he wanted and she transferred her attention to his marvellous body, stroking his bottom and testicles, leaning forward to kiss and nibble at his nipples. At the last possible moment, he withdrew from Belle and Ella grabbed at his penis, pressing it down with the flat of her hand as he worked it against the top of Belle's buttock crease. To share this much in his final ejaculation was a delight to her, almost as much as if he had penetrated her own body. His creamy white sperm shot out from the red tip of his solid rod with immense force, spattering over Belle's back. Ella flung herself forward and clasped Belle's body with both arms as she frantically licked at the Master's offering of power, absorbing his essence into herself and rejoicing in the moist heat of it. When she was satisfied that there was no more to be found on Belle's body, she ran her hands over her own breasts and stomach, lest some should inadvertently have strayed there, licking her fingers in the hope of transferring some further small scrap of his potency.

Then, suddenly, it was all over and it was time to return to some semblance of normality after the heady madness. With a strong sense of disappointment and loss, Ella allowed Miss Doyle to help her up and lead her away. Miss Doyle took her to the far end of the audience chamber, where there was a large couch against the wall and, having indicated that she should sit, took her place alongside her.

'I think you enjoyed that?' Miss Doyle said.

Ella, her mind still reeling from the force of recent emotions, could only nod.

'I think you have enjoyed everything you have seen heard and done here.'

'Yes, very much!'

'Would you, then, like the opportunity to stay?'

Ella stared at her. 'Stay? You mean for the rest of the day?'

'No. Permanently. For ever.'

'You mean ... You mean become as the others are?' The idea was simultaneously frightening in its immensity and enormously appealing.

'I do. You are being offered an extraordinary opportunity; a gift from the Master himself. You may, if you choose, become one of the Sisters of the Light – one of his Disciples. The Master would use his best endeavours to train you into enlightenment and, perhaps, if you are very fortunate indeed, into immortality.'

Ella was overcome with awe. She had not dreamed that such a prize could ever be hers. She had envisaged her visit to the Temple of Pleasure as a delightful interlude; an experience not to be repeated, followed by a return to the humdrum life of the outside world with all its many problems. Here, in this place, she would be surrounded by love. She would truly belong at last in a way she had never belonged to anyone.

She opened her mouth to express her glad acceptance, but Miss Doyle stopped her with a gesture. 'Before you decide, I must once more point out to you the cost of such a step. You would have to detach completely from all worldly things. If you have friends or family outside this place, you must never attempt to contact them or respond if they try to contact you. Such an earthly contamination of the spirit that the Master would be trying to build in you would be disaster. Can you do that?'

Ella thought about her life at *The Globe*, which now seemed unutterably mundane. Paula was the only person she might have claimed as a friend and even that friendship paled into insignificance when compared with what she was being offered here. 'I would do that gladly.'

'You cannot achieve enlightenment while burdened with possessions. You saw how difficult it was for Belle to separate completely from such things. As a Sister of the Light, you would own only a gown and such toilet articles as are necessary for cleanliness. Everything else must go. Your bank accounts, your flat, your car. You must give them all up.'

Ella thought about her flat, where she had so often known loneliness. What need would she have of a car when she was permanently in the Temple of Pleasure? What need of money when everything that was worth having would be supplied in abundance? 'I can give them all up,' she said, 'but that will take time to arrange.'

Miss Doyle shook her head. 'All will be taken care of. We are well used to such procedures. We will go now and make out the necessary papers. You will need a letter of resignation which makes it clear that you do not wish to be disturbed in your new, happier life. As for the other things, your signature will ensure that all assets are converted into cash. That is paid into a special fund which the Master uses for the good of the less fortunate in society. Is it not a pleasant thought that, in seeking your own true happiness, you will be bringing a little joy into the lives of others?'

It was a most pleasant thought. Ella glowed with inner satisfaction, a little relieved that she was not, by her decision, being entirely selfish. 'When do I actually become a Sister?'

Miss Doyle smiled. 'It is already accomplished. You became one of us when you agreed to the terms of a Disciple's life. You are now Sister Ella. I am your

Sister, Martha, and you shall refer to me as such in future. Come, kiss me. We are Sisters of the Light! The love of one Sister for another is as boundless as the ocean! The love of all Sisters for the Master is as great as Creation!'

Nine

Paula Matheson was worried. When Ella had not reported for work on that first day, she had assumed that some important development in the story Ella was working on had detained her. On the second day of absence, she had remembered Ella's shivering fit and decided that she had, in fact, come down with the flu, though it really was too bad of her not to telephone and say so. Paula made up her mind to give her a good talking to about that. Now, this morning, had come this extraordinary letter. Seated at her desk, Paula pulled it towards her and read it again, although she almost knew the contents by heart.

Dear Paula,
For some time now, I have been discontented with the way my life is going. I feel I need to get away and have a long think about my future. Please accept my resignation from The Globe. *Please pay any salary due to me into my current account, which I shall soon be transferring to Yorkshire. That is where I have decided to make my new life. I have deliberately not given my address there as I wish to make a clean break from everything in my past . . .*

Angrily, Paula pushed the thing away from her as if, by doing so, she could dispel the cloud of concern that had descended upon her when she first read it. It was, on the face of it, a perfectly ordinary, if totally unexpected, letter of resignation. Had it been anyone else, she would have simply snorted with disgust, filed the thing and set about recruiting another junior reporter. However, she could not rid her mind of the recollection of Ella's reluctance to return to Interplay. She had said that she was to be punished by some man. Paula had made light of it at the time, but now that threat took on a much more menacing aspect. She cursed herself for not taking it more seriously, for not having taken Ella off that story, in which she was obviously getting too deeply and personally involved, and replacing her with a more mature and cynical member of staff.

Well, there was something she could do about it. She could ease her conscience by making such enquiries as would satisfy her about the authenticity of the letter. She pushed back her chair, got up and put on her coat. Putting her head round the door of the Press Office, she said, 'I'm going out and about for a while to follow up a story. Mind my phone for me while I'm away.'

The young man who was the sole occupant of the office looked up from his keyboard and blinked. Paula going out on a story? That was newsworthy in itself! He shrugged and nodded, 'OK, Paula,' then returned to his piece about soggy supermarket bacon.

Paula's first stop was Ella's flat. As she mounted the common staircase, her unease grew. Two men were carrying a couch down the stairs. That must be the reason for the removals van outside. She thought she recognised the furniture as belonging to Ella. When she reached Ella's floor, her suspicions were confirmed. The door to Ella's flat stood open and two other men were carrying out a table.

She stopped them. 'Excuse me, but what are you doing?'

The older of the men set his end of the table down and regarded her quizzically. 'We're millionaires travelling incognito, missus,' he said. 'Every now and again we get this sudden urge to hump bleedin' great chunks of furniture about, just to stop our hernias from healing.'

Paula smiled ingratiatingly. 'I'm sorry. That was a silly question. What I mean is that this is my friend's flat and I wonder if you could tell me where you're taking the furniture. To Yorkshire, is it?'

'Christ, I hope not! The old woman's expecting me home for lunch. No, it's going to the local auction rooms.'

'It's going to be sold?'

The man rubbed the roll of fat at the back of his neck. 'Well now, they don't confide in me about things like that. They just say to me, "Pick it up here and take it there," so I pick it up here and take it there.'

Paula made her way back down the stairs. At the bottom, in the hallway, there was a brass plate which announced the name of the agents in charge of the building. She noted the number and called them on her mobile. That proved to be no help. They confirmed that they had received Miss Costello's written instructions to handle the sale of her flat on her behalf and to arrange the removal and sale at auction of the furniture. No, they were sorry, but they had no forwarding address for Miss Costello.

Paula's next stop was at the local bank. She had known the manager for years and had established the sort of relationship that enabled her to extract snippets of otherwise confidential information. On the pretext that there might be some delay in paying a

197

cheque into Ella's account, she found that it was, indeed, about to be transferred on her written instructions to the main branch in Leeds. That didn't help. It merely suggested that Ella's destination might be south-west Yorkshire – a not inconsiderable area to scour. They had no forwarding address other than the bank in Leeds.

In her car outside the bank, Paula lit a cigarette and scowled at her reflection in the driving mirror. The resignation checked out. It was all above board and legitimate. That ought to have been the end of it, but it wasn't. She could not shake off her unease. It was useless to go to the police. Even given her close acquaintance with the chief constable, there was no way they would take an interest. As far as they were concerned, Ella would be just someone who had got fed up and decided to move on, having first taken the precaution of setting all her affairs in order.

She started the engine and put the car in gear, intending to return to the office. For some reason that she could not afterwards explain, she did not do so. Seemingly of its own volition, the car negotiated the necessary turns that would set it on the Fernham Road. That was stupid. There was absolutely nothing to be gained by going out to the old Rodley place. She would never get past the gates. What was she going to do? Stop outside and bellow, 'Yoohoo! Ella! Are you in there?' As she drew near the great iron gates which led to the rambling mansion, the futility of what she was doing seemed even greater. If she sat outside and kept watch she would, in that open countryside, be as conspicuous as a boil on an elephant's bum. Well, she supposed it would do no harm to drive past, then turn around as if lost and drive back again. As she had surmised, there was absolutely nothing to see. Any gate guards were out of sight in the stone lodge inside the gates. She went about a mile further up the road, then found a convenient cart-track in which to reverse before retracing her route.

This time, as she approached the gates, her heart gave a great leap of relief. There was Ella, driving out in her unmistakable little red Fiesta. Paula tagged along behind and when she was out of earshot of the gates, poised her hand over the horn to claim her friend's attention with a toot. Suddenly, she removed her hand. It wasn't Ella in the car, but a man! Her mind raced to provide a sensible explanation. Perhaps Ella had sold her car as well as her flat and her furniture? That made no sense. Surely she would need a car in Yorkshire, of all places? And if she had sold it, was it not a remarkable coincidence that the guy who had bought it was a visitor at the old Rodley place? Paula eased her foot off the accelerator and allowed her car to fall back to a discreet distance. Once into the outskirts of Arton, it became easier to tail the Fiesta unnoticed, by allowing a couple of other cars for separation. When the Fiesta stopped at a small grocery store, Paula stopped too, a few yards behind, and waited. The man who got out was of medium height and sturdy build, tanned and muscular. His very black hair was sleeked back, but his most distinguishing features were his thin moustache and rather absurd black goatee beard.

Paula reached into her glove compartment and pulled out her miniature camera. She really didn't know why she still carried it. Probably a relic of her cub reporter days that she could not bring herself to part with. She made sure that it was ready for action and waited. When the man came out of the store carrying a brown paper bag, she fixed him squarely in the viewfinder and fired. The buzzing click of the tiny mechanism confirmed that she should have at least ten good pictures of him before he reached the car and got in. For good measure, Paula fired again, associating him with the car and the registration plate, then watched as he drove off.

Getting out of her car, she strolled into the store. A thin, pale girl in a soiled white overall who appeared to be about thirteen years old was listlessly thumping prices into the cash register at the only check-out.

Paula went up to her. 'Excuse me . . .'

'You'll have to wait!'

Paula lingered patiently until a stout lady customer had paid and departed.

'Excuse me, the man who was just in here . . .?'

'What man?'

'About five foot nine. Black moustache and beard.'

'If you say so, I don't look at people. I only take the money.'

Paula controlled herself with an effort. 'Your last customer, then. What did he buy?'

'Dunno! Oh, wait a minute. Cigarettes and toothpaste, I think.'

'Ever seen him before?'

The girl eyed her suspiciously. 'What you want to know for? You the Old Bill?'

'No, I think he might be a friend of a friend. Has he been in before?'

'Might have been. Can't say as I remember.'

'Did he pay by cheque or credit card?'

The girl shook her head vigorously, releasing a cloud of dandruff which drifted down onto the rubber belt beside her. 'No. Cash.'

'Thanks a bunch!' Paula said. 'You've been a great help.'

Back at the office, she approached the young man in the Press Office. 'Kevin!'

He had not heard her come in and jumped nervously, instinctively pressing the space bar on his keyboard which would return the screen from Blackjack to his story. 'Yes?'

She tossed the camera to him. 'Get that developed. Duplicate prints. Let me have a set, then get out and about to see if you can find anyone who can put a name to the face. Perhaps you'll be luckier with that than you are at the gaming table.'

Kevin blushed and went to obey.

Paula threw herself down in the big chair in her office. Surely she had now done enough and her conscience could rest. She pulled a piece of copy towards her and tried to sub it, but her mind would not stay on the job. She was filled with a restless urge she had not felt for years and knew exactly what it was. This was no longer a matter only of her concern for Ella's safety. All her reporter's investigative instincts had been piqued. Here was a mystery to be solved; a story to be unravelled. She knew that she could not bear to wait for a period of days, perhaps weeks, before her photographs bore fruit in the form of a name. She must do more. A completely ridiculous plan occurred to her and she thrust it from her contemptuously. It would not go away, but kept niggling at her brain until it eroded her common sense away to nothing. She sent for an Ordnance Survey map and spent some time poring over it.

That evening, in her flat, she dressed with care. Black ski-pants and black sweater. Black leather gloves. She fleetingly considered blacking her face, but rejected the notion as compounding that which was already farcical enough. She stared with disdain at her reflection in her long mirror. Perhaps, she chided herself, she should take a box of Cadbury's Milk Tray with her? She let herself out and went down to her car, carrying a bulging, clinking, plastic bag under her arm.

Along the Fernham Road, about a mile short of the Old Rodley place, Paula slowed the car and crept along at a snail's pace, staring intently at the roadside as revealed in the glare of her dipped headlamps. Even at that speed, she missed the overgrown and narrow entrance to the cart track she had selected on the Ordnance Survey map and had to back up before she could turn into it. With all the car's lights out, progress was minimal until her eyes became adjusted and what had seemed to be pitch blackness took on varying shades of dark grey. Even then, extreme caution was necessary to avoid missing the track altogether and becoming ignominiously bogged down in a ditch. Consequently, it took almost half an hour to reach her destination, an old barn in the corner of a field just outside the wooden fence that marked the boundary of Interplay's property.

Paula drove her car into the lee of the barn, close against its crumbling, wooden structure. She got out, bringing her plastic bag with her, then operated the central locking system. She walked a few paces away and looked back. The black car against the black barn was practically unnoticeable in the darkness, even viewed from this side. From the other side of the barn, it would be quite invisible to anyone looking out from the old Rodley place. Satisfied, she turned to go, then, as an afterthought, came back, feeling in her pocket for her spare keys. She took a slender pencil torch from her plastic bag and hunted around in the debris close against the wall of the barn. Next to a rusting harrow, there was a lichened roof tile, so recently fallen as to crush the grass beneath it and not yet be overgrown. She placed her spare keys underneath it, dusted her hands and, with a final look around, set off for the boundary fence.

The fence was no obstacle at all, consisting of posts and rails which made climbing over it simple. Not using her torch, but relying on night vision, Paula made her way towards the looming pile of the old house, stumbling now and again over a tussock. Close to the house, open field gave way to occasional clumps of rhododendrons and azaleas, obliging her to thread her way between them. Suddenly she froze. A few yards ahead of her, an Alsatian dog was blocking her path, ears pricked and hackles raised. A low, grumbling growl emerged from its throat and, even at a distance and in the gloom, she could see the white glint of canine teeth as its upper lip curled back menacingly.

Holding her breath and moving a fraction at a time, Paula reached into her plastic bag and withdrew a large lump of steak. Very slowly, she held it out in front of her and, in a voice that belied her lack of confidence, whispered, 'Here, boy! Good doggie! Dindins!' The Alsatian advanced a couple of paces. Was that a good sign, or the beginning of an attack? Hoping desperately for the former, Paula whispered, 'Hungry? Mmm! Yummy! Doesn't that smell good?' The dog regarded her thoughtfully, head on one side to obtain a better perspective of her intentions then, to her utter relief, trotted forward and sniffed at the meat. Greatly daring, she reached out her hand and ruffled the hair between his ears before dropping the steak on the grass. As he trapped the meat with his front paws and began to tear at it with slavering intensity, Paula patted him affectionately. 'Good boy! Whose a greedy little sod, then!' she said, and moved on.

As she neared the back of the house, details of its construction began to emerge. She saw an iron fire escape and made for it. She followed it upwards past a series of large, sash windows, trying each one in turn. They were all locked. She stopped. No point in going higher. It was time for a bit of burglary. Shielding her torch with her hand, she inspected the catch on the sash bar of the nearest window. It did not appear to have any security device to prevent it from being operated. From her bag, she took a roll of Sellotape and applied the sticky surface to one of the Georgian panes of glass next to the catch and thumped the centre of it with her gloved fist. It gave way with hardly a sound and bowed inwards. Working carefully, she pulled the tape away with the shards of glass still adhering to it and laid it on the fire-escape. She reached through the gap and opened the window catch, which moved easily. Even the sash was co-operative, moving up silently when she tugged at it. She put one leg over the sill and listened. All was silent. She brought the other leg inside, stood up and closed the sash behind her.

The shaded beam of Paula's torch revealed to her that the room she had entered seemed to be some sort of office to judge by the huge desk. She made that her first target, opening one drawer after another, hoping to find some sort of paperwork that would either identify the occupiers or give some clue as to what had happened to Ella. She was kneeling, searching a bottom drawer when the door opened; a switch clicked and the room was flooded with light.

Paula sprang up, looking around desperately for a speedy means of flight, cursing herself for having closed the window. The woman who confronted her was very thin and her long, dark hair hung down past her shoulders. She wore a pale blue housecoat. While her appearance was no cause for undue alarm, the presence of two hulking, uniformed security guards just behind her was.

'What are you doing?'

Now that, Paula thought, was definitely a silly question. How was she supposed to answer? She was tempted to say, 'What does it look like, you silly cow? I'm breaking into your house!' There was, though, on closer examination, something about the woman's eyes that made such an answer seem unwise. When in doubt, tell the truth. 'I'm looking for my friend.'

'Oh? Who are you?'

'I am Paula Matheson.'

'Good morning, Paula Matheson. I am Miss Doyle. I run this establishment. And what would your friend's name be?'

'Ella Costello. She works for me. I'm her editor on *The Globe*.

'Ah! Ladies of the Press. That explains a lot. Ella? Yes, she is staying with us. Did you have to break in at dead of night to have me tell you that? Could you not have rung the doorbell during daylight hours and obtained exactly the same information?'

Paula had the good grace to blush. She felt extremely foolish. After all, the woman was right. There was absolutely no reason for her to have indulged in such ridiculous tactics. She should have listened to that inner voice which had scoffed at her Girl Scout plan when first it entered her mind. Wait a minute, though – what reason was there to believe what this woman was telling her?

Paula said, 'I'd like to see her, please.'

'Of course.'

Paula blinked. 'I may?'

'Most certainly, but not tonight. Ella works hard during the day and I cannot permit her sleep to be disturbed. You will have to wait until tomorrow.'

'Oh.' That sounded entirely reasonable. 'I'll come back tomorrow, shall I?'

Miss Doyle's voice was ominously smooth. 'It would not be very sensible of me to allow you to walk out just like that. After all, you are, to all intents and purposes, a burglar. I have only your word for it that you are a friend of Ella's. You had better stay here tonight, then Ella can verify your story in the morning.'

'Thank you, but I'd rather go home.'

Miss Doyle's voice was even smoother. 'You will stay.'

Paula was scornful. 'Or else what? Will you get your heavies to beat me up?'

Miss Doyle sighed. 'How melodramatic! I shall simply summon the local constabulary. They will be most interested in your method of entry and your reluctance to stay to see the friend you claim to be the reason for your visit.'

Paula winced. She could just see the headlines in her own newspaper. 'Very well. I'll stay.'

'Good! I'll find a room for you. Now, if you would just remove your clothes . . .'

Paula's mouth dropped open in amazement. 'What? Are you mad?'

'Not at all. This is not a prison. I have no secure rooms and you have made your burglarious skills apparent. Having no clothes will help persuade you that it is a good idea to stay inside the house.'

'And if I refuse?'

'Your method of attempting entry to the house was ingenious, I confess. I have no idea why you should have done so, although your occupation provides a clue. Perhaps you had heard rumours about our totally respectable club and were snooping around, hoping to photograph some important person in a compromising situation – another of the paparazzi at your dirty work. I'm sure I can find a suitable camera if you don't happen to have brought your own. How unfortunate that, having reached the very top of the fire escape, you leaned over to peer into a window, lost your footing and fell all the way to the flagstones underneath.'

Paula's blood ran cold. On anyone else's lips, such a scenario would have sounded improbable. On Miss Doyle's, it sounded much less unlikely.

'You're bluffing!'

'Try me.'

The two women eyed one another, each judging the determination of the other. In the end, it was Paula who capitulated. 'All right,' she said. 'Just send those men away first.'

'And leave myself unprotected? Certainly not! You placed yourself in this embarrassing predicament, not I. Now, it's late; I'm tired and rapidly losing patience. You will strip now – right down to the bare skin – or take the consequences.'

Paula searched her mind for further means of prevarication but found none. She had brought this on herself by her impetuous stupidity and now she was going to have to take her medicine. Given her dominant personality, it was particularly galling to have to take her clothes off just because Miss Doyle commanded it. It was made worse by the fact that two men would watch her do it. Men had often stripped at Paula's order – never the other way about.

Reluctantly, she removed her gloves and laid them on the desk. She crossed her arms and peeled off her black sweater over her head, then kicked off her light shoes and eased down her black ski-pants, placing those on the desk as well. She had on only a black brassière and black panties. Paula cast an imploring glance at Miss Doyle, but received neither sympathy nor mercy.

Miss Doyle pointed. 'Those too. I know my men would be bitterly disappointed not to get a good look at your tits and arse.'

Paula's face flamed, well aware that Miss Doyle had chosen her coarse words in order to humiliate and embarrass her. The heat in her face was not entirely caused by shame. She was enraged at the display she was being forced to give and frustrated at her inability to do anything about it. Any shame she felt was reserved entirely for her own weakness in giving this woman the satisfaction of seeing her glance of supplication. Well, that wouldn't happen again! She faced her tormentor, unclipped her brassière and slipped it off, then wriggled her panties down over her hips and stepped out of them. Totally nude, she parted her legs, put her hands on her hips, stuck out her breasts and, by her pose, dared anyone to stare.

The trio came towards her. While the guards stopped alongside her, Miss Doyle went around the desk to the rifled drawers. She came back with a pair of leather cuffs joined together by a short chain. 'Hands behind, please.'

'What? No! No, you don't . . .!'

Paula's protests were in vain. She found herself grasped and held firmly by the guards, who forced her hands behind her back while Miss Doyle buckled the cuffs about her wrists with an ease which bespoke long years of practice. When she was released, Paula wriggled and strained, tossing her upper body about in an effort to free her hands then, realising the futility of that, stood still, waiting to see what would happen next.

Miss Doyle came and stood close in front of her, making it obvious that she was examining every detail of her nudity. She reached out and took one of Paula's nipple-rings in each hand twisting and pulling a little.

'You favour body piercing? Excellent! So decorative! Anywhere else? Ah! That expression gives me the answer, but I'll check just the same. Open your legs a little. Come along, be sensible! Either you do it or my men will. Frankly, the latter might be more entertaining, so I don't mind which you choose.'

Fuming, Paula parted her thighs then squirmed as she felt Miss Doyle's bony fingers intruding upon her most private places.

Miss Doyle stepped back, smiling and nodding. 'As I thought. Enough fun for one night, though. We all need some sleep. I will tell you in advance that my drawers also contain dog leads and that your nipple rings will make admirable fixing points for their clips. So, when I say that you are to follow me, I expect you to do it.' She led the way into the room next door, observing out of the corner of her eye that Paula followed her without hesitation. Once inside, she pointed to a bed. 'You may sleep there. You will be a little uncomfortable with your hands cuffed, but that can't be helped. You'll find a bathroom through there. How you manage anything you need to do is your problem. I will call you early in the morning.'

Miss Doyle went out and closed the door behind her. Paula heard the key turn in the lock, then went for a short, exploratory patrol around the room. Nudging the heavy curtains aside with her nose, she satisfied herself that there was no way of escape through the window, trussed as she was. She wriggled onto the bed, fell over onto her side and lay there, thinking about what had happened. Certainly, she had scant regard for Miss Doyle and her methods. There was one person, however, whom she respected even less and that was herself. What a dim bulb she had proved to be!

In spite of her confinement, Paula slept heavily, so

that it was Miss Doyle's hand on her shoulder that woke her next morning. She rolled over onto her back, groaning at the stiffness in her shoulders.

'Do I get to see Ella, now?'

'Certainly, but wouldn't you like to take a shower first?'

'Yes.'

'Roll over onto your face, then, and I'll unfasten you. Don't get any ideas. My men are just outside.'

Paula turned onto her face as instructed and felt Miss Doyle's fingers loosening the buckles that held her. The pleasure and relief that washed over her at being able to move her arms again was immense. She sat up, stretching high and wide, careless of her nude state, then wriggled to the edge of the bed and sat there, chafing her wrists.

'You'll find everything you need in the bathroom.'

Paula took the hint and got up to take a shower. When she came back, wrapped in a towel, Miss Doyle was sitting on the bed, waiting for her.

Paula had spent some time in thought while showering. 'You really are going to let me see Ella, aren't you?'

'I said so.'

'Yes, but I mean, really see her. I want to talk to her alone.'

'Naturally! I expected no less. You shall have more than enough time alone together.'

There was something here that Paula did not understand, but she could not think of a question that would clear up the confused jumble in her mind, so she left it, contenting herself with drying her hair.

'May I have my clothes back, now?'

'No.'

Well, that was straight answer if ever there was one. Paula shrugged. 'All right. Can we go and see Ella, now?'

'First I must fix your arms again.'

'Is that really necessary?'

Miss Doyle said, 'If you want to see Ella, it is. We have to go through parts of the house that are private. I don't want you to be free to break away and roam about. Now stand up and turn around.'

There was no point in arguing. Miss Doyle held all the aces. Paula allowed her hands to be cuffed again.

'Now open your legs!'

'Why?'

'I have to put you on a leash, to make sure you don't run off.'

'There? You're actually going to clip a leash to my . . . to those?

'Remember this is what you wanted. I didn't invite you here. If you want to visit Ella, you will do it my way.'

Paula opened her legs and Miss Doyle stooped in front of her. Paula felt her fumbling, then heard and felt the click as the clip on the end of a dog-chain was passed through both her labial rings. Miss Doyle stood up, holding the leash, then deliberately dropped it so that the weight of the chain tugged at the rings, swinging and dangling between Paula's legs.

'When we go through the first part of the house, it may be that there will be people there who might recognise you. I take it that you would prefer not to be recognised.'

'Yes, of course.'

'I can help you there. Sit down on the bed.'

Paula stared uncomprehendingly at the object Miss Doyle held in her hand. It looked like four hooks, heavily coated in rubber and joined together by an octopus of black, elasticised shock cords.

'What's that for?'

'You'll find that it will completely alter your appearance.'

211

'How?'

Miss Doyle held up the apparatus, picking up the hooks two at a time to illustrate her description. 'I shall hook these two into your nostrils. Their two cords go up on either side of your nose and over your head to the back, then these other two cords come around either side of your face and their hooks go into the corners of your mouth. Don't look so worried. I assure you that it's quite painless and that, while you're wearing it, even your own mother wouldn't recognise you. Now, are you going to hold still while I put it on, or do you want me to get the guards to help me?'

Paula sat with her head bowed while she thought about this, within a fraction of saying that she did not want to see Ella that badly. Unfortunately, she knew that this was not true and that she would not be able to rest until she had satisfied herself about her friend's fate.

She sighed, heavily. 'All right. Carry on, if you must.'

She grunted as she felt the first two hooks inserted into her nostrils. Given their thick rubber coating, they were not painful, but the sensation was very strange and made her want to sneeze. The upward pull of the elastic as it was tightened distorted her nose and made her tilt her head back, then the other two hooks were in the sides of her mouth, distending it into a wide, fixed grin. She shook her head violently. There was no way she was going to be able to get rid of it without her hands free. Such release was entirely at the whim of Miss Doyle and she felt the full weight of the humiliation of submission descend upon her. Her face was so much a part of her personality that what had been done to it was far more of a restraint than the handcuffs. It seemed to make captive her very soul.

'Ready, now!' Miss Doyle smiled at her prisoner. 'Just have a quick look in the mirror before we go to make sure that's done what you want it to.'

Paula got up and crossed to the dressing table mirror, her chain leash trailing on the floor. The reflection that stared back at her was an obscene gargoyle, like the face some ghastly child might pull. Her nose was flattened and distorted as though pressed against a sweet shop window, while that gruesome smile was the stuff bad dreams were made of. She realised that Miss Doyle's invitation to look in the mirror had nothing to do with checking the completeness of her disguise and everything to do with making her understand the full extent of her helpless subjugation.

Miss Doyle picked up the leash and gave it a little tug. 'Come along.'

The journey along the corridor and up the staircase to the Temple of Pleasure was purgatory for Paula. They passed several male guards who, although they gave no sign of emotion, could clearly see her bondage and every detail of the humiliating things that had been done to her. She felt better once they were inside the audience chamber and Miss Doyle removed the hated distorter and the leash. She left the cuffs in place, but Paula did not particularly care about those any more. She moved her jaws about and delighted in the fact that she was no longer tethered to Miss Doyle, either physically or mentally.

Miss Doyle was beckoning to one in a group of young women in gauzy white. She left the group and came towards them. Paula did not recognise her at first. Her blonde hair was pinned up in the Grecian style, but that was not the reason. Her face bore an expression Paula had never seen before. On anyone else's, it would have been merely calm and serene. On

Ella's it was exquisitely beautiful, as though she were some untouchable work of porcelain art.

When she smiled, it was as at some deep, inner secret. 'Welcome, Paula. I had been told that you would visit.'

'Ella?' Paula began. 'What ... Why ...?' She turned to Miss Doyle. 'You said that I might speak to her alone.'

'So you shall,' Miss Doyle replied. 'Sister Ella, perhaps you would show Paula to your room?'

'Of course, Sister Martha. This way, Paula.' Ella led the way out of the audience chamber and along the corridor until she reached her own door. She opened it and stepped aside to allow Paula to precede her.

Miss Doyle followed them into the room. 'You will be Paula's warden during her visit, Sister Ella.'

'With pleasure, Sister Martha.' Ella opened the front of her gown and exposed her breasts.

Miss Doyle passed her a pair of tiny, gold padlocks. 'You may do the honours, Sister.'

Ella smiled at her. 'Of course, Sister Martha. Come closer, Paula. Closer than that. Really close!' Reaching between their two bodies, she clipped Paula's nipple rings to her own.

Paula looked down at her new confinement. 'Hey! What have you done? What's this for?'

Miss Doyle said, 'I will leave you together now. You may chat all you like. Sister Ella will be glad to answer all your questions, Paula. I will come back later.'

Paula heard the door behind her close and knew that she was alone with Ella. She was a little disconcerted. She had envisaged this confrontation and planned to stride up and down, demanding explanations and now and again crashing her fist into her palm to emphasise a point. This was something completely different. Ella's face, with its silly grin, was only inches from her own and there would certainly be no striding up and down.

'Look here, Ella. What the hell is going on?'

Ella put both arms around her friend and hugged her close. 'Isn't it marvellous, Paula? I have been selected by the Master to be one of his Disciples. I shall have the privilege of serving him all my life and, if my dreams of immortality come true, for ever and ever.'

'Disciple? Master? Immortality? What are you babbling on about? Have you slipped your trolley? What about your job?'

'Oh, Paula. I'm so sad for you. You are still trapped by earthly mortal things; by possessions and relationships. But you're here now. I'm sure that if you work hard and can pass through the Portal of Pain, you too will find the Path to Enlightenment.'

'What on earth are you talking about, Ella? Have they drugged you? Are you high on something?'

Ella's smile was saintly. 'Not in the way you mean. I'm not ordinary Ella any more. Now I am Sister Ella, united in love and treading the same path as my Sisters here. The love of one Sister for another is as boundless as the ocean! The love of all Sisters for the Master is as great as Creation!'

Paula blinked, shaking her head as though, by doing so, she could remove the cloudy cobwebs that Ella's ramblings had created. 'Look,' she said, 'I think you'd better start at the beginning and tell me absolutely everything.'

It was unfortunate that their close coupling prevented them from sitting. Several times during Ella's discourse, Paula felt the deep need to sit down. At the end, she said, 'Are you telling me that you and all the other Sisters have sold everything? Your flat? Your car? You've handed over all your money to this bloke, wossname?'

'The Master.'

'Cunning bastard, more likely! Wake up, Ella! You've been conned. He's no more immortal than my Uncle Arthur and he died of drink three years ago.'

Ella was unshaken. 'I understand and sympathise, Paula. I was told that you would be armed by the Devil with lies to tempt me away from the Path of the Light. It's not your fault. That's the way Lucifer works. If he can prevent the Master from bringing just one of his three pupils though the Portal of Pain to the Light of Immortality, he regains the Master's soul – a great prize indeed.'

Paula shook her head in wonderment. 'Barmy! Completely round the bend!'

Ella remained completely serene. She merely put her arms around Paula again, kissed her and stroked her hair. 'Don't worry, Paula. You're here with me, now. The love of the Sisters will save you from Lucifer's lying blandishments. Ever since I found out you were coming, I have been working on a scheme. My ingenuity and the love of the Sisters will allow you to escape.'

Paula's face lit up. 'Now you're talking. An escape plan! How and when do we leave here?'

Ella laughed. 'No, silly! Not a plan to escape from here. Why would you want to? A plan to escape from the entrapments of the outside world. You'll be able to leave all that behind.'

'I don't understand.'

'Oh, Paula, it's so wonderful that you're here. Now you have a chance that all those other poor people on the outside don't have. I can help you pass through the Portal of Pain and reach the Path of Enlightenment. You can stay here for ever with us, just loving the Sisters and the Master.'

216

Paula stared at her, unable to believe her ears. Ella clearly believed this drivel! She was in the grip of some sort of religious fervour. Either that, or she had completely lost her mind. 'Hey! Come on, Ella! It's me you're talking to. Get a grip! Get both oars in the water! You've been conned. Don't you understand that?'

Ella smiled complacently. 'It's all right, Paula. I promise you I understand. Lucifer has taken over your mind and blinded you to the truth. Enlightenment will allow you to see clearly again and you can only achieve that if I help you.'

'But ...' Paula got no further. The door opened and Miss Doyle came in, carrying an assortment of odd-looking leather apparatuses. Paula risked a certain amount of discomfort by half-turning to look.

'Well, you two. Have you had a cosy chat about old times?'

'Damn you!' Paula said. 'What have you done to her?'

'Done? I have done nothing. Ella has been fortunate enough to discover a great truth, haven't you, Ella?'

'Oh yes, Sister Martha. I've been explaining it to Paula. She needs the Sisters so badly, but she doesn't really understand. I'm so grateful to you for allowing me to be the one that brings her through the Portal to join us.'

Miss Doyle smiled indulgently. 'You must thank the Master for that. It was he who saw a spark of ingenuity in you that caused him to select you for this privilege. I have just been looking at the preparations you asked for and I must say that I am most impressed. I can see why he chose to favour you – a Sister who has only recently joined us. I think it would be all right to reveal a confidence and tell you

217

that if the procedure goes as well as I think it will, the Master is considering bestowing a further honour.'

'You mean . . .?'

'Well, I don't want to raise false hopes, but a naked coupling with him might not be out of the question.'

Ella beamed. 'Oh, Sister Martha. What a wonderful thought! Can we begin at once, please?'

'Of course, Sister Ella.' Miss Doyle put her equipment down on the bed and set about unfastening the padlocks that secured their nipples. Paula stepped back with a sigh of relief, but that relief was short-lived. Miss Doyle picked up one of the items. 'I'd like you to look at this and understand it, Paula.'

Paula stared at the thing. In appearance, it somewhat resembled the bottom half of a bikini, fashioned in soft leather, except where a normal bikini would have elastic or strings to secure it, this had stout leather belts. The part which would pass between the legs was connected only at the front, not at the back, so that the whole thing resembled a large T shape. It was not a single thickness of leather, but a bulky bulge, about two inches in breadth and thickness.

Miss Doyle held it up, turning it so that Paula could see the inside. There were three distinct protrusions. The centre one was clearly the head of a fairly large dildo, with the glans of the penis clearly delineated in the soft, pink, shiny rubber. Above that was a small, pink rubber bump, hardly bigger than a button. Towards the rear was another dildo, thinner and longer than the first.

'Let me show you how it works.' Miss Doyle pressed the bikini at the top, just below the securing belt. There was a soft hum of a battery-driven motor as the two dildos began to extend and retract, pumping rhythmically but travelling only about an inch up and down. The little pink button seemed to go out of focus as it vibrated briskly. 'You see?' Miss Doyle pointed to the thicker dildo. 'This one goes in the front. This one in the back, and the little button . . . Well, you can guess by its position what the little one does.'

Paula could and her horrified expression was eloquent of her thoughts.

Miss Doyle smiled. 'Don't look so alarmed. Many of the Sisters choose to wear one of these purely for the delightful sensations it produces. It is a mark of Ella's ingenuity that she has found a way to use it to help you through the Portal. Now, if you will just part your legs, I will put it on for you.'

'No fear!' Paula exclaimed. 'You're not putting that thing on me!'

Miss Doyle did not appear to be in the least put out. She smiled again. 'You don't seem to understand that I wasn't asking you to vote on the subject. You will open your legs because, if you don't, I will do something to your body that will make this contraption seem to you to be a very trivial embarrassment.'

Paula ground her teeth with rage. With her hands still cuffed behind her, there was absolutely nothing she could do to prevent this infuriating woman from doing anything she liked to her. She shuffled her feet apart a little and waited.

'Wider!'

Paula shuffled again and Miss Doyle buckled the belt of the bikini around Paula's waist, pulled it very tight and padlocked it into place, leaving the bulging leather hanging down over her pubic hair. Miss Doyle stooped and, with great care, inserted the tip of the larger dildo into Paula's vagina, between her labial rings, then held the bikini in place with the flat of her hand while she moved around to the rear.

'Bend forward a little! More than that! No, on

second thoughts, you'd better go all the way down.'
Miss Doyle administered a sharp slap on Paula's unprotected bottom. 'All the way, I said! Right over!'

Face aflame, Paula obeyed. The dildo that was already in place made itself felt as she bent in half, but worse than that was the knowledge of what was coming next. She felt Miss Doyle's fingers spreading her bottom cheeks apart and braced herself. She felt the tip of the smaller dildo against her anus. It was cold and wet and she guessed that Miss Doyle had lubricated it in some way. She gasped as its long coldness penetrated her inner warmth, then moved uneasily as she felt the rear part of the bikini being padlocked to her waist belt.

Miss Doyle slapped again. 'Up!'

Paula straightened, slowly and uncomfortably, trying to get used to this double intrusion.

'Now I'll just give you a little taste of how it works.'

'Don't bother,' Paula said crisply. 'I can guess.'

'Oh, but I insist!' Miss Doyle pressed against the leather at the front again and the little motor sprang into life.

For Paula, it was an amazing sensation. It wasn't that the imitation penises were particularly large, or that the penetration of them was particularly deep. In fact, it was that lack of deep penetration that made them all the more effective, working, as they did, against areas with a great number of nerve-endings. In combination with the vibration of the clitoral stimulator, the effect was sensational and she could not restrain a gasp of surprise and pleasure. After only a few seconds, another aspect of the matter occurred to her. Padlocked into this gadget and with her hands cuffed, there was nothing she could do to stop it. Already, she could feel her juices running freely and knew that it would not be long before she was forced to squirm about in very public acknowledgement of all she was feeling. When she did that, these two women would see the movement and know its cause. That was particularly humiliating.

To Paula's great relief, Miss Doyle pressed the front of the belt again and the motor stopped. 'I just wanted to be sure you understood what it will feel like while the motor is running,' she said.

'I do!' Paula replied, with considerable feeling.

'Good, then we can proceed.' Miss Doyle picked up another arrangement of leather. 'Open your mouth!'

'Why? What are you going to do?'

'Gag you,' Miss Doyle said calmly, as though such a procedure were thoroughly routine. 'Stop you from talking. Sister Ella and I know that your mind has been unhinged by Lucifer. We understand, but there is no need for the other Sisters to be offended by hearing his words coming from your lips.' She held up a head-harness that incorporated a bright red ball-gag. 'This time I have no need to threaten you with physical pain. If you don't open your mouth very wide at once, I shall simply switch on the motor, then go away and leave you. I believe it takes about four hours for the batteries to go flat.'

Paula blenched. That was a threat which carried real weight. The prospect of being forcibly and mechanically masturbated for that length of time was horrendous. She opened her mouth with alacrity, stretching it as wide as she could so that there could be no possible doubt about her compliance. Miss Doyle settled the cage of straps over her head and pushed the red ball into her mouth. From either side of the ball, straps ran up either side of her nose to join at the headband. Another strap ran through the ball and around to the back of her head. When all the straps were pulled tight and buckled, there was no possibility of coherent speech, although she was relieved to find that there was a hole through the middle of the ball which admitted ample air for breathing purposes, while any attempt to form words would produce only a cooing gurgle.

There was still one final indignity. A long, leather strap with a clip at each end was fastened to her nipples so that it hung down the front of her body in a large loop. At a signal from Miss Doyle, Ella picked up these reins and gave a little tug, indicating that Paula should follow her towards the door. Until that moment, Paula had not realised that she was to be taken out of the room and the prospect of being observed by others in her gagged, cuffed and tethered state was hideous. She tried to indicate her unwillingness by digging in her heels, shaking her head and making the only noise she could.

Miss Doyle intervened. 'You must understand that it is the custom in this place that a person passing through the Portal of Pain for the first time, does so in the audience chamber in the presence and with the assistance of the Sisters. It is a privilege that you should not resent. Therefore, Sister Ella will be fully justified in putting all her weight into hauling you there by force, if necessary. I'm sure it won't be necessary, will it?'

Paula shook her head and, when Ella tugged gently again, followed meekly with a rather undignified, waddling gait caused by the thickness of the uncomfortable apparatus strapped between her legs. After all, she reasoned, how bad could it be to have a few little orgasms, even if there were people watching? Even the gag had its advantages. At least the thing rendered her practically unrecognisable. In spite of this self-reassurance, she shuddered inwardly, knowing in her heart that she was not looking forward to the unspecified torments that awaited her in the audience chamber. The only thing that was certain was that they would be severe, if Miss Doyle and this mysterious Master had anything to do with it. She suffered herself to be led by her nipples like some sacrificial animal towards her time of trial.

Ten

Paula stood obediently where she had been placed by Ella at the end of one line of a double row of Sisters, all turned half inwards, facing the far end of the audience chamber.

'We await the Master's waking,' Ella explained. 'He will commune with the Old One and then begin his teaching. When he does that, you will understand his powers better. While he is still at that end of the room, he will appear beside us. To the Master, the constraints of time and space are nothing.'

Being quite unable to speak, Paula nodded to show that she understood. When the curtains at the end of the chamber drew back, she watched with close attention. The first appearance of the ghostly outline of the Master, sleeping on his throne, caused the hairs at the back of her head to prickle. Then she became interested in the materialisation and forgot to be awed. Something stirred at the back of her mind. She could not put her finger on it, but stored the sensation away by force of habit. That is what she had done all her adult working life in the newspaper business. With such a huge input of information, it was quite impossible that every tiny snippet could be remembered in such detail as to be produced just when it was needed. Nevertheless, she had come to recognise an instinct in herself which sometimes told her that, if she sifted hard enough through half-forgotten items, something relevant to a contemporary experience would crop up. When the vague figure of the Old One appeared beside the Master, that tiny finger of recognition tickled exactly the same spot that had been stirred before, reinforcing her certainty that what she was seeing was related to something she had seen or read about before.

His conversation with the Old One over, the Master looked out at the assembled Sisters.

'Sister Ella?'

Ella threw off her gown and dropped to her knees, displaying her body to him with hands clasped behind her head. 'Master, I hear your call.'

'Have you brought someone with you?'

'I have, Master.' Ella half turned and, with her elbow, nudged in the direction of Paula's naked, fettered and gagged figure.

'With what intent?'

'I propose to bring her through the Portal of Pain to your own Path of Enlightenment, Master.'

'Will you do that alone?'

'No, Master. It will be done by the love of all the Sisters. The love of one Sister for another is as boundless as the ocean. The love of all the Sisters for the Master is as great as Creation.'

– The Master nodded. 'That is good. But I understood that you would use great ingenuity in your method. I see only the Belt of Pleasure in use. I don't understand how you propose to use that to produce the torment necessary to open the Portal.'

'Will you allow me to show you, Master?'

'Very well.'

Ella got up and signed to two Sisters further down the line. They went to the door behind the curtain at the side of the audience chamber and brought back the trolley to which Belle had been secured. The frame had been removed and, in its place, were two upright poles in the centre at either end. Each pole was about five feet high and at their tops were pivoted rods, facing inwards. There were iron weights at the ends of the rods, pulling them down so that they rested against the poles.

The Master frowned. 'I see, but I still don't understand.'

Ella stepped onto the platform and stood between the poles. She stretched out both arms and lifted the weights so that the rods to which they were attached were horizontal. 'Master, Paula's cuffs will be taken off. She will be perfectly free to roam about as she likes. However, these rods are connected to an infrared device which sends a signal to the Pleasure Belt. When the weights are held up, as I am doing now, the belt remains inactive. If just one weight is released, the belt is switched on and remains on until both are again in this position.'

The Master smiled broadly. 'Ah! Now I understand. There comes a point where pleasure becomes unbearable. If Paula wishes to spare herself that, she must stand with arms outstretched, supporting the weights. Truly a torment of the mind as well as the body. Excellent! How heavy are the weights?'

'Only two pounds each, Master, but there are other, smaller weights which may be bolted to the rods. Every time that Paula allows the weights to sink down, the Sisters will add a weight to each rod so that, when she lifts them again, they will be progressively heavier than before and she will be able to hold them for a shorter and shorter time.'

'You have done well for your first attempt, Sister Ella.'

Ella beamed. 'There is more, Master. The pain of

strained muscles is not the only torment. The Sisters will help Paula to pass more readily through the Portal of Pain by whipping and slapping her. She may, of course, choose to protect her body with her hands but, if she does, the belt continues its work and the weights get heavier still.'

The Master's smile broadened into a laugh and he shook his head in admiration. 'Very well, Sister Ella. You may begin.'

Ella went behind Paula and unbuckled her cuffs. As her hands came free, Paula brought them in front of her body and explored the outline of the fiendish Pleasure Belt she wore. A moment of touching and feeling was sufficient. There was no way she could rid herself of the thing and it was strapped so tightly to her that she could not ease it away from her crotch by sliding her fingers inside it. She felt the leather cage over her head which held her gag in place, only to obtain the same depressing information. She would not be able to free herself from that either. At that moment, someone activated the infra-red device. Paula was the first to know about it, because the thing between her legs ceased to be a lump of neutral, padded leather, and became an instrument of simultaneous irritation and enjoyment. She turned her mind away from the probing, vibrating movements it was making. She would stick it out. There was no way in the world she was going to humiliate herself by standing on that platform and holding up those weights, exposing her nudity to the lashes of the Sisters.

After a very short space of time, Paula detected a serious flaw in her plan. She had grossly under-estimated the sort of stimulation the belt provided when it operated continuously. She felt the onset of orgasm and fought to prevent it, frowning in concentration and bending herself double, trying to cross her

228

legs. Involuntarily, she squeezed her breasts hard and would have cried out had the gag not prevented it. Her orgasm was not huge and overwhelming, but it served to further sensitise her vagina and clitoris, so that now the actions of the belt seemed to be magnified. In addition to that, Paula saw activity at the poles and realised that the Sisters were adding weights to the rods. She had not reckoned on that and it made up her mind for her. She made her way as quickly as the belt allowed to the platform of the trolley and stepped onto it. She stretched out her arms and lifted both weights. She was comforted to find that they were not as heavy as she had thought they would be. Surely she could stand like this for a long time? A sharp slap on her bottom disillusioned her. A Sister on her left was smacking her buttocks; not particularly hard, but with sufficient force to sting and with a rhythm which made it clear that she did not intend to stop for a long time. Paula became acutely aware for the first time of the true nature of the torture that was being inflicted upon her. The ache that was beginning to make itself felt in her shoulders was bearable. Her spanking was bearable. What was much more difficult to endure was the self-control she was obliged to exert in order to prevent herself from moving her arms to protect her bottom during the awesome, yawning eternity that stretched before her. No time limit had been placed on her punishment and there were plenty of Sisters to take over spanking duties when one got tired. If she decided to drop her arms and accept the different torture of the Pleasure Belt, how long would that go on for? Miss Doyle had said that the batteries lasted four hours! Could she possibly endure four hours of that excessive sexual goading, even if it were split up into shorter periods. She thought not.

It was no good. Paula just had to drop her arms. She allowed the weights to fall down and stepped off the trolley, becoming immediately conscious of the fact that the effect of the Pleasure Belt's evil manipulation of her vagina, anus and clitoris seemed to be enhanced after so short a break. She felt herself rising to climax before she had covered more than a few paces. She stopped, head down and hands on knees, bracing herself to tough it out, groaning softly through the hole in her gag. She could see her own thigh muscles twitching and trembling with the strain, while her belly was leaping and jumping galvanically, as though electrically charged.

The throes of her peak slackened and she rested briefly, panting with whistling breaths through her gag. The thing was not going to leave her alone, though. Already, she could feel its subtle movements taking her up the slope of lust towards yet another orgasm. She couldn't stand any more. At a stumbling run, she made for the platform which was her only means of respite. Two Sisters were adding weights to the rods and Paula shook her head frantically, trying, by her cooing noises, to beg them to desist. She took her place again, extended her arms and accepted the burden of the weights in either hand.

The bliss of the cessation of the Pleasure Belt's movement was quickly overtaken by the stings of repeated slapping. This time, though, there was a fresh torture to be borne. Two Sisters mounted the platform in front of her and each selected one of her breasts, lifting them so that they could suck and gnaw at her nipples. The impulse to protect herself with her hands became almost too much for her self-control to deal with. With an extra effort of will, she forced herself to remain in the degrading, crucified pose which allowed such ready access to her whole body. To distract herself from what they were doing to her, Paula looked over their bent heads and beyond them. Ella and the Master were together and both were naked. As Paula watched, the Master lay down on his back on the floor, his penis rampantly erect. Ella straddled facing him and lowered herself, feeling for his organ beneath her. Paula watched the whole length of it slide out of sight until their pubic hair entwined. The sight of Ella's naked posterior and her stretched vulva working its way up and down the Master's rigid shaft was erotic in the extreme. That, coupled with what was happening to her breasts and bottom induced Paula deliberately to lower her arms a little so that the Pleasure Belt came into operation. She could tolerate it only for a short while, now, and bubbled quickly into orgasm.

Paula was going off into a sort of daze. When a naked, masked man appeared from somewhere behind her and passed her on his way to the couple on the floor, it hardly impinged upon her consciousness. He stooped over Ella's bare bottom, his erect penis in his hand. From where she stood, Paula had a clear view between his legs and past his testicles. She saw him centre his manhood on Ella's sphincter, then thrust violently inside, so far up her that his testicles slapped between her thighs. Paula heard Ella scream, but could not tell if it was a scream of pain or joy. She imagined what Ella must be feeling with those two stiff organs working inside her, separated only by a thin membrane of sensitive flesh. That thought was too much and Paula felt an urgent need to allow the weights to drop again, so as to satisfy her own sudden sexual craving. Orgasm struck her at once like a lightning bolt. The audience chamber whirled before her eyes. How curious! She had thought the wall hangings were grey, but now saw that they were red. No, they weren't! They were a glowing yellow, as far as she could tell with all this fog. Silly the way one's mind worked; prompting one to remember . . . to remember . . . What was it that she had to remember? Italy . . .? Something about Italy . . .? Too hot to think about Italy . . . Did it matter? It was all too difficult. That would be because it was so cold and the Pleasure Belt was . . . Italy . . .? Strange! Those wall hangings were not yellow at all. How could she have made such a silly mistake? They were . . . They were . . . black!

Paula slumped into unconsciousness and would have fallen, had it not been for the Sisters about her, who caught her and lowered her gently to the floor.

Paula's return to awareness was slow at first. She stirred uneasily and moaned then, feeling her wrists cuffed behind her again, jerked to full alertness and tried to sit up. She found herself lying in what she recognised as Ella's room, on her narrow bed, and was relieved to find that the Pleasure Belt, at least, had been removed. Ella herself was sitting on an upright chair, staring at her with an expression of concern that relaxed into a smile when she saw that her friend was awake.

'Oh, good! You've been asleep for such a long time that I was getting quite worried about you.'

Paula shook the last remnants of muzziness from her brain. 'How long have I been out?'

'About an hour. Do you notice the difference?'

'Difference? What do you mean?'

'You have begun your journey to Enlightenment. I remember how it was for me. So exciting! I felt like quite a different person afterwards.'

Paula caught the subtle nuance of that word 'begun'. There was more of the same, or similar, to follow. She was cuffed again and, as long as she remained that way, she was powerless to prevent anything. 'Er . . . Oh! I see what you mean. Yes, of course I feel different. Quite wonderful, in fact.'

Ella beamed. 'There! I told you so! You begin to feel the power of love all about you, don't you?'

'Just what I was going to say. Now I understand. The love of one Sister for another is . . . is . . .'

'As boundless as the ocean,' Ella prompted.

'Exactly. I can understand why no one would ever want to leave. I certainly don't, now. Not after that wonderful experience.'

Ella clasped her hands and laughed excitedly. 'Oh, Paula. Do you really mean that you want to become a Disciple?'

'Oh, absolutely! Look, can you take these cuffs off so that we can hold one another. I'm so excited that I want to hug you.'

Ella shook her head. 'I'm afraid I'm not allowed to do that. Sister Martha can, though.'

Paula struggled into a sitting position and swung her legs over the edge of the bed. 'Do you think you could go and tell her about me, then? Tell her I want to be one of the Sisters.'

Ella jumped up. 'Of course! I'll go at once. Is there anything else you need?'

'Are the Sisters allowed to drink?'

'Silly! Of course we are.'

'OK, then. Tell Sister Martha that a large brandy would go down very well.'

As soon as Ella left the room, Paula got up off the bed and began a tour of inspection. That didn't take long. The room was small and there was very little furniture. By turning her back to the small chest, she managed to open the drawers, one by one. She could not rummage, but had a quick look at the general contents. There did not seem to be much there that would be helpful. She pushed the drawers closed with her bottom and went to the window. That was latched, but did not appear to be locked. With her hands cuffed, there was no way she could open it, but it looked promising for later. The fire escape she knew so well was just outside and, in the far distance, she could see the old barn which, hopefully, still hid her car. By the time Ella came back, Paula was sitting on the edge of the bed again.

Ella was not alone. She had brought with her not only Miss Doyle, but the Master. Miss Doyle was carrying a bottle and some glasses, which Paula eyed hungrily, but only for a second or two before her gaze transferred itself to the Master. This was the first time Paula had seen him at close range and, as she took stock of him, she was impressed. It became easier to see how this man could turn someone's head – at least someone as gullible as Ella.

Miss Doyle said, 'Ella tells me that you have seen the error of your ways and now understand the value of the Portal of Pain.'

'Oh, yes, Miss Doyle! I just didn't understand before, but after what Ella did for me . . . Well! It was just a revelation.'

Miss Doyle nodded approvingly. 'In that case, I can offer you an extraordinary opportunity; a gift from the Master himself. You may, if you choose, become one of the Sisters of the Light – one of his Disciples. The Master would use his best endeavours to train you into enlightenment and, perhaps, if you are very fortunate indeed, into immortality.'

Paula bowed her head. 'I don't deserve it, after the things I said. I will try to be worthy of the Sisters.'

'Before you decide, I must point out to you that you would have to detach completely from friends or family outside this place. Such an earthly contamination of the spirit the Master will be trying to build in you would be disastrous. Furthermore, you cannot achieve enlightenment while burdened with possessions. As a Sister of the Light, you would live in a room like this and own only the bare essentials. Everything else must go. Money; house; everything. You must give them all up.'

'I understand. I would still like to go on.'

'Excellent! Ella told me that you would like a drink. We can make it a celebration. From now on, I shall call you Sister Paula and you must call me Sister Martha.' Miss Doyle set her bottle and the glasses down on the chest of drawers and poured four drinks. She offered one to Paula, who shrugged and, by shoulder movements, drew attention to her pinioned wrists.

'I'm afraid I can't, Sister Martha – the cuffs!'

Miss Doyle paused, drink in hand. 'Ah! Sister Ella – you may remove Sister Paula's cuffs for a while.'

The lightening of spirit Paula experienced on being free again was out of all proportion to the degree of extra movement obtained by being uncuffed. She actually began to feel hopeful again. She took the brandy, drained the glass at a gulp and handed it straight back for a refill. The cognac warmed and heartened her.

Throughout all this time, the Master had said nothing, which was a little unnerving. Every time Paula looked at him, she found him staring at her with a peculiar intensity that made it seem that he could read her thoughts. When that happened, she tried to let her eyes pass on around the room quite naturally and not let it appear that she was looking away shiftily.

When they had all finished their drinks, Miss Doyle said, 'There is paperwork to be done and made ready for your signature. In the meantime, you may wait here with Sister Ella.'

'Do I have to be cuffed again?'

'No, of course not. However, Sister Ella must still be your warden and, for her sake, you must have no opportunity to roam about.' Miss Doyle brought out the familiar little gold padlocks and Paula's heart sank, knowing what they meant.

Paula smiled. 'That's no hardship, Sister Martha.' She stood up and held out her breasts, supporting one in each hand and moving close to Ella. She watched as Ella opened her robe to expose her own breasts then felt and heard the click as the padlocks united their nipple-rings once more.

Alone with Ella, Paula leaned forward and kissed her on the mouth. 'Isn't it wonderful, darling? Now we're really Sisters and can love one another properly. Isn't that exciting?'

Ella returned the kiss with compound interest. 'You know that you have always excited me, Paula. That's why it's so wonderful to have you here with me. Shall we try leaning back and hurting one another's nipples? That's what Sisters do, here. They assist one another to the Light by shared pain.'

Paula hugged her enthusiastically. 'Better than that, Ella. Do you remember how I slapped your bottom, once? I'll do that again now, shall I? Would that help you towards the Light?'

'Oh!' Ella breathed. 'Would you do that for me? That would be so generous of you. I could slap yours afterwards, if you like?'

Paula slipped her left hand down between their bodies and found Ella's clitoris, massaging it. With her right, she reached around Ella's body and began to spank her buttocks as hard as she could. Ella jerked and wriggled in ecstasy.

After a few slaps, Paula stopped. 'I can't get any force into it this way. Why don't we see if we can get free of one another, then I could get enough space to swing my arm properly.'

Ella went pale. 'Sister Paula – we mustn't. That would be against the rules.'

'Yes, Sister Ella, but in a good cause. Think how much more enlightened you would be if I could only spank you harder. The Master would want that, wouldn't he? And, besides, I could put my finger in your bottom, just the way I did before.'

'Well . . .' Ella said, doubtfully. 'I suppose, if you put it like that . . . But how?'

'That's the spirit,' Paula said hastily, before wavering could become outright refusal again. 'Just shuffle over to the chest with me.'

She wrapped her arms around Ella and propelled her sideways until they were standing beside the chest of drawers. She reached down and opened the top one, taking out the tiny manicure set she had seen there during her brief exploration. She unzipped it and her heart gave a leap. She had hoped to find a nail file, but there was something inside which was much better. She took out the short nail clippers and, squinting a little, fixed their blades around the hasp of one of the gold padlocks. The soft metal parted with a click and she quickly did the same to the other. They were two separate human beings again, instead of being one rather clumsy one.

'There.' Paula said. 'Isn't that better? Now I can do to you all those naughty, painful things you love so much. First, I'd better cuff you, hadn't I? You like that.'

'Yes, but . . .'

'No argument! Slip out of your robe and turn round. There!'

'Oh, Sister Paula. What are you going to do to me?'

'All the things you like, darling Sister Ella. Now

237

open your mouth and let me put this gag on you, just as I was gagged. No, don't thank me. It's the least I can do.' Paula adjusted the leather cage arrangement, making sure that the buckles that held the red ball in place were really tight. She pulled the bedclothes and mattress off the bed, leaving the bare springs. 'On the bed, face down. That's right. Let's have that naughty bare bottom of yours in the air ready for a thrashing and a good length of wriggling finger.' Quivering in pleasurable anticipation, Ella obeyed, squirming a little as her bare breasts and stomach came into contact with the cold metal.

Paula picked up a sheet and, with a swift rip, tore a long strip off one end. She wrapped it securely around Ella's ankles and tied them to the springs. Working quickly, she secured further strips across her knees, waist and shoulders, binding her securely in place.

Paula picked up Ella's discarded robe from the floor and put it on. She went to the window and slipped the catch before pushing up the sash. She put her head out to reconnoitre before turning to look at Ella who had turned her head to watch with as much of an expression of amazement as the gag would permit.

'Sorry, chum,' Paula whispered. 'Sometimes, you have to be cruel to be kind. One day, you'll be glad I did this.' She put one leg over the sill, then drew it back. Going across to the chest, she selected one of the glasses left there and, to avoid holding it on the outside, picked it up by putting her fingers inside and expanding them until they gripped. She went back to the window, carrying the glass, stepped out onto the fire escape and, silent in her bare feet, ran down towards the garden and freedom.

Dennis Philps was feeling good that morning. He had every reason to. A very pleasant little transaction had taken place earlier that morning which had made him several thousand pounds better off. It had not even been dishonest. He had always intended to play a part in approving that planning application, anyway. He settled himself further back into his chair and watched appreciatively, as Mavis, his secretary, leaned over to put his tray of tea and biscuits beside him. Her young breasts jiggled against her crisp, white blouse every time she performed this service for him and it never ceased to please him. As on many occasions before, he resisted the temptation to run his hand up the back of those shapely young thighs, so conveniently positioned. Perhaps now that he had a little windfall cash to spare, a bracelet or some other piece of jewellery might make an appropriate gift. Better make it a necklace. It would be only polite for her to allow him to put it on for her, then he would get the opportunity to touch the back of that long, slender neck with its attractive wisps of hair that refused to be imprisoned in the rest of her upswept style.

'What?' Mavis had said something to him which his pleasant daydreams had not permitted him to absorb.

'I said that Paula Matheson is here to see you.'

'Paula? What does she want?'

'How would I know? Why don't you ask her?'

Mavis was too cheeky for her own good. She was asking for it and, one day, she would get it. What she deserved wasn't a necklace. It was to be put across his lap, have her knickers taken down and be spanked on her bare bottom. Her young, white, delicately rounded, shapely . . . Dennis stirred uneasily, reaching into his pocket for his handkerchief. 'Show her in!' he said, more gruffly than he intended.

As Paula came into the office, Dennis got up and

came around the desk, hand extended. 'Paula! How nice to see you again. Not in trouble with the press, are we?'

Paula smiled and took the proffered hand. 'Of course not, Dennis. You're much too good a source of information for that. A distinguished councillor; Head of Planning for the whole of Arton and District. Why would I want to upset you, particularly in view of our close acquaintance?'

Dennis looked uneasily about him. 'Steady on, Paula. Walls have ears. You know that was strictly a one-night thing and we'd both had a bit too much to drink. Why bring that up again?'

'Because of Italy, Dennis, dear.'

'Italy? I don't understand.'

'Yes you do. Remember the argument we had about that birthmark on your bottom? I said it looked like a map of Italy, but you said it didn't. Mind you, you turned out to be right, after my cane had finished with it.'

Dennis reddened. 'For Chrissake, Paula! Not in the office! Someone will hear you.' He crossed to the door peered out to see that the outer office was empty. Mavis must have gone for one of her numerous coffee breaks. He came back and gestured to a chair. 'Sit down. What made you suddenly think about my birthmark after all this time?'

'Someone saw it.'

'I still don't understand.'

Paula took out a cigarette and lit it, fixing him with a stare as she blew out the first stream of smoke. 'Think back to yesterday afternoon, Dennis. Yesterday – when, no doubt, your dear wife supposed you to be hard at work in the office, here. Think about where you really were and what you were doing.'

Dennis began to bluster. 'I don't know what you're

. . . I was . . . I was . . .' His face crumpled and, for a moment, Paula thought he was going to burst into tears. 'You mean, someone saw me?' he whispered hoarsely.

'Not only saw you, but took photographs, Dennis,' Paula lied with total sincerity.

'Oh, my God!'

'Now, Dennis. Don't take on so. I told you I haven't come to cause any trouble for you. I just need a little favour, that's all.'

He eyed her with deep suspicion. 'What sort of a favour?'

'Nothing dishonest. Just a little bending of the rules to get some information I can't get for myself. You're a great mate of the chief constable, I believe? Arton Golf Club and all that male bonding stuff.'

'Yes, what of it?'

Paula opened her hand bag and brought out a plastic bag in which there was a brandy glass. She set it on Dennis's desk. 'I want a name and other details to go with the fingerprints on this glass.'

He stared at it as though it were a snake. 'I can't ask Claude to do that.'

Paula picked up the object and put it back in her bag, closing the clasp with a snap. She got up. 'Such a pity, Dennis. I wonder how the paper will deal with the photographs. Much too rude to print. Perhaps we could still make some use of them, though. What would be a good headline, do you think? THE PHOTOS WE DARED NOT PRINT. COUNCILLOR'S LOVE TRYST. COUNCIL OFFICIAL PLANS REAR ENTRY.'

Dennis's face was the colour of his white blotter. 'All right! All right, Paula! You win. I'll try.'

Paula smiled sweetly and placed the glass on his desk again. 'You'll do better than try, Dennis. You'll succeed. If you're really unlucky, the prints will be illegible. That will count as a failure, so take great care not to mess them up.'

Back at *The Globe*, Kevin in the Press Office was the next one to have his day spoilt. Paula came in so swiftly that he had no chance to switch off his Casino screen.

'Paula! You're back! Where have you been? Old Flatt . . .'

'Old Flatt can wait. This is hot. Research, Kevin! Get that cute little arse of yours in gear. I want everything on file about the great illusionists of the past, particularly those who worked with black backgrounds and mirrors. I know I've seen it at some time, but it could be years back.'

'Illusionists? I don't . . .'

'Don't know what an illusionist is, Kevin? It's someone who makes you think something is real when it isn't. Something like a decent day's work, for instance. The sort of illusion you create, Kevin. Now get your finger out and let me have all that stuff on my desk in an hour or reality is going to catch up with you and it will be your cushy job that becomes the illusion.'

'Yes, Paula.'

She called after his disappearing shape, 'And if it's not in our files, get yourself down to the library. One hour, Kevin. This story is red hot!'

Greylands Retirement Home for the Elderly was set in large and pleasant grounds. As Paula drove her car up the approach road, she summed up the building ahead of her. Whatever else it might be, the word 'home' seemed inappropriate. It was too new; too clean and neat to be that. She parked tidily and went inside to speak to the matron, who proved to be a clinically efficient lady of indeterminate age with a large expanse of white-aproned bosom. The hand which shook Paula's was as cold and clammy as the accompanying voice.

'Mr Jocylin? Number thirty-six? I told him you'd made an appointment to see him, but I'm not sure he'll remember. His mind is going and that gives us a lot of trouble.'

Paula smiled, concealing her instant dislike of a woman who could refer to another human being as 'Number thirty-six'.

'Oh well, perhaps I'm wasting my time, but I may as well see him now I'm here.'

'Certainly. Will you come this way?'

The matron led the way down corridors too shiny and disinfected to be friendly until they arrived at a conservatory which jutted from the main building into the garden. In one corner, by a potted palm, there was a white-painted wicker armchair in which the sparse figure of a man reclined, apparently asleep. The matron approached him and shook him by the shoulder.

'Mr Jocylin? Mr Jocylin! There's someone here to see you.'

The old man opened eyes that were wildly vacant and confused. 'Eh? Who's that? Gracie? Is that you, Gracie?'

The matron caught Paula's eye, pursed her lips and shook her head. 'No, Mr Jocylin, it isn't Gracie. Your wife's dead. Why don't you listen? This is Miss Matheson. She's come a long way to see you, so behave yourself for a change.' She turned to Paula. 'I have to get on. I'll leave you with him. He may get more sensible when he wakes up a bit.'

Paula nodded her thanks and settled herself into a matching chair opposite the old man. She had hoped for more, but was prepared to battle through his senility, if she could, to obtain the information she needed.

She leaned forward and touched his knee. 'Mr Jocylin,' she said gently, 'I'm Paula Matheson. Are you . . . Were you, at one time, Prospero the Magnificent?'

The rheumy blue eyes regarded her unsteadily, without recognition, and her heart sank. In this old man's body, the porch light was on, but nobody was home.

'Has she gone?'

'What? The matron? Yes, she's gone.'

'Good!' The old man straightened, easing his neck muscles and wiggling gnarled, stiff fingers. Suddenly, his eyes were no longer unfocused, but clear and piercing; much younger than his apparent years. 'Editor of the Arton *Globe*. That's what you said. I remember Arton well. That's when it was a real town. Even had an Empire. I suppose you're too young to remember the Moss Empires, aren't you?'

'Yes.' Paula sat back, taking stock of him. 'Why do you do that?'

'Do what?'

'Pretend to be daft. There's not a daft bone in you.'

He cackled unexpectedly, revealing uneven and discoloured teeth. 'Drives 'em crazy! Don't begrudge an old man his only bit of pleasure. Besides, when the Mothers' Union organises community singing with tambourine accompaniment, it's useful to be too senile to remember to attend. Now, what do you want of me, young woman? I didn't think I was newsworthy any more.'

'I'm doing a piece on the great illusionists of the past. I'd like you to tell me how your illusions were achieved. You were the greatest . . .'

'Am the greatest!' he interrupted. 'Do you know why?'

244

'No.'

'All the others are dead. Outlived the lot of them, I have. But you can't expect me to reveal my secrets.' He drew himself up in a way that made it seem as though he were standing, instead of sitting. 'The mystery of my illusions dies with me.'

'That's a great pity,' Paula said. 'I have a bottle of vintage port in my purse. I planned to open it to celebrate getting what I need.' She locked eyes with him.

'Hmm! Vintage, you say? You've done your homework. Sure it's not supermarket horse-pee?'

Paula shook her head. 'Not at the price I paid for it. Do you want to see it?'

He looked sharply about him. 'Not here! Better come along to my room. I have some mementoes there that would interest you, anyway.' He rose, with some difficulty, and reached for a slender, silver-topped cane. 'Arthritis,' he explained, then slowly and carefully led the way out of the conservatory.

His room was not in the least what Paula had expected. Any element of clean brightness attributable to the modernity of the architecture had been submerged in a positive rat's-nest of tatty furniture from many different periods. Theatrical posters left very little of the wall-colouring visible.

He removed a pile of yellowing theatre programmes from the seat of a faded, overstuffed, Victorian armchair and gestured for Paula to sit down. She did so gingerly, looking around her with interest.

'Like it?' he asked, seating himself in another chair opposite hers.

'Erm . . .'

He chuckled and his dark eyes twinkled in a surprisingly youthful way. 'One of the advantages of being barmy,' he said, 'is I get to keep it the way I like it. If they try to change it, I throw a tantrum and they humour me.' He waved a thin arm in an expansive gesture which embraced everything about him. 'You see before you a lifetime of theatrical digs. Countless grubby dressing-rooms. Here, in this atmosphere, I can keep my audiences with me. So many places. So many faces. We should drink to that, don't you think?'

Paula grinned and delved into her bag for the bottle of port. 'Glasses?'

'Toothmugs on the washstand, dear lady. Will you get them? My knees only go from sit to stand a few times a day now.'

Paula fetched the glasses, poured generous helpings of port into them and handed one to him. He raised it to his nose and tested the bouquet, nodding and smiling appreciatively before taking a large gulp.

Paula took out her notepad. 'About your illusions?'

He took another gulp of port and sighed with deep satisfaction. 'Before I begin, may I ask you to do me a great favour?'

'Of course. Do you want me to fetch something else for you?'

'No. If you wouldn't mind, I'd like you to take off your clothes.'

Paula had often read of people's jaws dropping in amazement and had assumed it to be creative licence on the part of the writer. Now she felt her own do the same thing and, totally bereft of words, she not only allowed it to happen, but exaggerated her gape as an indication of her immediate reaction while she fought for words.

'You want me to . . . to do a striptease for you?'

He shuddered delicately. 'Absolutely not! Perish the thought. All that crude wriggling about. Most unladylike. No, I just want you to undress quite normally and let me look at you.'

Paula laughed at his brazen effrontery, still not really able to believe that this conversation was taking place. 'Why, you randy old sod!' she said, almost in a tone of admiration.

'Oh, not at all, dear lady,' he said. 'I promise you that there is absolutely no sexual connotation to my request.'

'Says you!'

'No, really! Let me explain. There are certain advantages to great age. The fires of youth burn low. Vulgar passion is replaced by an appreciation of those qualities in a woman which get overlooked when bedding her is the prime motivation. You have come bearing a beautiful treasure. It is as though you had a work of one of the master painters or sculptors with you and it is presently covered with cloth. If you did, indeed, have such a thing and I asked you to uncover it, you would surely not refuse me the pleasure of seeing it?'

'But I'm not a painting or a statue.'

'You are not,' he agreed. 'You are much more beautiful than either. Won't you allow me to admire you?'

Paula eyed him, weighing his request in her mind. 'And if I don't agree, I suppose I don't get the secrets of your act?'

He shook his head. 'This is not part of some tacky bargaining process. You will get your story, whether you undress or not. All I'm asking you to do is to make a generous gift to an old man who has no opportunity otherwise to gratify his taste for the exquisite.'

Paula thought about that. If the matron's chunky figure were the best that the Home could offer, he was indeed deprived. And there could be no possible risk. She was quite certain that she could walk faster than he could run. She stood up. 'Mr Jocylin,' she said. 'You are a silver-tongued old devil.' She unbuttoned her jacket and took it off. In a matter-of-fact way, she disposed of the rest of her clothes and stood naked in front of him, her hands at her sides.

He leaned forward in his chair. Placing both hands on the top of his cane, he rested his chin on them and stared at her intently. Paula found his gaze curiously disturbing, because she could read in his eyes the truth of his claim that there was nothing sexual about his request. For the first time in her life, her nude body was being looked at by a man who had absolutely no ambition to own it. So far from being embarrassed, the evident admiration in his eyes was having the opposite effect. She felt proud of her body. Not the sort of pride she had felt many times – that of being able to use it to arouse passion. This was quite different.

'I wish you could see what I can see,' he said.

Paula smiled gently, encouraging him. 'What do you see?'

He straightened his back and looked into her eyes. 'Youth; vitality; energy; suppleness. They don't last, you know. You think they will, but they don't. I see a life-span too. A future I don't have any more. So many things clamouring to be done and, for you, there is time to do them. And do you know where all that is contained?'

'No,' she said softly, mesmerised by his eyes and his voice. 'Tell me, please.'

'Better than that; I'll show you. Go and stand in front of that long mirror over there. Get between the mirror and the window so that the light is behind you. Now turn a little to your left, so that you see one breast in profile, silhouetted against the light. Stretch your right arm up and put it across the top of your head, reaching for your other shoulder. Look at the line made by your arm, breast, waist, hip and thigh. Is that not the most exquisite set of curves you've ever seen? Pure art, isn't it? They communicate every scrap of your youth and beauty and say it all far better than any words could. Now you can see what I mean about a painting or a sculpture.'

And she did see the resemblance. It was exactly as he claimed it. This was ridiculous, Paula thought. She was actually getting turned on by this skinny old man. But it wasn't a sexy turn-on. That was the extraordinary thing. It was an emotion she had never felt before. An ability to detach herself from her own sexuality and feel the same pure and clean excitement as he.

She broke her pose and came back to stand in front of him. She wasn't quite sure why she felt she would have liked to kiss him. She didn't. That would have meant breaking the spell; descending from the heights of aestheticism by making banal physical contact.

'Thank you for that generous gift,' he said simply.

'I'm not sure who gave and who received, Mr Jocylin,' Paula said, and meant it.

'You can put your clothes back on now.'

'There's no rush.' Paula sat down again and picked up her pad. 'Now, you old rascal. About these illusions . . .'

The audience chamber was beginning to fill with the gowned figures of the Sisters. To Ella, that was the signal that the first half hour of that day's punishment was at an end and that the second stage would soon begin. Every day, for the past three days, since Paula had left her helpless and tied to her bed, she

249

had been brought, naked, from her room by the other Sisters. Half an hour before the Master was due to wake, they had lifted her and draped her across the vaulting horse used for beating. They had lashed her straddled legs and spread arms to the legs of the horse on either side, then left her there to contemplate the strapping that would begin as soon as the Master woke. That was only fair and just. She deserved it. She had been entrusted as warden to Paula and she had betrayed the Master's trust. She was only thankful that she had been offered this alternative to expulsion.

She kept remembering the shame and humiliation of being discovered by Sister Martha. No explanation was demanded and she was sure none would have been accepted, if offered. Sister Martha had simply gone away to fetch a cane. Gagged, cuffed and lashed immovably, face down, her bottom had been an obvious target, Ella had no choice but to accept her punishment. She not only accepted it, but welcomed it. Every burning slash chipped away a little of the guilt she felt and she was grateful to Sister Martha for realising that and for prolonging the caning. Had Ella not been gagged, she would have cried out for the beating to continue when Sister Martha finally stopped. Remaining tied face down all night, unable to rub her stinging buttocks, gave her the opportunity to reflect on her error and to hope that further punishment would help her back to the Path to the Light.

So it was that, when the curtains drew aside to reveal the blackness in which the spirit of the Master slept, she rejoiced at his coming. Perhaps, this time, the strapping she received would finally assuage her blameworthiness and restore her to the Master's favour. His shape was becoming more distinct. Soon, he would speak with the Old One. Would she intercede on Ella's behalf? Tell the Master how sorry his erring pupil was?

The misty outline of the Old One appeared, little by little, yet she did not speak. The Master glanced at her sharply. The Old One moved a little from side to side, her imprecise shape wavering. Suddenly, the white veil that covered her from head to toe fell in a crumpled heap on the floor. Ella blinked. Where the Old One had been was the unmistakable figure of Sister Martha, wearing her shiny, black dominatrix outfit. Her hands were out of sight behind her and on her head, she wore the leather cage of the gag with which Ella was intimately familiar, its red ball distending her mouth into an expression of surprise. Around her ankles, obvious white cords made it clear why she remained where she was.

There was a murmur of consternation from the assembled Sisters which turned immediately into a gasp of surprise as Paula's head suddenly appeared, floating in space behind Sister Martha's right shoulder. A moment later, the rest of Paula's body began to appear from the neck downwards, little by little, until she was completely revealed, dressed in white blouse and brown slacks.

'What the . . .!' The Master gripped both arms of his throne, preparatory to rising, only to be thrown backwards by some invisible force.

'Thank you, Kevin. I'll take it from here.' Paula moved swiftly to the side of the throne and took both ends of a rope which had, miraculously, appeared across the Master's chest. She knotted them quickly, securing his upper body to the throne. The Master raised his right arm, but the centre part of it became suddenly invisible and it fell onto the arm of his chair, where Paula tied it in place. Passing behind the throne, she dealt similarly with the other arm.

'All right, Kevin, you can take it off now.'

The head of a fair-haired young man appeared alongside Paula's and the rest of him followed quickly as it became apparent for the first time that he was removing a black, velvet overall and hood that had covered his everyday clothing completely.

'Don't be alarmed, Sisters!' Paula stooped and picked up a big, red book. She opened it and turned to face the Master. 'Harry Flack, alias Prince Rashid, also known as Sardo the Magnificent, this is your life!'

'Damn you!' The Master struggled furiously to get free, kicking his legs.

'Shut up a minute, Harry. The Sisters will want to hear this. Born in a small town in Wisconsin, Harry served time in a young offender's correctional facility for car theft. After working as a carnival roustabout and shill for a while, he developed an act as an illusionist, Sardo the Great, ably assisted by none other than Dolly Doyle here, whom you all know and love as Sister Martha. Jailed for statutory rape, he gave up the magic business when he came out and became Prince Rashid, Hindu mystic and beloved leader of a rich and faithful flock of true believers. Just ahead of the IRS and a warrant for fraud, he disappeared. No one knew where he was. Now they do. Anything to say, Harry, in that great English accent you developed?'

The Master shot her a glance of pure hate. 'Go to hell, you bitch!'

Paula addressed herself to the Sisters. 'Look, girls; I know this has come as a bit of a shock to you all, but you've been ripped off. Harry, here, wasn't a bit interested in your immortality, or your souls, though he was certainly willing to have a lovely time with your bodies. What he was after was your money. The

252

charitable fund he told you about was his own pocket. That's where the proceeds of your bank accounts and the sale of your property went. The police are due to raid the place soon, but I wanted to come on ahead and be the one to break the news to you in this particular way. That's why I got Kevin to help me to break in again. I knew I'd read about that sort of show before and as soon as I found out how the Master managed to appear and disappear, I knew the only way to convince you that he wasn't divine was to steal some of his props and give a show of my own.'

The reaction to her words among the Sisters was mixed. A few looked angry but most were either distraught or just plain bewildered. They had just seen something they believed in with all their heart and soul crumble to dust before their eyes.

One gave voice to the common feeling. 'But what shall we do?'

'Do? Well, first I suggest that you get that silly cow, Ella, down off that contraption. She looks ridiculous with her bum stuck up in the air like that. Then you just go home and try to pick up the pieces of your lives. Any of you that feel cheated and want to stay to watch what I'm going to do to Dolly Doyle's backside can do so.'

Released from the horse, Ella went over to a large sofa at the side of the room and sat down on it. She buried her face in her hands and sobbed. Presently, Beatrice joined her. They embraced, then sobbed together.

Paula spared them little attention. She was directing the work of a group selected from the more disgruntled of the Sisters as they brought the trussed Miss Doyle down from the stage. She was wriggling like an eel as they carried her, but her attempts at escape were futile. They laid her down, none too gently, at Paula's feet, where she squirmed in impotent rage.

'Naked, I think,' Paula said. She smiled down at Miss Doyle. 'That's the way you like your women, isn't it? Well, that's the way I like mine, too, particularly when I'm going to do to them what I'm going to do to you. All right, Sisters. Hang onto her arms and legs when you untie them, then strip her off. You can take the gag out, too, now. I want her to be able to scream.'

Paula watched the operation with a satisfaction made all the sweeter by Miss Doyle's reaction to what was happening. She yelled and struggled all the while. Even when stripped and held face down on the floor, arms and legs securely pinned, she continued to wriggle every part of her body that was free to move.

'Up on the horse with her, like Ella was fixed,' Paula ordered.

The Sisters dragged Miss Doyle to her feet. She tried to break away from them, her face turned appealingly to Paula. 'Not that! Please not that! You mustn't. I can't stand pain.'

Paula waved the group away. 'You should have thought of that before you inflicted so much of it yourself.'

The Sisters lifted Miss Doyle easily and draped her over the vaulting horse. They spread her arms and legs wide and strapped them to the legs of the horse so that she was doubled over it, her bottom taut and strained, high in the air.

Paula was struck by a sudden thought. 'Where's that belt thing?' she asked. 'The one I had to wear.'

'You mean the Pleasure Belt,' Belle said. Her eyes gleamed with vicious delight. 'What a good idea! I'll fetch it.'

'No!' Miss Doyle moaned. 'Not that, please.' Her efforts to see what was going on behind her were almost comical. With her head hanging far down, she could see underneath the horse. A view of feet and legs told her that a small knot of the Sisters were gathered behind her. She could not raise her head far enough to see what the upper parts of those bodies were doing, but the sensation in her vagina and anus soon informed her that the Pleasure Belt was being fitted and locked into place.

'Who knows where the remote switch is?' Paula asked.

'It's all right,' Belle volunteered. 'It has a little switch of its own. Would you like me to turn her on?'

'Yes, please.'

Miss Doyle could not fail to hear this exchange and knew exactly what was about to happen to her. Her moaning and sobbing increased in intensity and Paula felt a sympathetic twinge in her own vagina as she vividly recalled the unbearably sweet sensations that gadget was capable of producing.

Belle squeezed her hand between the leather of the horse and Miss Doyle's stomach, groping for the switch. A loud shriek told everyone that her search had been amply rewarded and that Miss Doyle was feeling the full effects of the massaging penises inside her.

Paula watched as impassively as her inner turmoil would allow, noting the obvious signs of sexual stimulation. Miss Doyle's small breasts were not concealed by the horse and the extent of her nipple-erection was apparent. As her torment continued, the soft flesh directly beneath her nipples hardened and swelled into truncated cones from which her teats protruded obscenely, marking her state of total arousal. She held out well, considering the excessive provocation she was experiencing. Her moans were quieter as she ground her teeth in an effort to fight off orgasm. As Paula knew well, it was a battle she could only lose. The quivering of her stretched thigh muscles was the first indication of the approaching storm. Her moans became staccato grunts until her whole body was jerking and shaking with pent-up stress. Then, with a scream, she strained her head upwards, her eyes vainly seeking a means of release before succumbing to the need for climax and slumping, breathing heavily.

There was no respite, as there had been none for Paula. The Pleasure Belt went about its work methodically and without compassion. Miss Doyle's second orgasm was achieved more quickly and was more evidently forceful than the first.

Paula went around the horse and grabbed Miss Doyle's hair so as to be able to lift her head and look into her eyes. 'I'll switch it off as soon as you beg me to beat you,' she said. 'Would you like me to start now?'

Mouth open and panting, Miss Doyle shook her head.

'Please yourself,' Paula said and stepped back, folding her arms as though content to wait all night. Having experienced that belt herself, she was perfectly sure of eventual capitulation.

Two more orgasms came and went before Miss Doyle raised her head wearily. 'All right. You win. Do it.'

'Do what?' Paula asked, innocently.

Miss Doyle's voice was almost a whisper. 'Beat me. Do it now. I can't stand any more.'

'Strap or cane?'

'What?'

Paula said, 'I'm offering you a choice. Do you want to be beaten with a strap or with a cane?'

'Bitch!' Miss Doyle yelled, finding sudden energy, then her head dropped again. 'Oh God! I'm coming again. I can't . . . I can't . . . Oh God! Beat me with a strap. Please!'

'If you're sure,' Paula said. 'Belle. Switch off, please, and hand me that big strap.'

Smirking with pleasure, Belle passed across the broad, thick piece of leather with which the Master had beaten Ella. Paula flexed it between her hands, then, without further ado, slapped it across the backs of Miss Doyle's thighs. Again and again she struck, covering an area from waist to knees with red welts while Miss Doyle screamed loud and long. When her arm tired, Paula handed the belt to Belle. 'Keep it up,' she said. 'When you get tired, switch her on again while you rest.'

Paula went across to the sofa where Ella and Beatrice were now seated side by side, still sniffling. She sat down between them. 'What's the matter with you two?' she asked. 'I would have thought you'd be pleased to be free of that slimy bastard.'

'Don't call him that,' Ella wailed. 'We love him. You've ruined everything. Our lives were just perfect until you came along and spoiled them.'

Paula snorted. 'Spoiled your lives? What are you talking about? All you were getting here was a lot of pain and you were paying handsomely for it.'

'It was what we wanted. You don't understand. Pain cleanses. It heals the spirit. It takes you into the light. It can make you one of the immortals.'

'Oh, come on!' Paula protested. 'You can't possibly believe that any more. Not now I've shown you that all this was just conjuring tricks.'

Ella sniffed, dabbing her eyes. 'All right. Perhaps immortality wasn't certain. But we never thought it was. We would have had to be much better at loving one another. Where shall we find the same love and appreciation of the pleasures of pain? You have closed the door of the Portal to us. Beatrice and I are going away together. We'll wait for the Master, no matter how long it takes; then we'll all be together again.'

'What will you live on while you're waiting?' Paula enquired, shrewdly practical.

'We'll manage somehow.'

Paula rubbed her chin thoughtfully. 'How's this for an idea? I won't try to destroy your faith in the Master. I can see you're both too far gone for that at the moment. Since it was my fault that you lost him, so to speak, it seems only right that I should make amends. There's a spare bedroom at my place that you can both share. When you feel ready, Ella, you can come back to work. Whether Beatrice works or not is up to the pair of you.'

'That seems fair,' Ella said, reluctantly. 'What do you think, Beatrice?'

Beatrice cupped her hand and whispered in her companion's ear.

'She says that we must continue on the Path to the Light if we are to remain faithful to the Master,' Ella confided.

Paula snorted. 'You mean you've both developed a taste for having your bottoms beaten.' She thought for a moment. 'You reach this Path of yours through the Portal of Pain thing, don't you, Beatrice?' she asked, more gently.

Beatrice nodded. 'And by loving one another.'

'There you are then,' Paula said. 'Tell her, Ella. Am I good at inflicting pain, or am I not?'

Ella nodded. 'She is, Beatrice. Really.'

'If you doubt it, ask Miss Doyle over there.' Paula jerked her head over her shoulder towards the shrieks

258

of torment which were just as loud as ever as Belle plied her strap. 'As for loving one another, that can be arranged.'

'Are you sure?'

Paula ran her eyes over Beatrice's lush curves, comparing them with the perfection of Ella's so close alongside.

'Quite sure,' she said. 'Doubly sure, in fact. Come along. Let's go home.'

Bonded by Fleur Reynolds
September 1997   Price £4.99   ISBN: 0 352 33192 5
When the beautiful young Sapphire goes on holiday and takes photographs of polo players at a game in the heart of Texas, she does not realise that they can be used as a means of revenge upon her cousin Jeanine. As the intrigue mounts, passions run ever higher – can Sapphire hope to avoid falling prey to the attractive young Everett, or will she give in to her libidinous desires?

Silent Seduction by Tanya Bishop
September 1997   Price £4.99   ISBN: 0 352 33193 3
Bored with an unsatisfying relationship in her home village, Sophie enthusiastically takes a job as a nanny at a country estate. She soon finds herself embroiled in sexual intrigues beyond the furthest reaches of her imagination. A series of passionate encounters begins when a mysterious, silent stranger visits her at night, and she sets about trying to discover his true identity.

There are three Black Lace titles published in October

French Manners by Olivia Christie
October 1997   Price £4.99   ISBN: 0 352 33214 X
Gilles de la Trave persuades Colette, a young and innocent girl from one of his estates, to become his mistress and live the debauched life of a Parisian courtesan. However, it is his son Victor she lusts after and expects to marry. Shocked by the power of her own lascivious desires, Colette loses herself in a life of wild indulgence in Paris; but she needs the protection of one man to help her survive – a man who has so far refused to succumb to her charms.

Artistic Licence by Vivienne LaFay
October 1997   Price £4.99   ISBN: 0 352 33210 7
Renaissance Italy. Carla Buonomi has disguised herself as a man to find work in Florence. All goes well until she is expected to perform bizarre and licentious favours for her employer. Surrounded by a host of desirable young men and women, she finds herself in a quandary of desire. One person knows her true gender, and he and Carla enjoy an increasingly depraved affair – but how long will it be before her secret is revealed?

Invitation to Sin by Charlotte Royal
October 1997   Price £6.99   ISBN: 0 352 33217 4
Beautiful young Justine has been raised in a convent and taught by
Father Gabriel to praise the Lord with her body. She is confused
when the handsome wanderer Armand offers her the same pleasure
without the blessing of the church, and upon sating her powerful lusts
is banished in disgrace from the convent and put into a life of servi-
tude. She must plan her escape, and decide whether to accept
Armand's invitation to sin. This is the second Black Lace novel to be
published in B format.

NEW BOOKS

Coming up from Nexus and Black Lace

There are three Nexus titles published in September

Amanda in the Private House by Esme Ombreux
September 1997   Price £4.99   ISBN: 0 352 33195 X
When Amanda's housekeeper goes missing, she travels to France in an attempt to find her. During the search she meets Michael, who awakens in her a taste for the shameful delights of discipline and introduces her to a secret society of hedonistic perverts who share her unusual desires. Amanda revels in her new-found sexual freedom, voluntarily submitting to extreme indignities of punishment and humiliation.

Bound to Submit by Amanda Ware
September 1997   Price £4.99   ISBN: 0 352 33194 1
The beautiful submissive Caroline is married to her new master at a bizarre fetishistic ceremony in the USA. He is keen to turn his new wife into a star of explicit movies and Caroline is auditioned for a film of bondage and domination. Little do they know that the film is being financed by Caroline's former master, the cruel Clive, who intends to fulfil a long-held desire – to permanently make her his property.

Eroticon 3
September 1997   Price £4.99   ISBN: 0 352 32166 0
Like its predecessors, this unmissable collection of classic writings from forbidden texts features some of the finest erotic prose ever written. In its variety of people and practices, of settings and sexual behaviour, this exhilarating anthology provides the true connoisseur with the flavour of a dozen controversial works. Don't miss *Eroticon 1, 2* and *4*, also from Nexus.

Sherrie and the Initiation of Penny by Evelyn Culber
October 1997   Price £4.99   ISBN: 0 352 33216 6
On her second assignment for her enigmatic master, Sherrie acts as instructress to the unhappy writer Penny Haig, initiating her into an enjoyment of the depraved and perverse games the writer has never before dared to play. Penny soon becomes a fully-fledged enthusiast, revelling in humiliating ordeals at the skilled hands of expert disciplinarians.

Candida in Paris by Virginia Lasalle
October 1997   Price £4.99   ISBN: 0 352 33215 8
Naughty Candida has a new mission – one very much in keeping with her lascivious sensibilities. She is sent to investigate a clandestine organisation providing unique sexual services for wealthy Parisians, and soon finds herself caught up in a secret world of orgies and hedonistic gratification. She cannot resist the temptation of sating her prodigious lust – but does she underestimate the danger of her task?

NEXUS BACKLIST

All books are priced £4.99 unless another price is given. If a date is supplied, the book in question will not be available until that month in 1997.

CONTEMPORARY EROTICA

THE ACADEMY	Arabella Knight	Oct
AGONY AUNT	G. C. Scott	Jul
ALLISON'S AWAKENING	John Angus	Jul
BOUND TO SUBMIT	Amanda Ware	Sep
CANDIDA'S IN PARIS	Virginia LaSalle	Oct
CANDY IN CAPTIVITY	Arabella Knight	
CHALICE OF DELIGHTS	Katrina Young	
A CHAMBER OF DELIGHTS	Katrina Young	Nov
THE CHASTE LEGACY	Susanna Hughes	
CHRISTINA WISHED	Gene Craven	
DARK DESIRES	Maria del Rey	
THE DOMINO TATTOO	Cyrian Amberlake	
THE DOMINO ENIGMA	Cyrian Amberlake	
THE DOMINO QUEEN	Cyrian Amberlake	
EDUCATING ELLA	Stephen Ferris	Aug
ELAINE	Stephen Ferris	
EMMA'S SECRET WORLD	Hilary James	
EMMA'S SECRET DIARIES	Hilary James	
EMMA'S HUMILIATION	Hilary James	
FALLEN ANGELS	Kendal Grahame	
THE TRAINING OF FALLEN ANGELS	Kendal Grahame	Dec
THE FANTASIES OF JOSEPHINE SCOTT	Josephine Scott	
HEART OF DESIRE	Maria del Rey	

EROTIC SCIENCE FICTION

RETURN TO THE PLEASUREZONE	Delaney Silver	

ANCIENT & FANTASY SETTINGS

CAPTIVES OF ARGAN	Stephen Ferris	Mar
CITADEL OF SERVITUDE	Aran Ashe	Jun
THE CLOAK OF APHRODITE	Kendal Grahame	
DEMONIA	Kendal Grahame	
NYMPHS OF DIONYSUS	Susan Tinoff	Apr
PYRAMID OF DELIGHTS	Kendal Grahame	
THE SLAVE OF LIDIR	Aran Ashe	
THE DUNGEONS OF LIDIR	Aran Ashe	
THE FOREST OF BONDAGE	Aran Ashe	
WARRIOR WOMEN	Stephen Ferris	
WITCH QUEEN OF VIXANIA	Morgana Baron	
SLAVE-MISTRESS OF VIXANIA	Morgana Baron	

EDWARDIAN, VICTORIAN & OLDER EROTICA

ANNIE AND THE SOCIETY	Evelyn Culber	
BEATRICE	Anonymous	
CHOOSING LOVERS FOR JUSTINE	Aran Ashe	
DEAR FANNY	Aran Ashe	
LYDIA IN THE BORDELLO	Philippa Masters	
MADAM LYDIA	Philippa Masters	
MAN WITH A MAID 3	Anonymous	
MEMOIRS OF A CORNISH GOVERNESS	Yolanda Celbridge	
THE GOVERNESS AT ST AGATHA'S	Yolanda Celbridge	
THE GOVERNESS ABROAD	Yolanda Celbridge	
PLEASING THEM	William Doughty	

SAMPLERS & COLLECTIONS

EROTICON 1		
EROTICON 2		Jun
EROTICON 3		Sep
THE FIESTA LETTERS	ed. Chris Lloyd	
NEW EROTICA 2	ed. Esme Ombreaux	

NON-FICTION

HOW TO DRIVE YOUR WOMAN WILD IN BED	Graham Masterton	
HOW TO DRIVE YOUR MAN WILD IN BED	Graham Masterton	Jul
LETTERS TO LINZI	Linzi Drew	

Please send me the books I have ticked above.

Name ....

Address ....

....

....

.... Post code ....

Send to: **Cash Sales, Nexus Books, 332 Ladbroke Grove, London W10 5AH**

Please enclose a cheque or postal order, made payable to Virgin Publishing, to the value of the books you have ordered plus postage and packing costs as follows:

UK and BFPO – £1.00 for the first book, 50p for each subsequent book.

Overseas (including Republic of Ireland) – £2.00 for the first book, £1.00 for each subsequent book.

If you would prefer to pay by VISA or ACCESS/MASTER-CARD, please write your card number and expiry date here:

....

Please allow up to 28 days for delivery.

Signature ....